Love from Scratch

KAITLYN HILL

DELACORTE PRESS

Text copyright © 2022 by Kaitlyn Hill
Jacket art copyright © 2022 by Ana Hard

All rights reserved. Published in the United States by Delacorte Press, an imprint of Random House Children's Books, a division of Penguin Random House LLC, New York.

Delacorte Press is a registered trademark and the colophon is a trademark of Penguin Random House LLC.

Visit us on the Web! GetUnderlined.com

Educators and librarians, for a variety of teaching tools, visit us at RHTeachersLibrarians.com

Library of Congress Cataloging-in-Publication Data is available upon request.
ISBN 978-0-593-37916-5 (trade) — ISBN 978-0-593-37918-9 (ebook)

The text of this book is set in 11.5-point Adobe Garamond Pro.
Interior design by Cathy Bobak

Printed in the United States of America
10 9 8 7 6 5 4 3 2 1
First Edition

For Stephen, who always makes me feel heard, respected, and adored—and who looks great in an apron

Chapter One

The man in front of me has a bee in his bonnet and cat hair on his coat. I know these things because from where I stand—smooshed into the back of a crowded elevator in the downtown Seattle skyscraper where my internship is located—the sleeve of his suit is only inches from my face. As such, I can see the white strands plain as day against the black fabric while he grunts at the phone in his hand—plus feel the tickle in my nose that says I'm dangerously close to a sneeze.

Lordhavemercy, I think, one big compound, catchall word I inherited from my mamaw and so many other Southerners, religious or not. It's what you say when you're in company too polite to say something worse.

Mr. Business is testing my limits, though. He just couldn't be bothered to use a lint roller, could he? Nor to give me any personal space back here, in the midst of whatever turmoil he's dealing with in his email inbox. I hope my nose breath is making him hot. I press my tongue to the roof of my mouth, a trick I saw online somewhere to help put off sneezing, watching the floor numbers tick higher.

Finally, the *ding ding* is for my floor and I adjust my grip on the tray of to-go cups I'm balancing in the crook of my arm, reaching for my badge to swipe into the office with the other hand as I make the quiet, "pardon me, sorry" noises required to edge my way out of the crush of bodies. It's made a little easier today by the human Grumpy Cat, whose office must also be on floor forty-two, thus allowing me to slink through the wake left by his wide frame.

That plan is working flawlessly, right up until he steps off the elevator and—I don't know—needs a moment to collect himself, or realizes he forgot to feed Fluffy or something. He stops short, with no regard for my or anyone else's presence a half step behind him.

And because I do not stop short, I run smack into his cat-hair-covered backside, coffee tray first, sending hot brown lava into the air, onto the floor, and all over myself.

"Whoa, careful there," the man grumbles with an errant glance over his shoulder. He's already turning to head down the hall toward the entrance of some investment firm, leaving me gaping and covered in gourmet bean water.

I should be careful? Oh, for the love of—

"Reese! Oh my God, are you okay?"

Teagan, receptionist at Friends of Flavor, comes rushing out

2

of the glass double doors that face the elevators, through which I guess she just witnessed the accident.

"I'm fine," I say in the least grumbly voice I can manage, peeling my once-lavender shirt away from where it's clinging to my stomach and chest. I'm never dressed in the blacks and grays of most of the businesspeople who work in our building, but of course I had to go all-pastel today. "Can't say the same for the drinks, though."

I peer over the to-go cups, which have all miraculously stayed in their designated slots, and to my relief find that my own hot tea might be the only total loss. *Gourmet leaf water,* I mentally correct myself, with regard to what's soaked me. I've never felt so betrayed by my favorite beverage. The bean waters kept their lids on and lost a little foam at most. Small victories.

"What an asshole," Teagan blurts, nodding in the direction of my new nemesis, who has by now disappeared. I nod my agreement but keep my mouth shut; she's been here a couple of years and is so well liked that I don't think anyone would bat an eye at her outburst. I've been here less than two weeks and would rather not be tossed out on my tea-soaked rear for losing my temper.

"You go on in, I'll wipe the rest of this up," she continues, shooing me away. I would argue, but she probably knows the time and therefore realizes that I'm already cutting it close, so I thank her profusely and get on my way.

Rounding the lobby corner, I shift the ill-fated tray to my other hand just in time to hold it out of the way of someone passing with a wheel of cheese so massive he nearly has to walk sideways to fit it through the hall. I pass by one of the ingredient pantries and catch a guy who looks like he stepped straight out of the Discovery Channel dropping live crabs into a tank. When I've almost reached the little alcove off Prep Kitchen 2 where my team works, a cooked strand of spaghetti sails just past the end of my nose and sticks to the wall beside me.

"Sorry! Didn't see you there," calls out an embarrassed kitchen assistant. I wave him off and bite my bottom lip to keep myself from saying something snippy. Not seeing me there seems to be the theme today, doesn't it? But honestly, they seldom "see me there," and that's fine. So long as I'm noticed by the people who matter—the people with my future in their hands.

This is how it goes at Friends of Flavor. It's the second full week of my internship, and I'm only just getting used to the organized chaos that characterizes these "culinary content creators." There is constant hustle and bustle, chefs and kitchen assistants and art directors and camera crews and more rushing around to get the next recipes made, the next episodes shot for the various series, the kitchens cleaned so it can start all over. I'm merely a background player, an intern on the marketing team, and I have no desire to be anything more attention-grabbing—for now. If I can just keep my head down, work hard, learn from the pros, and do a good job on the tasks I'm given this summer, it could be the beginning for me. My entry into their flagship semester-long culinary internship in the fall, and from there . . . who knows what else? Once I have my degree, I'm angling for something full time in marketing or maybe on the production side—wherever my skills can be best put to use. If all goes according to plan, hopefully I'll have a chance to stay in this weird and wonderful world long term.

Working at FoF has been my dream for years now, ever since my best friends back home in Kentucky, Natalie and Clara, pulled me out of a seriously self-pitying funk our freshman year of high school and into the home theater at Clara's house with a dozen FoF videos queued up. It was the start of our shared obsession with the channel and the charismatic chefs who make its culinary magic. On countless nights when our schoolmates went to parties and football games, we stayed in, smooshed together on someone's bed or couch, catching up on all the episodes of FoF's cooking series. We fell in love with Katherine's easygoing competence on *Fuss-Free Foodie*. We got to travel the US with Rajesh in *Cross-Country Cookery*. We dreamed of one day competing against other amateur chefs on *Good Chef/Bad Chef*. The prep kitchens and studio where most shows took place seemed like Narnia to us, as aspirational and dreamy and seemingly out of reach as that wonderland through the wardrobe.

I never imagined Narnia having quite so many copy machines, though. After rounding the corner near one of the mechanical beasts, I'm finally in the marketing team nook. I hand off the surviving cups to each of the team members I work with, who mumble their under-caffeinated thanks, then take a seat at my makeshift TV-tray desk. If anything, I suppose I can be thankful that the shock of the hot liquid down my front has given me the jolt of energy that I won't be getting from a beverage this morning. I see a lock of dripping blond hair hanging in my periphery and try my best to discreetly wring it out above the trash can before pushing it back into place. I snap a quick picture of the results of the spill to Natalie and Clara with the caption "#OOTD #professional." Their responses come quickly and are highly on-brand.

> **Clara:** yikes! hope you have stain-fighting detergent. my mom uses tide

> **Natalie:** Wet t-shirt contest?? LOVE that for you!

Laughing as I pocket my phone, I decide to put the annoyance of the coffee-tea-tastrophe to rest so I can get on with my day. I take out my laptop and open it, tucking my backpack neatly against the wall—as neatly as it will go, anyway, in a space barely big enough for a small trash can, let alone a whole human and her possessions.

Dream internship, I remind myself. Living the dream.

The dream that wasn't so out of reach, as it turns out. Friends of Flavor is a real business, with real offices, where they hire real people to do real work. I had no idea the extent of the labor it takes behind the scenes to make twelve minutes of "Rajesh Prepares Chef Grant's Deconstructed Chicken Cordon Bleu" look so clean and flawless. But the world of food media is complex, with many cogs that keep the machine running. It's appealed to me since I first started watching FoF's shows, and they're producing the best work in the business. I love food and enjoy cooking, but my culinary chops are mostly collected from time spent in my mamaw's kitchen throwing extra butter into everything and learning her recipes and techniques by example. Without any professional kitchen experience, I always figured that my graphic design skills from years on the school newspaper staff would have to be my in.

And when I started browsing internships for the summer before college and saw that the big streaming service that hosts Friends of Flavor had a spot open in its marketing department for a recent high school grad with minimal experience to their name? A chance to get away from my hometown and to my new city as soon as possible before I go to the University of Washington in the fall, to start anew away from all the people and baggage of my past, to work with some of my favorite creators in the whole wide web? I barely even considered what the day-to-day would look like, or that it might be anything other than a dream come true. Truly, I don't think I've ever clicked a button so fast in my life.

I've done quite a bit of clicking buttons since then, though, like I do now as I open up the usual tabs in my browser. Button clicking is one of my main responsibilities here, along with getting morning coffee when the boss decides to splurge on some from outside the staff break room. Every Friends of Flavor social media page is at the ready on my computer, waiting for me to tend to the replies and reposts and favorites appropriately. In other words, to click some buttons.

On Instagram, I like everyone's comments that I can. This is a never-ending task, as there are thousands of comments per post and they are constantly multiplying. Half of them are just people tagging their friends so they'll see the post, but as my boss Margie says, we still have to show that we "appreciate their engagement." I reply to a handful that I deem reply-worthy, like if they ask a genuine question to which I can find an answer—

> **@sw3et.c4rolin3e3:** What brand of brown sugar did Nia use in her drop cookies?
>
> **@friendsofflavor:** Domino, but any kind will do!

—or if they say something that gives me a chance to be quippy—

> **@MrZtoA1:** I accidentally melted my butter instead of softening it OOPS
>
> **@friendsofflavor:** BUTTER luck next time! ;)

Quippy comments always get more engagement and are the most fulfilling for me personally. My food pun repertoire is vast and always growing. Those almost balance out all of the comments I have to delete and users I have to block for inappropriateness. Why anyone would come to a page for a *cooking channel* to post racial slurs is beyond me, but then so is posting that garbage anywhere. I think of it as my daily taking out the trash, and it's sort of cathartic. Block, delete, block, delete, block, block, block.

Twitter and Facebook are more of the same, though the latter is increasingly bogged down with accidental comments by older folks who were clearly trying to type in the search bar, bless their hearts. Where we get the most engagement, and therefore where I spend the bulk of my time, is in the comments on our actual video content.

It's impossible to keep up with all of the comments on the Friends of Flavor channel on our host streaming service, Ulti-Media. The UltiMedia website is busy as it hosts a wide variety of original scripted and unscripted content on its different channels. There are channels for every interest—sitcoms, dramas, romantic movies. But Friends of Flavor's culinary reality series make it one of the most popular channels of all. Everyone likes food, right? And honestly, most people seem to like our videos.

UltiMedia has a comments section under each video, and each channel has an account that can monitor and reply to comments—a lot of my job is managing Friends of Flavor's. But there are so many episodes within each of the different series getting a minimum of thousands of new views daily, it's all I can do to give the occasional "Thanks for watching!" to every 217th commenter. Anything to show we care, I guess. It's one of

Friends of Flavor's biggest priorities to remain as approachable to the over four million viewers of each new video as they were to the first fourteen, and as a loyal longtime fan myself, I appreciate it.

I've been at it for a couple of hours when I hear Margie abruptly scoot her chair back behind me. I peek over my shoulder, though I know she's likely only taking a bathroom break. But to my surprise, she's gazing at her cell phone as she gets to her feet and gestures for me to get up, too.

"Aiden texted. Impromptu meeting in PK 1. Why don't you join me, see what's up?"

I nod, knowing it's more of an order than a suggestion, and close my laptop. I fight the urge to tuck in the flyaway strands of Margie's long, gray-brown braid as I trail her down the hall. While Margie has her shit together more than most people I know, the state of her braid always suggests otherwise. And somehow, I seem to be the only one who notices. It's like these people didn't grow up with a mama who would lick her fingers and pat into submission any individual hair that dared to step out of line.

When we reach Prep Kitchen 1, I'm pulled out of my hair reverie by the tall, stressed-out head of operations of Friends of Flavor—and cohost of *Good Chef/Bad Chef*—looking even paler than usual. Aiden, whose blond-haired, surfer-bro looks I might find attractive if not for every word that comes out of his mouth, paces back and forth. He has one hand on his hip and the other scratches aggressively at his neck, his intense gaze snapping toward us—well, toward Margie—when we enter.

"We have a problem," he announces.

"So I gathered," Margie replies coolly. She has at least a couple of decades of age and experience on Aiden and the rest of the Friends, and it mostly stands out when anything has gone wrong.

"The six of us have to fly to Chicago this afternoon. Jules Veronique had an opening in his schedule come up for tonight, and his assistant just called me, and they've finally agreed to let us film the crossover episode at his new restaurant. Everyone's schedule is cleared, the suits okayed it, and flights are booked, so we're going. Because we have to go, right? So we're going. We need to leave any minute."

He pauses, giving Margie an opening. "So . . . what's the issue?"

Aiden sighs, pulling a hand through short, platinum locks. "We were going to film a regular episode of *Piece of Cake* this afternoon, but Nia will be with the rest of us in Chicago. We have advertisers already scheduled and expecting an episode tomorrow, but now we won't have our pastry chef here to *film that episode.* Since you're marketing and have experience in the saving-face stuff, I thought you might . . . I don't know, have an idea."

Margie nods slowly, sucking her cheeks in. I feel a bit touchy on her behalf at the clipped way Aiden talks to her. Maybe it's my respect-your-elders upbringing. Maybe I'm still thinking of Mr. Cat Suit and I'm projecting onto Aiden. Or maybe it's just that I'm over men's condescension toward women who are their equals—not that I'd ever express such opinions to these two.

After a moment of staring blankly into mid-distance, Margie opens her mouth to speak.

"Yo, A, was this the sourdough starter you were looking for? It kinda looks like a baby vommed in this bowl. Kinda smells like it, too, but—"

The speaker who isn't Margie stops short and sets the bowl he's holding on the counter, looking at our small crowd in confusion. I haven't seen him before. He's definitely an intern; if the fact that he looks about my age hadn't given him away, the general air of doesn't-know-what's-going-on-in-this-office-or-the-world would.

"He could do it."

It's Margie who speaks this time, and it feels like all eyes in the room turn to her in surprise.

"Our *intern*?" sputters Aiden.

Sourdough Guy crosses his thick arms over his apron-clad chest, looking a little defensive even though he doesn't know why yet. He's significantly shorter than Aiden, barely my height, but a lot bulkier. It'd be hard not to notice that he clearly works out when he's not in the kitchen. I try not to judge appearances, but muscles combined with the backward baseball cap on his head are making it difficult. Another dude-bro.

Margie shrugs. "Sure. It'll be different. '*Piece of Cake* Makes Macarons, Featuring the Intern.' Better than nothing."

Aiden steps closer and lowers his voice nowhere near enough to keep Sourdough Guy from hearing him. "I don't think so. He really—he's not ready to do a video. Not on his own, anyway."

"Reese can do it with him."

I don't even register at first that Margie is talking about me. The stressed-out chef doesn't either, but that's because he hasn't bothered to learn my name.

"Who?" he asks.

"Reese. Marketing intern." Margie puts a hand on my shoulder and nudges me forward as if presenting me for inspection. I open my mouth to protest, but I can't seem to produce any sound.

Aiden barely glances at me before wiping a hand over his face. "Margie. Please. Intern plus intern does not equal chef."

She matches Sourdough Guy's stance, though it looks less aggressive on her. "No, but it does equal a solution to your problem, which is what you asked me for. It'll be fun and different, and if it's a bomb, we'll never have to try it again. Don't you have a plane to catch?"

The expression on Aiden's pale face is grim, and I'm sure my own is similar, because what the *devil*? After another tense moment, Aiden sighs heavily. "I'm trusting you with this, all right? Can you manage this for me?"

In spite of my reluctance to do what Margie has suggested,

I'm secondhand offended again when he speaks to her like a child. But she just pulls her braid over her shoulder and starts smoothing it with her hand like she has all the patience in the world.

"I've got it. Give Jules my best."

Chapter Two

The next couple of hours are a blur of following Margie around the office as she makes the necessary preparations and adjustments for the sudden change of plans for Nia's baking show, *Piece of Cake*. Consulting people in various kitchens and cubicles, and even a few over the phone, she makes a bunch more decisions than it seems should be needed for a video of two people doing some baking. But I imagine I don't even understand the half of it.

My eyes have glazed over and my head is spinning when Margie finally turns to me, sometime after the lunch break we've skipped. It's the first real acknowledgment I've gotten since we were standing in front of Aiden.

"Have you seen the other intern recently?"

I look around and shake my head. "I can go look for him if you want."

She just turns and waves for me to follow her, calling out as we walk back through the prep kitchens, *"Intern!"*

In Prep Kitchen 3, a backward-cap-covered head pops up from beneath the counter.

"Me?"

Margie beckons him over with two fingers. "Yes. I assume you have a name?"

He flips a kitchen towel over his shoulder and wipes his hands on his apron before holding one out to her. "I'm Benny."

"Margie." Their hands meet in one brisk shake before he drops his and offers it to me.

"Reese," I say, still in a daze. I am totally dead-fishing our handshake, but he doesn't seem to notice.

"Like Reese's Cups, the best candy in the history of the world?" He gives me a lopsided grin and I blink back at him.

"Uh . . . no. Like Reese Witherspoon, patron saint of Southern ladies who watch too many romantic comedies."

Benny laughs so loud, it startles me.

"Right." Margie smirks between us. "You two ready to get started?"

This is the closest anyone has come to asking if I *want* to be in a video to be viewed by millions on one of my favorite cooking shows of all time. But still, it doesn't feel like I have much choice. I nod as Benny gives an enthusiastic "Let's do this!" He's like the FoF equivalent of the spirit chair on my high school's student council, who had to get the crowd going at pep rallies. I hated pep rallies.

Margie leads us to a counter in Prep Kitchen 2 where

some kitchen assistants have set out bowls of ingredients. A videographer—Charlie, I think—sets up a camera on the opposite side of the counter. There are a couple of other people bustling around the kitchen testing recipes or something of the sort, and no one seems too interested in the fact that two inexperienced teenagers are about to be trusted with the most precious of Friends of Flavor content.

"First, these. You're both eighteen, right?"

Margie slides some forms toward Benny and me. Waivers, consent to be filmed, and all that. We both nod—we have to be eighteen to work here in the first place. Benny barely even looks at the papers before dropping his signature onto the designated line. I'm reminded of the scene in *The Little Mermaid* when Ariel signs her voice away to Ursula, and I try to skim for any major life-altering clauses. But I feel the pressure of everyone waiting on me and quickly sign my name, kissing my fins goodbye.

"Great," Margie says. "So this should be pretty easy. The premise is that—true to reality—Nia had to step out for the day with the rest of the Friends, but she left you with all these ingredients already on the counter and asked you two to take over. À la *Chopped* but with fewer ingredients and less direction. That's all we give you to go off, and we'll see what you two come up with. We're calling it *Piece of Cake: Amateur Hour.*"

Benny crosses his arms again, and his thick brows knit together under the edge of his hat. "Gotta say, as the *culinary* intern, I resent the word 'amateur' a little."

Margie looks amused. "We'll talk about a title change once you've had any formal training whatsoever."

I clear my throat, sensing an out. "As the *marketing* intern, I accept that word. Completely. Like, are you sure you want me to be part of this? Because my kitchen skills aren't too refined just yet, and—"

"I think it's even better that way, honestly. But that reminds me"—Margie's eyes flick down to my shirt, which now looks like the result of a sad attempt at purple-brown tie-dye. "We do need to grab you an apron. Lose the sweater. Be right back."

I blink at her retreating messy braid before sense returns to me. I slip my cardigan from my shoulders and hang it on a coat hook on the wall. There's a dress code at Friends of Flavor and I'm careful not to push the boundaries. Fortunately, today's tea-stained top at least has short sleeves. I feel Benny watching, which makes me self-conscious about my—*gasp*—scandalously bare arms. I must have forgotten to check my internalized self-consciousness from years of sexist school dress codes at the door today. That shit runs deep.

I feel fabric brush my arm and turn to find Margie holding out what looks at first glance like a burlap sack but is actually an ugly brown apron. Still an improvement over what's currently happening across my torso.

"All we had left are the ones we give to guest stars. Sorry," she adds with a shrug that suggests she's less than concerned. I take the apron anyway and pull it over my head, freeing my hair from the neck strap before I tie the strings behind my back. It fits much like a burlap sack would, too. Feeling better and better about my first and probably only brush with internet fame.

Maybe I can come up with a fake name for the video so it won't follow me forever when anyone Googles "Reese Camden." Better yet, if people who already know me stumble across the video, they'll just think I have a doppelgänger.

As Benny and I wait for further direction, I notice that his apron actually looks good on him. It should, since he has to wear it every day, but does it have to look *that* good? The off-white accentuates the tan on his muscular arms, and the muscles themselves are accentuated by the second skin that is his tight T-shirt.

I mean to look away, but my eyes catch on his, and on the cocky smirk playing over his face. *Ugh.* He knows he's objectively attractive, and now *he* knows that *I* know. I narrow my eyes at him, but his prideful look doesn't falter.

"Now just relax and have fun with it," Margie tells us. "Introduce yourselves however you want, then, Benny, why don't you explain the scenario and kick off the rest of the show? It's okay if it's awkward or you fumble with words or whatnot, just keep going. We'll edit all the extraneous stuff out later. Ready?"

No. Not even close. Those are the vaguest instructions that have ever instructioned. And I have to carry them out with a guy who, as far as I can tell, is a tool. Who thought this was a good idea?

Margie. Margie, my boss, who I very much want to like me.

"Yep!" My voice comes out as a squeak.

Benny's gaze slides to me before he answers. "Lights, camera, action, baby."

Okay, Spielberg. I barely curb my eye roll before Charlie the cameraman mumbles something that sounds like "That's my line," then starts counting down from three on his fingers.

The camera's red light comes on.

We're rolling.

"Hey, y'all, I'm Reese, marketing intern here at Friends of Flavor," I say with a wave. I'm shocked that I'm even saying words. I have essentially mimicked the way my favorite Friend, Katherine, does her intro on *Fuss-Free Foodie*. Plus a "y'all," because I can't help it.

"Hey, y'all," Benny says in a high-pitched, exaggerated Southern accent. My eyes dart to him and my jaw drops, but he just laughs and eases back into his normal voice. "I'm Benny, culinary intern. We're stepping in today because Nia and the other Friends had to run off to tend to some very important . . . food . . . things. But don't worry: we are total nonprofessionals with very little experience, and they left us with zero direction."

He's good at this. Too good. I feel the instinct to clam up coming on and do my best to fight it. *Channel Katherine.*

"We met just a few minutes ago and he's already making fun of how I talk," I say. "All required ingredients in a recipe for success."

"Don't get your petticoats in a twist, Scarlett O'Hara," Benny shoots back. "I'm twice as rude to people I actually know. Now, let's check out our ingredients."

Oh, this is a game he wants to play, is it? Scarlett O'Hara? I just—I won't even begin to engage with that. Nope. This guy is getting nothing from me. Only the minimum amount of interaction to get through this video and not make myself out to be a total bitch. And maybe afterward I'll figure out a literary character to whom he would least like to be compared and throw it back at him. All in due time.

"Looks like we have some eggs," I start, naming the most obvious ingredients first. "Green food coloring . . . flour . . . sugar . . . or maybe it's salt, I can't tell."

Benny takes a pinch and tosses it in his mouth. "Sugar," he declares, then reverts to his imitation accent and adds with a wink, "Darlin'. And some other not-yet-identifiable stuff, but from first pass, I'd guess they want us to make green eggs and ham."

I cross my arms, ignoring his cheekiness. "There's no ham."

"Ah, good catch. Back to the drawing board."

"What if we—"

Before I can finish my thought, Benny plunges his fingers into the remaining bowls and licks the contents off one at a time.

"This one's powdered sugar, not flour," he says, then licks a different finger. "This one's flour."

Lick. "Vanilla"—lick—"salt"—lick—"*butter*, yum"—lick—"mmm, cream of tartar?"

I don't even know what that is, let alone what it tastes like. With a flourish, he uses his clean hand to reach over and pluck a nut out of the last bowl. "Pistachio," he declares, smiling obnoxiously at me with gross bits of green smeared across his teeth.

"Please go wash your hands," I reply with a frown.

He turns to the sink, remarking over his shoulder, "You won't get my cooties, Reese's Cup."

I roll my eyes at the camera. "We're not at nickname level yet."

Benny returns to my side, wiping his hands dry on his apron. "I'm sorry to report that we are. Benny's my nickname."

"Really? Then what's your re—"

"Let's get started on these macarons, eh?"

He doesn't want to talk about his real name. Duly noted. I'll bring it up if he calls me Reese's Cup again.

"How do you know that's what we're making?" I ask.

He puts a hand to his chest. "Chef," he says in the same tone with which you would say *duh*. When I raise a skeptical eyebrow, he adds, "In training. And it was a hunch based on the stuff laid out for us. Plus, it's the example Margie used when pitching the video earlier. Enough chitchat, let's shake 'n' bake!"

Benny rubs his hands together excitedly and starts pushing bowls my way. I have no idea what to do with any of them, and while I hate to look like the student in this little production, he seems to actually know what he's doing. Or he's confident enough to fake it well.

"So I should probably just tell you I'm about as green as these pistachios when it comes to macaroons. I've never even eaten one, let alone made—" I begin self-consciously, but Benny cuts me off.

"Macarr*ons*," he says, throwing his hands up emphatically and rolling the *r* for longer than seems necessary. "Not macar*oons*. Important distinction, Reese's Pieces. Two different cookies."

I shake my head on an exhale, trying hard to keep my composure. "Right, well. Painful as it was to admit it the first time, I'll repeat that I've still never had a macar*on,* so you've gotta, like, tell me what to do."

Benny grins at me, then looks directly into the camera. "It would be my honor."

He shuffles around more bowls and I mock-whisper to the imaginary audience, "Apologies in advance to, well, feminism as a whole."

"Did you say something?" Benny teases, pushing the pistachios toward me with finality. "There are just so many recipes, so much knowledge in my head that sometimes it's hard to hear anything outside it, you know?"

"Keep it up, Benjamin," I say in the warning tone that my mamaw would use to tell my papaw that he should very much *not* keep it up.

"Not my name," he says, pointing a finger at me. "Blanch those nuts."

I cock my head to the side. "Do what now?"

He reaches for the flour and a sifter. "You're in charge of the filling, and first you'll need to make pistachio paste. Fill a pot with water and bring it to a boil."

Something tells me this is going to be a long and involved process. I've always known that even a supershort episode on Friends of Flavor is a highlight reel of footage that can take anywhere from hours to days to prep and film. But this is the first time I've considered what that could mean for Benny and me. I'd feel better about the prospect if I'd eaten lunch.

Benny tells some stories about trying macarons in France when he visited while spending the summer in Italy with his grandparents. I'm half listening while I wait for the water to boil. But mostly, his stories add to the insecurity I'm feeling right now. He knows complicated recipes off the top of his head; he's traveled around Europe. I'm good at button clicking, sure, and I can handle my familiar comfort food recipes, but I don't have his ease around a kitchen. And so far, I've felt in over my head in Seattle. I've never resented the fact that I haven't been far out of the Southeast before, not when I've had the internet at my disposal for all kinds of armchair travel and self-education. For most of high school, I was desperate to leave—it's why I applied to UW, just about as far as I could get in the States without having to fly over an ocean—but that was because of the people around me, not the place. I love Kentucky and dare anyone to hate on it to my face. But I have to admit to myself that right now, my upbringing makes me feel like some country bumpkin who's out of her depth.

Benny recaptures my attention once the water is boiling and gives me the next few instructions. Put the pistachios in the pot, take it off the heat, let it sit a couple of minutes before draining. Then I should be able to rub the flaky brown skins off with ease.

"Easy there, Girl Scout, you're not trying to build a fire. Gentle." He puts his big, floury hands over mine and delicately flicks the skin off a pistachio to demonstrate. I flinch at the contact, momentary as it is, then let up on the pressure I've been applying to the cluster of nuts between my palms. They really do come apart with the lightest touch.

I'm pouring the nuts into the food processor when I notice Benny is already pulling a bowl out from under the stand mixer and starting to fold in dry ingredients by hand.

"Why do I feel like you're way ahead of me?"

He gives me that lopsided smile. "Mine still have to bake. Relax, it's not a competition. But if it were, I'd probably win."

I push the processor button aggressively, like I'm trying to tune out his voice, but in my haste make a fatal mistake. Okay, not fatal, but messy.

I don't get the lid fully locked in place.

It's secure enough that the food processor still starts, but in the two seconds my finger is on the button, the lid goes flying across the counter, sending pistachio bits in every direction. Mostly, it seems, toward me. They're in my eyes, nose, mouth, and all across the front of my ugly apron. Forgetting the nuts are edible and probably even taste good, I sputter and try to spit them out, stepping back from the counter as if the damage isn't already done. As my senses return, I hear Margie, Charlie, and Benny . . . well, losing their shit.

After a moment, I drop my head and start to laugh too. The tears that come to my eyes help flush out some of the stray pieces that are stuck in my lashes, and I try to wipe off the rest of my face with the bottom of my apron. It takes a couple of minutes for everyone to regain composure. Benny is the first one to address me.

"You good, Hurricane Reese?" he asks, stepping closer and swiping once at his own eyes.

"Aside from being covered in green chunks and hugely embarrassed? Sure," I offer with a reluctant smile.

He takes another step closer and my smile drops. Our faces are less than a foot apart. But before I can react, he reaches up and his fingers are on my face . . . pulling a piece of pistachio from my eyebrow.

"There," he says softly, stepping back. "There's still more where that came from, but mostly in your hair. And might I say, green is your color."

I let out a choked cough, still surprised by the close contact with this near stranger and not impressed by his poor attempt at flirtation. I turn away and gather my blond-with-temporary-green-highlights locks up into a high ponytail. I can write off any remaining chance of looking cute in this video.

Clearing his throat, Benny asks, "Would this make you feel better?"

I look over in time to see him dipping a finger in his light green batter and smearing it like war paint in a single stripe under each of his eyes. I laugh in spite of myself and shake my head.

"You look like you're fixing to play a St. Patrick's Day football game, while I was caught in an explosion at the Planters factory."

His head falls back as he laughs and before I know it, he has more batter on his fingers and reaches over to put two stripes under my own eyes. "When the nut factory explodes at noon but you have to play in the big game at one."

I shake my head, but I'm fighting a laugh, too. I notice Margie twirling a finger in a "wrap it up" motion, so I try to regain control of the situation.

"Okay, we can do this," I say, shaking myself to refocus on the task at hand.

Benny takes a deep breath and turns back toward his side of the counter. "Yep. Your 'stach stash is down by about half, but that's fine. They'll just be more creamy than nutty."

I finish processing the pistachio paste with the lid fully on, and Benny starts piping his batter onto a cookie sheet in neat little circles, giving me further instructions as he goes.

The rest of the prep goes off pretty smoothly. He supervises cream production while the cookie parts of the macarons bake, and both finish almost simultaneously. While the cookies are cooling, the camera keeps rolling. Margie and Charlie are talking with each other and not really paying attention, so Benny and I both relax a bit. We use the time to pick at the cookies with air bubbles that cracked while baking, popping little bites in our mouths. They are light, sweet, and delicious.

"These are good," I admit before I can stop myself. I clear

my throat and try to backtrack. "I mean, seriously, did they give you a recipe before this? Believe me, I'm not trying to pump your tires any more, but there's no way you just knew all the steps on the fly."

One side of his mouth quirks up, a dimple appearing in his cheek. I blink back down toward the cookies quickly. Up close like this, the boy's face is dangerous. Which he absolutely knows.

"No recipe, thank you very much. My parents own an Italian restaurant in San Francisco, where I'm from. Pops runs the kitchen for the most part, all the entrées and stuff, but desserts are all Ma. Her specialty is cannoli because, y'know, Italian, but she went through a French pastry phase a couple of years ago. Our kitchen at home was like a macaron factory for months while she perfected her recipes, and my brothers and I were her line workers. I'll probably remember how to make macarons even if I get to be old and decrepit and forget my own name."

I smirk at that. "So what you're saying is that you got lucky."

"Oh, extremely. No matter what ingredients were here, we would've had to find a way to make 'em into pasta or pastries. It's all I got." He pauses, then adds, "But with your newfound skills at putting the lid on the food processor, who knows what we're capable of?"

"Cute," I deadpan, feeling around my hair for a piece of debris. When I find one, I throw it at him.

Benny laughs as he dodges, then leans over to check on his cooling cookies. Margie and Charlie return their attention to us.

"All right," Benny says finally, rubbing his hands together. "I think we're ready to pipe."

I hold the frosting bags while he spoons the cream in, then we each take a bag and half the cookies. I watch as Benny does his first couple, hesitant that I might mess something up again.

"Learning from the master, eh, Reese's Cup?" he says cockily without lifting his head from his work.

I roll my eyes and lean over to start doing my own. I'm about to squeeze out the first dollop when Benny's voice cuts the silence again. "The trick is to be fearless. The macaron can smell your fear."

"I think my only fear was making a fool of myself, and that one already came true, so . . ."

"Nothing to lose!" He fist-pumps with the hand not piping.

I start piping, *fearlessly*. In a matter of minutes, we've each made our own share of little cookie-sandwich-y macar*on*s. Without planning it, we both pick up one of the delicate desserts and turn to each other.

"Cheers, *y'all*," Benny says with a wink that looks to be more for me than the camera. I narrow my eyes again, but tap my macaron against his and we each take a bite.

And for a dessert made by one near-novice and one semi-apprentice working entirely from memory? They turned out damn good.

I say so through a mouthful, then slap a hand over my mouth, cheeks reddening. "You probably can't say 'damn' on a video, right? Cut that out, please. My mama will fly to Seattle to stick a bar of soap in my mouth."

Benny makes a sound halfway between a cough and a laugh. "Wait, are you serious? That's a little 1800s. She never actually did that, did she?"

"No." His shoulders relax before I continue. "'Cause we never swore in front of Mama. But I don't want to try my luck now."

He looks appalled. I don't *really* think Mama would wash my or my siblings' mouths out with soap, but it was her favorite threat. Truth be told, she used it way more often for all my lord-have-mercies and oh-my-lords, especially after I stopped going to church with my family a few years back. But it's kinda funny to see Benny riled up, so he can think what he wants.

"I think we've got about enough, if one of you could just tie it all together for us," Margie says.

Benny looks to me. He did do the introduction, and I am feeling a little more used to the whole camera thing now. I nod.

"Thanks for watching as we made a total mess of the kitchen, and some macarons to boot. I'm Reese, he's Benny, and this has been *Piece of Cake: Amateur Hour*. We'll see y'all . . . well, probably never again, because we weren't hired for this and we're kind of a train wreck. Have a flavorful day!"

I wave after dropping the signature ending line, and Benny chuckles beside me as he lifts a hand, too.

"That was excellent," Margie declares, surprising me with her praise. "Editing will have fun with it, huh, Charlie?"

He grumbles in agreement as he starts to disassemble the camera, and I'm gathering that grumbling is just his standard mode of communication. Some of the kitchen assistants appear to whisk away the dirty dishes, and Benny and I clean up our workstation. Margie says we can go home for the day whenever we're finished, then retreats to the marketing office.

Once the mixers and processors are put away and the counter clean of flour and pistachio debris, we stand there looking around and seem to mutually decide there's nothing left to do.

"Well," Benny says, turning to me with a hand outstretched. "It's been a pleasure, Reese."

He adds my name as an afterthought, deliberately not using an annoying variation of the only nickname he's come up with. I shake his hand, meeting his strength instead of limp-noodling this time. The macaron batter stripes on his face are cracking, even more so when he smiles and gets little creases around his eyes. The whole effect is . . . a lot. I feel the beginnings of a blush coming on but hope the mess on my own face distracts from it.

"Likewise, Benvolio."

He laughs. "It's short for Beneventi, actually. My last name."

I notice we're shaking for an oddly prolonged time, and I slip my hand out of his. "So you're not going to tell me your real first name?"

"We don't speak of it" is his mock-stern reply.

"Mysterious," I deadpan.

"Keep the ladies wanting more, I always say."

I roll my eyes, unable to come up with an appropriately snarky retort. "Well, um . . . see you around, then." I turn away from him to retrieve my sweater, untying the apron as I go.

"I hope so," he says, and it's like I can hear the crooked grin in his voice. "Hey, actually, what are you doing this weekend? We should have lunch."

My arm slips through my cardigan sleeve and I pull the sweater tight across my front before turning back to him.

"Lunch?" I say, the word loaded with as much skepticism as if he'd suggested we hit up a nightclub. *What's your angle, Beneventi?*

"Yeah," he says, eye-smoldering at me. "The meal in the middle of the day. Or dinner, which happens in the evening. They have those where you're from?"

I feel my upper lip curl and I'm sure my face is the least attractive thing right now, but that's for the best. "Yes, we do. Just usually with people I actually want to spend time around."

There. That's for the Scarlett O'Hara comment. And it's true, anyway. I barely know the guy and what I know so far, I'm not sure I much care for. He's cocky, which I hate, whether it's earned or not. And perhaps even more frustrating to me is it probably *is* earned. He knows his stuff, and I don't like being made to look ignorant while he mansplains the difference between baking powder and baking soda. Logically, I know I can't blame him for being good in the kitchen nor for the fact that I'm less so. But I'm not trying to out-logic my intuition about this boy.

Benny puts one hand over his heart and stumbles back like

I've shot him. "Oof. You wound me, Reese's Cup. But c'mon. I don't really know anyone around here and—no offense—I doubt you do, either. We're the only interns, as far as I know. Don't you think we should be . . . I don't know, at the very least, allies?"

That's actually the very most I want from him. But his point reminds me of something important—we *are* the only two interns. I don't know if he's trying to work here long term, but as far as I know, we're the only two in-house candidates eligible for the fall culinary internship—the application for which states that "preference will be given to in-house applicants." He clearly has the upper hand in culinary experience, having done the restaurant thing. I've always played more of an assistant role for my mamaw, who works through the same recipes time and again and usually tells me what to do at every step.

So *is* he going for the fall culinary spot? That seems like something I should know. Something I could find out over, say, lunch. Along with other things about him that might be useful to me if we're in competition with one another. Like his weaknesses. Keep your enemies close, and all that.

Goodness, I'm thinking like a movie villain. Or maybe I'm just thinking like a woman who wants to get ahead and won't lie down and let her future happen without doing anything to sway it.

Benny interrupts my thoughts, adding, "My treat. Please?"

I scrunch my nose. Even a movie villain can cover her own bill, thank you. "No."

"No? That's it?" he scoffs. I get the sense he's not rejected often, and I want to make him sweat it out a bit more, but . . .

"No, you won't pay. I'll go, but I'll pay for myself. Lunch Saturday. Do you have your phone?"

That smug smile is back and I find myself regretting my decision already, but it's my own fault. He pulls his phone from his back pocket and hands it to me, and I enter my number.

"Reese Camden," I say as I hand it back to him. As if he has seven other Reeses in his contacts already. "Text me and we'll pick a time and place."

"No need to beg, now," Benny teases, leaning against the counter and folding those annoyingly nice arms over his chest.

I turn on a heel and start to leave the kitchen without another word.

"Looking forward to it!" he calls after me, and I feel my frown deepen. That sure makes one of us, bud.

Chapter Three

I'm feeling some semblance of calm as I walk to meet Benny on Saturday. I didn't see him at the office yesterday, but he texted last night suggesting a place close enough to the Seattle U dorm where I'm renting a room for the summer that I suspect he might be staying on campus, too. I was happy to agree this time, intimidated as ever by the what-do-I-feel-like-eating decision in a city where I don't know any restaurants.

I enter through the café's heavy glass door and a quick scan tells me that Benny isn't here yet. I hate to awkwardly hang around, pretending to look at stuff on my phone, so I go ahead and ask for a table for two. The hostess seats me by the window. I pull out the sketch pad and pencils that I always carry with me, hoping to play around while I wait, but something moves in my peripheral vision less than a minute later. I look up to find I have the perfect view of Benny jogging across the street my way.

I'm not a fan of the dropping feeling in my stomach when

I see him, like I'm on a roller coaster that's about to plummet. He's in a T-shirt and jeans again, the former of which clings to his broad chest and biceps. Seriously, they make shirts in bigger sizes. He has to know what he's doing. His head is covered again with a backward baseball cap, just the tiniest glimpse of dark hair peeking out in front. But it's probably his face more than anything. The face that seems to be in an easy perma-smile, usually one-sided, often with dimples. Dark eyes shadowed with unfairly long lashes.

I shove these observations out of my mind and my drawing stuff back into my bag as he enters the restaurant, and try to not notice the way his face starts doing that smoldering thing when he catches sight of me.

Oh, he is trouble.

But this is a fact-finding mission only. Information gathering. We are not friends. For some reason, my idiot body doesn't get the memo and decides to stand up when he approaches the table, meaning it now looks like I expect to be greeted somehow. I almost sit right back down again, but I feel like that would be weirder, so I stand there and hope he decides how to deal with my absurdity.

When Benny gets close, he starts to raise his arms the slightest amount and I see the hesitation on his face. Taking pity since I put us in this situation, I mimic the action and lean closer. The result is a loose, awkward half hug like we're two middle schoolers at church camp trying to leave room for Jesus.

"Hey, Reese," he says smoothly, giving me a wink as we both take our seats. The hug was *definitely* a mistake.

"Hey, how are you?" I reply in a monotone, trying to look totally unimpressed by him and very occupied with spreading my napkin across my lap.

"Can't complain. My neighbor—who I'm convinced must be a bullfighter who practices in his room, that's the only way he could possibly make that much noise—he must've been out last night. I slept like a baby for the first time since I've been here. How about you?"

"Fine," I say curtly. "Are you in Seattle U summer housing, too? I saw you walking here from the same direction."

Benny smiles. "The very same. Wait—are you my bullfighting neighbor?"

I give him a withering look, daring to look his stupid handsomeness in the eye again. "Doubtful. There was as much noise coming from my room last night as there usually is." I hear every which way he could run with that sentence and choke on my own spit. "Um, I mean, which is to say, very little noise. Because I'm quiet. And I live alone."

Benny presses his lips together and his eyes practically glitter, one eyebrow rising in a way that could mean a lot of things. Good gravy, can I *please* pull it together?

Before I can say or do anything else moronic, the waiter shows up to take our orders. Instinctively, I say, "Sweet tea, please."

The waiter—as they always do on this side of the country—

starts in on the standard, "We just have unsweetened, but I can bring you some sug—"

"Just water, actually. Thanks."

Benny holds up two fingers and he and the guy exchange nods before the latter goes to get our drinks. Across the table, Benny gives me a curious look.

"Not into self-serve sweetening, Reese's Cup?"

I shoot him another stern glance at the return of the nickname and start to fiddle with my silverware roll. "It's not the same as sweet tea."

He folds his bulky arms across his chest. I won't give him the satisfaction of staring, but I'm legitimately fascinated that he's able to keep up this body type while working in a kitchen. He's probably one of those guys who spends all his free time at the gym, lifting weights in front of the mirror, taking "progress" selfies. I smirk at the thought.

"Isn't it? Tea plus sugar equals . . ."

I let out a sigh. "It's like people outside the South don't understand how solubility works, I swear. With sweet tea, sugar is part of the preparation while it's still hot, so it gets all good and blended. Now, if he brought me a cup of what y'all call 'iced tea' and a couple packets of sugar, I'd have to stir for half the lunch to dissolve it, at which point it isn't even gonna taste the same *and* I'll have wasted all that time and effort. Thank you kindly, but pass."

Benny leans back in his chair and scratches at the light stubble along his jaw while amusement flickers across his face. "Solubility, huh? Seems I've touched a nerve. Maybe you can make me the real stuff sometime."

It's my turn to raise an eyebrow as I lean back, starting to feel like I'm holding my own in this back-and-forth. I guess that's just the power of my feelings for sweet tea. "I'm sure they sell it at the grocery store."

He laughs, as if I wasn't totally serious.

"I love your accent, by the way." He pauses, seeming to search for words and I focus hard on trying to suppress the weird, nervous-Chihuahua-shaking my heart is doing. The flirt game is too strong with this one. I can't let it distract me. "It, like, gives everything you say this . . . this sweetness but also sounds slow and smooth, like it's dripping with honey, or molasses."

Excuse me . . . *what?* I feel my mouth open and close a couple of times like I'm trying to catch flies. But I can't come up with the words to respond to . . . whatever that was.

And then I can't help but laugh. Benny tilts his head in confusion and maybe a little amusement, and I recover enough to say, "Oh good gracious. What a line! Has that—has that worked for you before? With the last girl you met from the South? Honestly, it felt a little clunky toward the end. I think it could use some refinement. Like honey. Or molasses."

Benny shakes his head, looking down at his lap with an almost sheepish little laugh. "Damn. You're not gonna give me anything, huh? I meant it as a compliment. I really like to hear you talk. In the most appropriate, workplace-safe way, of course."

He looks back up with a wink that suggests anything but

workplace appropriate, and I narrow my eyes. Tucking a lock of hair behind my ear, I shake my head. "Uh-huh, right. I'm not sure I buy that. No one's ever told me they like the way I talk."

He leans forward again and folds his hands on the table. "Yeah, no one's ever *told* you. I'm sure plenty have thought it."

Before I have time to respond, the waiter returns to drop off our waters and ask whether we're ready to order. Neither of us have even looked at the menu yet, but when Benny and I look at each other, it seems we mutually decide to make selections on the spot. He gets flatbread pizza and I pick the black bean burger.

The waiter takes our menus and Benny refocuses on me. "So, speaking of the accent. Kentucky, right?" I rear back in surprise. He's either an accent savant—doubtful—or he's done some snooping. Either way, I give a hesitant nod and he continues. "What brought you out here?"

I feel my brows draw together, confusion surely plain on my face. "Uh . . . Friends of Flavor?"

Benny waves a hand. "Yeah, yeah, but you know what I mean. Why Friends of Flavor? How'd you find it? What's your story and all that?"

His question raises my defensive porcupine quills. I've known this guy for all of forty-eight hours. I don't owe him my "story" yet. Honestly, I don't know if I'd tell him my full story if I'd known him forty-eight weeks. Painting the whole picture would make me revisit some painful parts of the past, parts only a handful of people in my life know. And I don't think Mr. Never Skips Arm Day here is gonna join that group.

"You first," I say, stalling.

His eyes do their twinkly amused thing again and he shrugs. "All right. Well, I told you about the family restaurant in San Francisco, right? Beneventi's. Family owned and operated for thirty years. Ma and Pops run a tight ship. I'm the youngest of four boys, and my brothers—Manny, Leo, and Enzo—are all in their twenties and working there full time. It was always my part-time gig after school and this summer, I probably would've started full time too, but I, uh . . . Well, I was curious about trying something a little different before I'm locked in to the family biz forever."

There's something about the way he says "forever," kind of low and distant, that makes me think there's more to that story. That plus the far-off look in his eyes for a few moments, before he seems to shake himself back to the present. *Ding, ding, ding.* I tuck the moment carefully into my mental (B)enemy intel file.

"So I found this! It's been cool so far, working with the Friends. I'd watched some of their shows before, obviously, but seeing it all happen live is something else. I've spent the most time with Seb and Aiden while they film *Good Chef/Bad Chef,* a little bit with Raj when he's not traveling, but they're all chill and fun. Mostly. Aiden has his moments."

He says this so casually, like he's not talking about my biggest celebrity crushes whom I've obsessed over for years. But to him, I guess they're no big deal. They're always in the studio or prep kitchens, where Benny works, filming, developing recipes, or workshopping new ideas for their respective series. But with my job so far consisting mostly of engaging on social media, there hasn't been any reason for me to take part in the actual content creation for the channel. I feel a pang of jealousy—the only Friend I've "met" so far is Aiden, and I wouldn't call it much of a meeting.

I clear my throat, and try to do the same with my wandering mind. "That must be fun. I spend most of my time at a desk. Or at a TV tray, pretending it's a desk, to be more accurate."

Benny laughs. "So is it everything you dreamed of, coming out to the West Coast for this big fancy internship?"

He's teasing, but since he did open up a little about his family and his reasons for being here, I feel like I can give him a crumb or two. If only to keep him from getting suspicious about my motives for coming to lunch today. "In some ways, yes. I've been a huge Friends of Flavor fan for years and a career with them has been a dream of mine, but I haven't had any culinary training outside of cooking with my family. So I knew if I wanted to work here, I'd have to find another in. I kind of couldn't believe my luck when the marketing position showed up. I did all the graphic design work—page layouts, ads, a bunch of web content—for my high school newspaper, and I also wrote a small food column, with restaurant reviews and new recipes I'd tried, and included my own illustrations. I sent a whole portfolio of samples in with my application. I thought I'd be doing more design stuff for videos and marketing campaigns and less of the social media maintenance they've had me on so far. But I'm just trying to work hard and make a good impression in the mean-time, and hopefully I'll get a chance to show what skills I have and learn more—especially around the kitchens."

Pausing over a sip of water, I remind myself—*fact-finding mission*. What can I drop in about my own goals to get Benny to tell me what I really want to know?

"I think I want to stay in marketing or something else behind the scenes long term, but they don't have many opportunities for someone without a college degree, and it would probably help to get a better grasp on the food side of things, too. I'm starting at UW in September," I add with forced casualness, "so I'm really hoping they keep me on for the fall semester culinary internship and see where that could take me."

"Same here," Benny says, leveling a steady look at me as he takes his own sip of water.

My breath catches. Is he saying what I think he's saying?

"Y-you're going to UW too?" I ask, crossing my fingers under the table.

He sets his glass down. "No. I want the fall semester culinary internship."

Even though I set us both up for this bomb, there's still a record-scratch sound in my head.

Our waiter returns with our food just then, and I could kiss his aloof little face. I don't know if the interruption has distracted Benny or if he senses the need for a change of subject, but as we start to eat, he pivots to asking me about myself outside of work.

43

I don't give him a whole lot to work with, conversation-wise. It's a lot of questions on his end and brief replies on mine.

"So, you have any siblings?"

"Yes."

"Brothers, sisters?"

"Two brothers."

"Older or younger?"

"Brian is fourteen and Elliot is twelve."

"Oh, nice."

Cue my nodding and eating in silence until he comes up with the next blandest topic to ask me about. Rinse, repeat.

Fortunately—for the purposes of getting through this lunch, not necessarily fortunate in general—Benny is good at talking about himself unprompted. Before long, he starts filling the silences I leave with stories about Italy and his family. He even talks about Seattle's weather.

But the whole time, the facts are running through my mind on a loop: one fall semester culinary internship, two of us. Plus, of course, who knows how many other, random applicants who don't have the leg up of already working at Friends of Flavor. All the descriptions of the fall internship, and even the onboarding materials for my current position, have *strongly implied* that the semester-long program is intended for those with previous FoF or UltiMedia experience. In spite of us being very different people with very different responsibilities in our respective roles, it looks like Benny is officially my competition. And frankly, given that he currently occupies the summer version of the position we're vying for, I'm not sure that I like my odds.

Taking another sip of water, I study the boy opposite me. He's gesturing wildly, telling some story about his parents' restaurant using his hands as much as his words. Is he preoccupied with thinking of me as his competition, too? Somehow I doubt it. I click buttons all day and generate pithy replies to comments. He pals around with the actual Friends themselves and is a natural in the kitchen. So far I've been banking on the hope that my range of talents will work in my favor, my well-roundedness outweighing whatever I lack in advanced culinary capabilities. But Benny's already a good cook, and who knows what kind of other skills he's hiding under that ball cap? His range might very well put mine to shame.

". . . and it's like, what kind of person pairs a red wine with scallops, you know?"

Benny pauses as if expecting a reaction from me. I haven't even heard most of what he's been rambling on about, but I have, like, zero thoughts on red wine *or* scallops. Never tried the former, might have sampled the latter once when my family took a vacation to Florida. Why am I such an uncultured swine?

"Totally," I mumble. He doesn't seem to notice anything amiss, though, and launches into another tale about his brother Enzo.

Temporarily freed from my conversational duties again, I sink farther into my seat and stew. Benny was *so* good filming our video the other day. We haven't seen the final product, of course, but it was obvious that it was his comfort zone and not mine. I felt awkward, worried about how I looked and sounded and how I would be perceived by viewers. Will they think I'm a dumb blonde for not knowing enough about cooking, for messing up with the food processor? Will they think I'm uptight and no fun for not going along with all of Benny's jokes and flirting? It seems inevitable that he'll be the audience favorite, as he fell so easily into the role of the guy who is somehow both in control and laid-back, who has the whole situation in the palm of his hand.

What a blessing it must be to be a good-looking, confident dude.

On the other hand, even if I had been better prepared or more knowledgeable, I probably wouldn't be accepted as easily as Benny. I'd be a know-it-all or bossy. If I laughed at all his jokes and went along with everything he said, I'd be a ditz or falling all over him. It's just another one of what seems like countless situations in life where as a woman, you can't win.

". . . and what's even the point in trying, right?"

Benny's words and subsequent pause stir me from my thoughts. It's almost as if he could hear me thinking, and the question feels like a challenge. Externally, I shrug noncommittally.

But internally, something is ignited. There's *so* much point in trying, no matter how much I try to convince myself that he already has an advantage. I'm not going to give up that easily.

The viewers of our brush with internet fame don't have to like me. Benny himself doesn't have to like me. Actually, Benny in particular probably *shouldn't* like me. Because my eyes are on the prize that is the fall semester internship. And that means doing everything in my power to make our bosses like me, respect me, and want to keep me around at least as much as they want Benny—preferably a whole lot more.

I've made the mistake before of letting my guard down too easily—letting the wrong people in and allowing them to see my vulnerable side, my weaknesses. I've been walked all over because I'm young and polite, naive and eager to please. But here, this summer, in the midst of the coolest opportunity I've ever been given, I won't fall into old patterns. I'll keep my focus on my goals. Make work a No Feelings Zone. I won't give anyone reason to see me as less than capable. I'll be so objectively good that they can't count me out.

Especially now that I have this smooth-talking, good-looking foil as competition. I wonder if Benny can tell how far my mind is from the café by the time we're finishing up and paying our bills. It's a dozen city blocks away at the Friends of Flavor offices, planning how to be the best intern they've ever had.

And planning to never again go out to lunch with a certain boy with dangerous levels of charm.

He aims said weapon at me once more as we're leaving the restaurant, sliding his hands in his pockets and giving me that one-sided grin. "Glad you decided to give me a chance, Reese's Cup?"

Oh, if he only knew how very quickly my feelings are running in the opposite direction.

"Sure, glad's one word for it," I murmur, letting my lips curve up in what hopefully passes for a smile. Other words for it include "remorseful" and "sorely-mistaken-but-won't-let-it-happen-twice."

Benny flashes a full smile at me then, one I can scarcely look at if I want to keep this newfound resolve of mine. We walk toward the dorms, and I repeat in my head all of the reasons I can't let this guy any closer than he's already wriggled in.

I have a feeling this summer is going to be a long and wild ride. Benny Beneventi had better buckle up.

Chapter Four

"**W**hat does 'ship' mean? Aside from a large boat."

This is how Margie greets me when I walk into the marketing office on Monday morning. I set my stuff down, then walk to her desk, where she has not yet looked up from her phone.

"Um. What's the context?"

"Your video went live this morning," she says, still scrolling, and my heart stops. I vaguely remember Aiden saying that it would, but I thought I'd have more time to mentally prepare.

With effort, I tune back in to what Margie is saying. "I check comments occasionally, just to see how people are responding, and there's a lot of 'new ship,' 'I ship it,' and so on. What is all that?"

I blink at her and feel the heat rising in my cheeks. Where's the accidental pistachio face mask when you need it?

"I . . . Uh. Let me, um, watch it and I—I'll take a look at the comments after," I say.

She nods, already distracted by some other task on her

computer. I walk back to my pseudo desk on shaky legs and open up my laptop. Of course I know what "ship" is, and I have a suspicion as to what's going on in the comments. But do I have even the faintest interest in explaining that to my boss?

I would rather put a bar of soap in my own mouth, frankly.

Before checking on whatever online horrors await me, I pull my buzzing phone out of my pocket. I've felt the texts piling up, and can only hope they might prepare me for the worst of it.

Natalie: OH

Natalie: MY

Natalie: GODDDDDD

Natalie: REESE CAMDEN, FRIEND OF FLAVOR!!!

Clara: wait what's going on I just woke up

Natalie and Clara are the biggest Friends of Flavor fans I know. Of course Nat's seen the video already. I put my clammy palm to my forehead. I should've told them what was coming over the weekend, but I got distracted by the whole Benny lunch scenario, then a "social platform management" webinar Margie assigned me, and plotting out my path to ultimate intern domination, and, well, the time got away from me.

Natalie has sent five screenshots in rapid succession from what I assume are different parts of the video, but I don't look too closely.

Clara: . . . excuse me what

Clara: is that real??

Natalie: YES CLAR I WOULD NOT CREATE FAKE
SCREENGRABS OF OUR BFF REESE IN AN ACTUAL
REAL LIFE FOF VIDEO ON THEIR REAL LIFE CHANNEL

Clara: ok can you stop yelling

Clara: but R, this is so sick!! tell us more!

Natalie: I WILL NOT BE FORCED TO TEMPER MY
EXCITEMENT AT A TIME SUCH AS THIS

Natalie: But my inner voice is getting tired so

Natalie: Reesey, explain yourself stat!!! I'll just be
watching this on repeat till you do

I have not had enough tea to deal with this yet. I reach into
my bag with shaking hands and pull out a pair of headphones,
discreetly plug them into the laptop, and pull up Friends of Flavor's page on UltiMedia. Welp, there's me. Front and center, in a
screengrab with the words AMATEUR HOUR superimposed under
Benny's and my smiling faces. Faces . . . that are smiling at each
other rather than at the camera.

Er. This isn't encouraging.

With a quivering hand, I push Play. My heart is pounding
and I feel the stress sweats coming on, just from seeing my face

on-screen. I'm really in a video on Friends of Flavor. A video that millions will likely watch, and judge, and comment upon.

Oh my stars. Oh no. Ohhh, what have I done?

The video starts, of course, with Benny's smooth intro. I notice that as natural as he seems in real life, he comes across even better on-camera. He looks confident and comfortable, talking with his hands in a way that would look like awkward flailing if I did it, but on him is cool.

The ten minutes that follow include a lot of our banter, even a fair amount that I thought would get cut. There's my screwup with the food processor played at regular speed, then again in slow motion, then slower motion, then one more time at regular speed for good measure. I have to fight really hard not to laugh out loud.

But besides that, I spend a lot of the video mesmerized. It's all moments that I remember. But threaded together the way they are, with zoomed-in shots on our faces or hands at certain moments and emphasis on lines one or the other of us said . . . Benny and I look like the two leads in a gosh darn romantic comedy.

I feel my face flaming red by the end of the ten minutes and thirty-two seconds.

We did *not* look that cutesy in person, right? I mean, my goodness. At times, it wasn't even just cutesy, like when he was cleaning pistachio off my face and then went on to draw on me with batter. His fingers weren't running over my cheeks that slowly, that *tenderly*, were they? Surely they added some weird effect there. And they kept making it look like Benny is watching me when I'm not looking. Not just watching, *gazing*. There are a few shots of me doing it right back, which I certainly don't recall.

And the banter seems so much more . . . I don't even know, *charged*. Was it charged when it was happening? Annoying at times, maybe, and definitely funny at others. But my gosh, we were making macarons! That was the main focus. The video would have you believing we were on a first date with some light pastry-making on the side.

I, for one, am appalled.

I'm even more scared to scroll down to the comments now, but since that is my actual job, I make myself.

Omg these 2 are the CUTEST . . .

wow I ship this so hard, is it creepy to ship a couple teenagers, idc

Benny is hot pls tell me he's legal

Didn't expect to find my new OTP in a FoF vid but here we are

Reese could get it, js

More Benny and Reese!!! Gotta see the romance play out!

When he painted her face I think it made me believe
in love again

"Reese's Cup" omg I SCREAMED he loves her

So they totally want each other, right? I'm not
imagining it?

SHIP IT. This is better than cable omfg

I slam my laptop shut and yank the headphones free. It makes more of a commotion than I meant to, and the others turn to look at me.

"Sorry," I whisper. Then I sink down in my seat and rub my temples.

Well, didn't see that one coming.

I can't believe I didn't think to let any of my family or friends back home know about this over the weekend. Of course Nat and Clara are shocked that I didn't give them a warning. They're the only ones who keep up with FoF, but that doesn't mean this won't find its way onto the phones or computer screens of everyone else I know by the end of the day. The internet is weird like that, and everyone in my community seems to know everybody's business, so if even one person comes across me in a video, it'll be everywhere. This might be okay if it was just a normal cooking show with normal amounts of charm and personality from the host, the kind of stuff most Friends of Flavor videos contain. But this? This'll have Mamaw starting to plan my wedding to Benny before the week is through.

I'm more concerned about what everyone else in my world will say, though.

Not to mention, the editors left my "damn" in. Even bleeped, you can tell there's an offensive word.

Hell's bells. This is so far above my pay grade.

I sit there in sulky silence for a few more minutes, processing what I just watched and read and how the devil I'm supposed to deal with it, both in the job and personal capacities.

I realize, rationally, that the video is perfectly innocent. There is nothing inappropriate going on between Benny and me, even with the clever editing and everything. But in my experience, people will take anything and run with it.

And as the comments have made clear, they already have.

I let my head fall into my hands, all of the unwelcome thoughts starting to flood in. Thoughts of what happened the last time I had much of an online presence. The last time I got involved with a boy and the outside world saw fit to comment on how I conducted myself with him. Of all the labels that stuck to me over the course of a few months during my freshman year of high school—*slut, easy, bitch.* Labels that kicked off a long list of judgments and names and presumptions.

I'm so careful about how I interact with the people around me, especially with guys. I know that I keep walls up, but those walls have kept me safe in the time since it all fell apart. I thought

I'd been keeping myself well and truly guarded in the time that I've been here, several thousand miles from my old life, but clearly I've already become too comfortable. I let myself get dragged into the brightest of spotlights that's ever been on me, and even let a bit of my real self show while I was at it. And now it's out there for strangers on the internet to think and say whatever they want. Reese Camden, happy, at ease, and, sure, having a little fun with a cute boy. The response is positive.

Up until it isn't anymore.

"Reese?"

My head shoots back up at the sound of Margie's voice. I twist around in my chair, feeling the blood draining out of my face.

"Yes, ma'am?"

She is leaning casually against her desk with her arms crossed. "What did I say about the ma'am thing?"

I give her a sheepish smile. "Oh, uh, sorry."

She studies me for a moment and I can't read her expression. "Everything good?"

That, I didn't see coming. Margie's been a perfectly nice boss so far; she never raises her voice or snaps at anyone. The only minor "issue" she and I have had was over my calling her "ma'am" during my first couple of days. A tough habit to break for one raised to be a polite young lady. But this is the closest we've come yet to any kind of personal conversation.

"Yep!" I say brightly, nipping said personal conversation in the bud.

She looks skeptical, probably because she's not an idiot. "Something wrong with the video?"

I swallow heavily and consider how to answer this. *Yes, the fact that I'm in it!*

"Um," I start, ever the shining beacon of confidence and clarity. "No, it's—I mean, I'm fine. It's just, er, hitting me that I'm in a video. On Friends of Flavor. Like, one that people are going to see."

There's a tinge of sympathy in the small smile Margie gives me. "Sure. I know it isn't what you signed on for. It turned out great, though, really. You did a wonderful job and it seems like everyone loves it so far."

"So far" is the operative phrase. But I nod and thank her, and she encourages me to take a lap and get some water before returning to my work for the day. I do, but to little avail.

Back at my computer, I decide to largely ignore comments on *Piece of Cake: Amateur Hour* for now. I don't know how Friends of Flavor can appropriately respond to comments about their eighteen-year-old interns' fictional relationship anyway.

There are some pictures from the Friends' Chicago trip on the other platforms, and I spend most of the day liking and replying to responses on those photos as well as answering some of the many random questions that come at us on a daily basis. On my lunch break, I text the family group chat with my mom, dad, and little brothers to tell them about the video. I make it sound like it's a good thing that I am totally excited about and that it is not at all sending me into a worry spiral. I don't know if they'll watch the video. Then I check the group text with Natalie and Clara. My phone has continued to vibrate with their incoming thoughts since I last checked it.

Clara: wow that was seriously cute, this is so exciting

Natalie: Um YEAH don't even get me started on the actual CONTENT too LATE you DID so here I go—you and ball cap Benny would be hot together

Clara: ^agreed

Natalie: Boy is allllll over you and I hope you've gotten some digits slash maybe you didn't tell us about this ALL EFFING WEEKEND because you were too busy making out with your new boyfriend

Clara: definitely sounds like Reese yep

Natalie: The chemistry! I feel it clear across the country! It is absolutely radiating from my laptop screen!!

Natalie: This is the most exciting thing that's happened to me all summer. Maybe all year. Acceptance to college? Pfft

Clara: same

That's where they've left off, and I laugh in spite of my inner panic. I halfway consider waiting until I'm back at the dorm to tackle this conversation, but honestly, I might need some best-friend encouragement if I'm going to survive the rest of the day.

> **Reese:** Hiii I'm sorry for not properly preparing you! But I've kind of been pretending it wasn't happening!

> **Natalie:** Why would you ever!!! You were amazing!!!!! I'm picking out names for you + Benny's children!!!

> **Reese:** Yeah that last one is why

> **Reese:** I'm freaking out, y'all. I never thought I'd actually be in videos and it happened really suddenly and now potentially millions of people could see me and judge me and it could be like high school x 1000

> **Clara:** deeeeep breaths, you know logically you're jumping to the worst possible outcomes right? much more likely, people will keep thinking you're cute and fun like they do in the comments so far and maybe it could help you get the fall internship

I run a hand over my face and follow Clara's advice, even if she didn't mean it literally, inhaling for a few seconds, then exhaling for a few more. Repeat. Repeat. I peek over my shoulder to check out any activity around the office. It's quiet, with my marketing coworkers tapping away at their computers. I see some folks hustling through the hallways, but it all looks the same as usual. No one is running around with a megaphone yelling, "ALERT! INTERNS' VIDEO HAS GONE LIVE! TOTAL DISASTER! EVERYONE PANIC!"

No, that's only happening within my own mind. But I'm comforted by how unaffected the rest of the world is, how this is clearly *only* a big deal to me. And maybe Benny. If I cared to interact with Benny any further, I might reach out, see where his head is at. If we were friends, that's what I'd do.

But we're not, and we never will be. I return to the two friends in my texts, who have always been and will continue to be the only ones I need.

> **Natalie:** This is NOT high school anymore!! We are DONE with that mess, a mess that was never even your fault to begin with, which I will keep reminding you forever and ever amen

> **Reese:** It just feels like the chances of this turning bad are higher than y'all think they are

> **Reese:** I don't even want people to think Benny and I are cute together or whatever, it's way too close to other less flattering things they could speculate about

> **Reese:** That's *not* helping my whole "pls take me seriously, bosses and coworkers" vibe

> **Clara:** I don't think you should even worry about that part. let this be a fun exciting thing ok? I know it's easier said than done but try to enjoy

Natalie: ^ what she said. Remember that post on TKM where Katherine talked about asking for a raise, and how in this case it was helpful to think "hey, a man wouldn't worry about x, y, z"? You know a dude would NOT care one bit if people thought he looked cozy w his hot girl costar

Natalie: Ik ik it's different but IT SHOULDN'T BE

Natalie: You just need to be proud of yourself for doing this cool thing!! Keep doin you and who knows where it could lead!!

She knows she's got me when she references TKM—the Kat's Muse, aka FoF chef Katherine's blog and our guide to existing in the world as the confident women we are, or at least want to be. Basically, a guide to becoming Katherine. We've been reading it as long as we've been following the channel, since we fell in love with her through her hugely popular series, *Fuss-Free Foodie*. Katherine's personality is as no-fuss as her food, her reddish-brown curls often thrown up in a topknot above one of her signature slouchy-tee-and-leggings ensembles. She somehow comes across like both the coolest girl in school and everyone's best friend.

I remember the post Nat's talking about; I'm pretty sure it's bookmarked on my laptop. Not because I plan on asking for a raise anytime soon—Lord knows I'm just trying to hold down this minimum-wage situation. But the post has a lot of advice that's relevant to the kind of driven, single-track mindset I want to have in my career, to shutting off the inner voice that wonders whether I'm good enough and projecting total confidence regardless of whether or not I feel it.

Yeah, I definitely do *not* feel it. Yet. But Natalie's right—I should try not to let my worries get in the way of enjoying this fun, unexpected success.

Reese: Y'all are right, per usual. I'll try to chill

Clara: you're doing your best, I know it's prob stressful

Natalie: Ok so now that you're chill . . . you've gotten Benny's # right don't lie

Reese: . . .

Natalie: YES MY QUEEN GET ITTT

Reese: Technically, I do have his number. But it is NOT like that, no matter what the video looked like. He's kind of a tool, knows he's hot, etc. Not into it

Natalie: Hmm . . .

Reese: I'm serious!

Clara: hmm . . .

Reese: Clara!! I expect better from you

Natalie: Jk, I trust your judgment and all that. But in case you change your mind, I will hold on to my list

Reese: List?

Natalie: Baby names

Reese: Oh ffs

I set my phone down and sigh. I wish it felt as simple to me as it does to them, to start over and have a casual thing with a guy. But Benny and I do not and will not ever have a *relationship.* Regardless of how some fancy camera tricks made it look.

Chapter Five

I'm sitting at my desk again for lunch, doodling in my sketch pad to try to relax while I half-heartedly pick at my sandwich, when Margie strolls in.

"Hey, Reese, sorry to bother you on your lunch break, but when you're done, can you meet Aiden and me in his office?"

My stomach drops. *No.* I've been at lunch for twenty minutes—what could have shifted so horribly in twenty minutes?

The petrification I feel must show on my face as I nod, because Margie gives me one of her cool smiles. "Nothing bad, I promise. You're a hit! See you in a few."

That does little to assuage my fears. I look around for some magical cure to my worries and decide to chug my full water bottle. People are always preaching the benefits of water, and I never drink enough. Maybe it'll purify my skin *and* cleanse me of the irrational shame and dread that seems to be embedded in my bones.

Aiden's office is, naturally, in one of the far corners of the Friends of Flavor side of the floor. I haven't been inside, but it was pointed out by Margie with more than a hint of envy when she gave me a tour on my first day.

I shouldn't be surprised to see Benny sitting on the cushy leather couch when I walk in, but I am. I lift a hand in response to his warm, easy smile. Aiden and Margie sit in the two leather club chairs in front of Aiden's desk, so the only seat left is on the couch with Benny.

Of course it is.

I settle into the other end, which leaves the middle cushion between us, and fold my hands in my lap in the hope that it hides their shaking. Aiden crosses one leg over the other and leans toward Benny and me, clearing his throat before he speaks.

"Benny, Reese. Thanks for coming." As if there was another option? "And thanks for your participation in the most recent episode of *Piece of Cake.* As you may have noticed if you've been checking in or if you've heard from Margie, it's . . . Well, it seems like you two are a huge success."

Benny's head—covered in yet another backward baseball cap—jerks back in surprise. I guess this is the first he's hearing of it. So he must not have spent the whole morning obsessing over the opinions of millions of people who woke up to our faces on the UltiMedia home page. Wonder what that's like.

"Seriously, we don't often get this much engagement within

the first twelve hours, between views, shares, comments, and the like. Margie's idea was a good one."

Am I imagining the flicker of pain across Aiden's face when he says that last part?

Margie takes over. "I told Aiden how smoothly filming went, too, and all things considered, we've been discussing the possibility of filming more content with you both."

Now it's my turn to be startled. They want us to make *more videos*? On some weird impulse, I turn to look at Benny just as he's looking at me. Having known each other for all of four days, our telepathy isn't flawless, but what passes between us is something akin to *what on earth are they talking about?*

That's what's going through my mind anyway.

"We still have a lot of details to work out, of course, but we wanted to run it by you, see where your heads are," Aiden says. "The suits—er, our CEO and other company executives who approve decisions like these, they're on board so far and pleased with how the first one went. We don't know exactly what an ongoing series with you two would look like, but it would likely be under the *Amateur Hour* name and involve a lot of improvisation, because you both did so well with that and the chemistry was great. On a more practical level, since we know this isn't what you signed up for with your respective internship roles, it would involve a change in day-to-day responsibilities and certainly a raise. You would still spend most of your time on your current duties, and we'd work filming new video content into your schedules here and there as we get the series planned out."

"As we said," Margie goes on, "more detail-oriented talks will happen down the road. But we want to hear any questions, comments, or concerns you might have. Do any immediately come to mind?"

Um . . . yes? Several?

I look at Benny again. He's staring at our bosses with an expression of amused bewilderment that he might have if they'd just stood before us in their underwear and done the chicken dance. But he nods after a moment. "Sounds fun."

Something is bubbling up in my throat that could be a laugh or a cry. I can't determine which. This was not on my agenda for today. Nor for the summer, or my whole life, really. I'm a behind-the-scenes gal all the way. My gut instinct is *no, No, NO!* If I make it through one video with minimal public fallout, that's more than enough. Why risk putting myself out there in a way that could do further damage to my life, my future, my psyche, for goodness' sake?

But then Aiden says the one thing to get me reconsidering. "It would also, of course, be a good trial period of sorts for further employment opportunities."

Oh good gravy. My ass is grass, isn't it? Of course the fall internship is on the line. And therefore of course I'm going to say yes to this proposal.

But . . .

"What if I have conditions?" I say, then immediately feel my face flame red because who the hell do I think I am? Anyone other than the brand-new, green-as-all-get-out summer intern desperate to make a good impression, apparently.

Margie and Aiden look equally surprised by my question. Margie's features settle back into a placid expression before Aiden's do and she gestures for me to proceed. "Share them."

Okay, brain, time to come up with your conditions. My main concerns, I guess, all center on being in the public eye and being privy to too many thoughts and opinions and critiques of me. And how I would rather not see any of them, if I'm going to stay focused on myself and my priorities.

So I improvise.

"See, I know that one of my main responsibilities is engaging with our audience on social media. But I was wondering if, possibly, in the case of videos that I'm in, I could . . . maybe not be responsible for reading and responding to those comments."

Aiden looks perplexed, like he can't understand why I'd ask such a thing, but Margie's face gives nothing away. After a moment she says, "Right. I think I understand your concern, and I could have someone else in marketing deal with engagement on your videos. But I do wonder about how you'll handle your own social media. Anyone who joins Friends of Flavor and starts appearing on our channel generally sees a substantial increase in their following on personal social networks. In other words, you would become a public persona and the public will want to follow your life off camera, what you post when you have a new episode up, et cetera. It's part of why each of the Friends is so popular—viewers develop an attachment to them. Are you prepared for that?"

I feel myself fidgeting an uncool amount, but I can't stop. "Um, well, it might not be as much of an issue since I don't have any personal social media accounts."

Now it's Margie's turn to match Aiden's befuddled look, but it's the latter who says, "You don't? That's something you'll need to fix."

I feel my whole body tense up but try to sound confident as I answer, "I would rather not."

I'm probably starting to sound like I'm on the run from the law or something. But is it really so ridiculous? I guess at a company that relies on the internet and social media—and where my entire job so far has been using social media—the answer is yes. I thought I got this role because of my graphic design abilities and other work at my school newspaper, though, and replying to comments and clicking Like has been easy enough that I've rolled with it.

Becoming an online personality was never part of the plan. Then again, neither was appearing on camera.

Margie raises an eyebrow and I fear I've completely blown it. I'm surprised when Benny cuts in. "I'm on all the, er, apps and sites, and I'm fine with people following me. And Reese and I hang out, so I can, you know, Insta-post with her or whatever if that'll make anyone feel better."

Margie and Aiden exchange a long look. Meanwhile, I'm

staring at Benny with my jaw slightly dropped. I wasn't expecting this kind of assist from him. And to say we "hang out" is a little generous for one lunch that will not be happening again. But I suppose I can appreciate the intent.

"All right," Margie finally says with a long-suffering sigh. "Anything else?"

Benny meets my eyes and I see the beginnings of a smile playing at the corners of his mouth. Sure, I'm grateful to him for backing me up, but why do I feel like there are going to be strings attached to his help?

The flicker of competitiveness ignites again within me and I press my lips together. If he thinks he has something over me for this or that I'm gonna go all soft after one nice gesture on his part, he's gotten me wrong.

"I think that covers it," I say.

Close to an hour later, my worries are more about whether this meeting will end before nightfall. Aiden appears to have done some brainstorming over the weekend and came back chock-full of ideas for *Amateur Hour*. He's all emphatic hand movements and white-blond hair standing on end.

Margie, meanwhile, calmly sips her coffee in the chair beside his. Every so often, she pulls out her phone to type something. Whether it's business-related or her texting someone "SOS get me out of this office," I couldn't say. I would be doing the latter if I had any seniority.

My boss seems to reach a limit, though, when Aiden starts

talking about having Benny and me sub for the fishmongers in Pike Place Market for a day.

"Let's perhaps table some of the creative discussions for now and get down to logistics," Margie cuts in, not a moment too soon.

The two superiors go on to explain where we'll go from here, getting paperwork drawn up for us and so on. It all seems to be happening quickly, with plans to film a second video this week getting tossed around. Margie and I split off from the guys before long and head back to marketing, and I try not to feel residual discomfort over my conditions, however small they are.

I get back to the usual grind for the rest of the day, but with a couple of fun extra tasks like picking out an apron online to order. Because, as Margie puts it, "as admirably as you pull off the burlap sack, you shouldn't do it long term." Each of the Friends has a signature apron or two that regular viewers come to recognize. But I never thought about how much pressure there would be to pick one out for myself.

Of course, some of the pressure I feel is only because Benny's plain off-white one looks so maddeningly good on him and there's this totally nonsensical voice in my head saying that I have to look better.

Ultimately, I decide on a soft-pink apron that the reviews describe as lightweight and comfy, and Margie gives me her company card to pay for it. And because Seattle is a magical place, it will arrive in time for our next video.

By the end of the day, I'm tuckered out and ready to crawl home for an ill-advised but hard-to-pass-up evening nap. I'm pulling my bag onto my shoulder and about to turn the corner when I nearly run smack into Benny.

"Hey," he says with a laugh, grabbing my shoulders to steady me as I stumble. "Didn't mean to sneak up on you. Just thought I'd see if you wanted to walk with me, since we're neighbors. But not next-door neighbors, because you don't make noise."

I shuffle awkwardly out of his grip and start heading down the hallway, nodding for him to join me. "Let's go, Eggs Benedict."

As we retrace my morning route—down the elevator, out the doors, and through the maze of busy sidewalks—it feels weird not to be making the journey alone. Benny and I fall into step down the block, walking in silence for a few moments before he glances at me. "So . . . that was something today, huh?"

I let out a laugh that sounds a bit deranged. "What, you don't become an internet sensation every Monday?"

"Listen," he says after a nervous pause, "I mean, I don't wanna pry, and by all means you can tell me to mind my own business, but since we *are* kinda together in this . . . are you really okay with doing a series?"

I tense at the question. "Yes, definitely. Why do you ask?"

Benny looks at me out of the corner of his eye. "I dunno, the social media thing? Not wanting to watch your videos or comments or whatever? You just seemed kinda nervous about it all."

Shit. Boy's got my number. But I don't want him to know it. On the one hand, it's kind of sweet that he's checking in with me, making sure I'm okay with everything. But on the other hand, I feel defensive. He doesn't know me, doesn't have any right to what's going on in my head. And I don't know *him* enough to trust that he won't use any of my weaknesses against me. I consider how best I can put off his questions without giving anything away.

"I'm a very private person," I start carefully. "I love Friends of Flavor more than, like, anything. But I didn't come here with any intention of becoming one of the Friends. I'm much happier behind a screen, keeping my head down, doing the less glamorous, more anonymous work it takes to keep the operation going."

"So you're saying you're more comfortable being on the same side as the thousands of people hiding behind their usernames, posting and commenting and tweeting their opinions about us," he says with a hint of a smirk. *Excuse me?*

"No," I protest. "I've always been a viewer, but never a commenter. I'm not even on social media."

Benny snorts a laugh. "So you said. And yet you're the *social media intern*? How does that happen?"

"I'm the *marketing intern*." I raise a finger to correct him, though the other title would be just as fitting thus far. "And I used to be on social media. I keep up with trends and stuff. I just didn't have the best experience with the . . . the public scrutiny, I guess. If you could call the couple thousand people I went to high school with the public."

"That's weird," he says with an earnestness in his voice and expression that catches me off guard, as much as the fact that he just called me weird. "I mean, not you. But the fact that anyone would 'scrutinize' you. What's not to like? You seem like Little Miss Perfect."

My cheeks flush. "Hardly. But I don't know, it—it's hard to explain. And it's not your problem anyway."

I all but spit the last part out, trying to reestablish some distance between us. Benny nudges my side with his elbow, a move that startles me so much I skip a step. He coughs, trying and failing to cover his laugh, then clears his throat. "You know, you can make it my problem if you want. That's what allies do, right? Help each other with their problems?"

There's a split second after his words settle in. Then I shake my head, picking up my pace to walk ahead of him up the next hilly stretch of sidewalk.

"Are we allies? I must have missed that somewhere between you teasing me about my accent and my name and a heap of other things."

Benny is jogging to catch up with me. "Hey, I said I *like* your accent and then you teased *me* for that. And if I remember correctly, one of the first things I ever said to you was that you share a name with the best candy ever. It's like all my usual charm goes"—he lets out a slow whistle and coasts one of his hands a few inches over the top of my head—"right over this lovely blond noggin."

I scoff, turning the corner onto the street with our dorms. The sky is getting uncharacteristically dark for an otherwise pretty summer day. "Listen, Benny. If we're going to work together, there's gonna be no more of this . . . *charm* offensive you're apparently trying to wage. It's not going to work. We are coworkers, and that is *it*. Not allies, friends, or anything else. You'd better get it through that irritatingly symmetrical skull of yours ASAP."

He raises an eyebrow suggestively, his crooked grin kicking up. "Oh? What's the 'anything else' you speak of, Reese's Pieces? I only offered allyship—any other ideas are all yours."

A disbelieving laugh escapes me before I can stop it. "You're gonna run out of Reese's candy varieties very soon, Benzoyl Peroxide."

Benny stuffs his hands in his pockets, his chest a little too puffed out as my building comes into sight. "Have you considered that maybe I can't help it, that I'm just effortlessly charming?"

"I haven't actually, because I don't care. You should quit it either way. I'm not interested," I huff.

We walk in silence for a few moments, the noise of the city fading into the slightly quieter buzz of the campus, but I swear, I can hear the wheels in his mind turning. I've almost reached my dorm's entrance when he pauses by the fountain.

Then he calls out, "Irritatingly symmetrical, huh?"

And he's on his way, splitting off toward his dorm.

I shake my head as I enter the building and climb the stairs to my room, but my own wheels are turning, and my pulse is picking up speed. And unfortunately, I'm thinking about the moment when he offered, not for the first time, to be my ally. If I'm totally honest with myself, I don't know that the offer is disingenuous. I'm starting to believe that, despite us angling for the same fall job, Benny might actually think we can and should be on the same little intern team this summer. Weirder still is that some part of me warms to the idea, if only for a couple of seconds.

But rationally I know that letting myself entertain the prospect of being his ally or friend is ridiculous. Our relationship will continue to exist firmly in the No Feelings Zone that is the workplace. At the end of the summer, only one of us will get to stay at Friends of Flavor, and it'd better be me.

Now, if only my rational head could get my racing heart on the same page.

Chapter Six

When I pull open the glass doors to Friends of Flavor the next day, Teagan excitedly waves me over to her desk.

"Oh my God, it's the newest star of Friends of Flavor! Can I have your autograph?" she trills at a ridiculously high pitch.

"Stop that!" I hiss, covering my face with my hands. "And I promise you don't want my autograph. My school didn't really teach cursive."

She mimes smacking her forehead with her hand. "Youths these days. How do they expect you to get jobs? To function in the world?"

I shrug with faux wide-eyed innocence. "I don't know. I did learn how to square dance in gym class."

"Now, there's a marketable skill. But seriously, your video was so cute! Have your family and friends back home been watching?"

"A few have," I say, eager to change the subject. "Margie and Aiden asked us to do more. Benny and me. Our own series."

"I heard—how exciting! And yeeeaaah, Benny," she drawls with a gleam in her eye. "What's his deal? Is he single?"

"Easy there, cradle robber," I tease, even though she's only a few years older than me. "I don't know, though. He's . . . a lot."

"Hmm. A lot, huh? A lot of arms and chest and probably abs, too . . ." She trails off, raising a suggestive eyebrow.

I roll my eyes and start to walk away. "Byyyeee, Teagan."

"You're a lot, too, you know! A lot of intelligence and beauty and class!"

I laugh as she keeps calling after me. Margie isn't at her desk yet, so I decide I should settle in and start the daily grind.

I only see a couple more references to Benny and me as I scan through social media and avoid checking our video. An old episode of Lily making shakshuka on her international-cuisine-focused show, *World on a Plate,* got some buzz over the weekend after a Food Network star tweeted about it, so I've had to rewatch it and do a little research on what the heck shakshuka is in order to respond to some of the comments. Then my mouth is watering, because holy yum.

I'm not sure how long I've been favoriting and replying to tweets and comments when a message from Margie pops up in my work email.

R -
Video shoot @ 11, PK 2.
Thx,
M

My shakshuka craving is displaced by a big ol' ball of nerves in my stomach. I confirm that I'll be there, then pull out my phone to text Benny.

Reese: You get the message about a video at 11?

Benny: Of course. They couldn't film without their star

It might be funny if it wasn't so on the nose. I grimace at my phone, considering a sassy retort. But he texts again.

Benny: Meet in PK 1 before?

Reese: Sure

My nerves still aren't settled by the time I set off to meet Benny. When I walk into PK 1, I don't see him. Instead, my eyes are drawn to the gentle giant working a ball of dough between his hands on the counter. He looks up as I approach and flashes me the most dazzling smile I've ever seen.

Seb.

Easily my favorite of the men on Friends of Flavor, he has the build of a professional athlete, but the softest demeanor and a gift for encouraging the aspiring chefs who come on his and Aiden's show. He's the titular good chef to Aiden's bad. They're FoF's answer to *The Great British Bake Off*'s famed judges, if Mary Berry was a tall, gorgeous Black man and Paul Hollywood regularly made competitors cry.

"Hey, you're Reese, right?"

He brushes one of his flour-covered palms off on his apron

and holds it out to me. I walk closer with what I'm sure is an expression of awe on my face.

"Yeah, hi," I manage quietly as my hand meets his.

"Sebastian." He gestures to himself as if I wouldn't know. "You can call me Seb. I saw your video from last week—nicely done!"

"Th-thank you," I stammer. "I've seen . . . all of your videos. I love you." Oh my *God*, Reese, could you be any smoother? I clap a hand over my mouth and he lets out a small laugh, then goes back to working his dough. "I mean, I'm a big fan. Of your show. I love your show."

"Wow, thank you so much," he says sweetly, grinning down at his work. "Maybe we'll get to collaborate sometime. Are you here for the summer?"

"Oh, that would be amazing. Yeah, through August—"

"Not recruiting yourself a new costar, are you, King-Size Reese's Cup?" Benny's voice comes from right behind me and he claps a hand on my shoulder.

I shoot him a menacing look. "I might if you use that mildly insulting nickname variant again."

"So Reese's Pieces was better?"

"Slightly. At least it doesn't comment on my size."

"Noted. Shall we, then?"

Seb glances between us with amusement. I reluctantly nod.

"We'll catch you later, Seb?" Benny asks.

"Maybe," the taller guy says. "I'm just prepping some dough

for Katherine before I head out to teach my yoga class. I'll be back after, if you're still around. Good luck with filming, though—both of you. Friends of Flavor is lucky to have you guys."

Why is he so pure and beautiful? Be still, my nontoxic-masculinity-starved heart. I manage to smile back at him before Benny says, "Later," and leads me away.

"Jeez, down girl," he mutters in my ear once we're out of the kitchen.

I swat at his stomach, which he has time to flex before I reach it. *Ugh.* "Hush, you. He's just such a sweetheart."

"Uh-huh. And a sweet face and sweet bod and—"

"And he's, like, thirty and married, so you can hop right off me."

"Riiight," Benny sniffs, and did he just *roll his eyes* at me? "All right, forget about your heartthrob for today. You ready for filming?"

I study his face with suspicion. There's something in it—in his words and voice, too—that seems off. If it was anyone else, anyone with a legitimate reason, I might almost detect something like jealousy. But it isn't anyone else. It's Benny, and that isn't us.

So I nod and answer, "As I'll ever be, probably. You?"

"Oh yeah." He waves a hand like this is nothing to him, and his expression relaxes again. "Nothing to worry about."

I sure hope he's right.

"You know what would be super convenient? If someone made this stuff and sold it at the grocery store like, I don't know, in a jar."

"Oh for the love of—" Benny pretends to smack his head against the prep kitchen counter, then looks back up, directly into the camera. "Forgive her, everyone, for she knows not what she says."

I smirk, not taking my eyes from the handful of mystery herbs I'm chopping, which will go in the pot with the garlic, onions, and tomatoes that I meticulously crushed, chopped, and diced by hand. "I'm just saying. I survived for eighteen years without ever having homemade spaghetti sauce and I've turned out fine."

"Aren't you a fan of this channel? Are you trying to implode the whole business model?" Benny teases, waving his floury hands in the air. They've thrown him another softball today, whether intentional or not, by providing all the right ingredients for gnocchi and homemade sauce. He practically cheered when he saw it all laid out on the counter.

"Anyway, you know what they call the stuff you're used to?" he asks. I raise an eyebrow. He's already struggling not to laugh at his own joke. "Impasta sauce."

I groan. "Oh lordy, I—no. That was so bad. You don't get to make fun of me anymore today. Taking away your privileges."

He just shakes his head, still chuckling. "You'll see what I mean when we're done. You haven't had marinara till you've had it homemade."

He does the thing where he rolls the *r*'s excessively as he corrects my terminology and I roll my eyes in turn, ignoring the little shiver that goes down my spine every time he goes all Italian on me. The latter reaction is very much involuntary and I'm very much *not* a fan.

Though we're only a little way into our second video, we've established our unspoken roles. Benny is Mr. Suave Foodie, happy to use his lifetime of experience in a restaurant kitchen to take charge of the cooking process and use all the right lingo. I, on the other hand, represent the Normals of the world—the newcomers who have watched a ton of Friends of Flavor but don't have any training outside a home kitchen. He teases me for not knowing everything about everything; I get to rib him when he gets too mansplainy.

I drag the knife slowly through another bunch of tiny aromatic leaves. I'm not especially efficient at chopping, but keeping my fingers is more important to me than speed. My fear of coming across as a dumb blonde is still in the back of my mind as I go through each motion deliberately. But I'm trying to embrace what I *can* offer, even if it's not loads of culinary knowledge and technique.

I'm not going to be a better cook than Benny by the end of the summer, if that's what Friends of Flavor is looking for in their fall intern, but I can supply an approachability that not all of the

FoF chefs have. Viewers want to feel like they're *friends* with the Friends of Flavor, and I happen to be your friend who's not the biggest culinary expert but is still out here trying her best.

This is what I keep telling myself anyway, while Benny strains every one of his prominent muscles by carrying this show on his back.

I can follow instructions like nobody's business, though, bar a couple of mishaps no bigger than the food processor lid. I pick up the cutting board and brush the chopped herbs into the still-warm saucepan where I sautéed the onions and garlic earlier, giving these the same treatment in order to, as Benny says, "release their flavor." I peek over my shoulder to see whether he looks ready to provide me with my next steps. He's just set his own pot of water on the burner to bring it to a boil. His back is to the camera and me, and he reaches up to readjust his backward ball cap, giving all of us a prime view of those ridiculous biceps stretching his tight T-shirt sleeves, back muscles rippling underneath the thin cotton just in case we didn't get the point already.

I whip my head back around, willing the blush from my face, and see that I've been brushing my hand over the empty cutting board for at least a few seconds. Boy, do I hope the camera didn't pick up on that.

"Looks great. Now let's bring it all together and add some heat."

I jump at the sound of Benny's voice from right behind me. He reaches around and takes the saucepan in front of me. He dumps the sizzling herbs into the tomato pot and moves the latter to the stovetop where he's been working, starting up the gas underneath it.

I belatedly step aside, trying to look unaffected as I tap my nails on the counter. "Just out of curiosity slash, um, in case viewers want to know . . . how much longer till it's ready?"

"Unclear. From here we kinda just taste test."

I suppress a groan at the exact moment that my stomach chooses to growl. There's a clatter and I turn to see Benny has dropped a spoon in the pot.

"That was not your stomach just now," he says, pointing a warning finger at me like I'm a kindergartner in danger of pulling a ticket.

"No, it was the voice of the troll that lives under the stove. He encourages you to feed me soon or he'll kidnap your firstborn."

Benny's head falls back, he's laughing so hard, and he runs his hands over his face. "Well, tell the troll we might not be in such dire circumstances if only *someone* had eaten *breakfast!*"

This morning, I woke up to a text from him sent half an hour prior, inviting me to grab breakfast with him on our way to work. As surprisingly friendly a gesture as it was, it also became Benny's first encounter with Morning Reese. I explained in brief, I'm-typing-this-half-asleep terms that I usually skip breakfast and sleep until the last possible minute when I'll still be able to get to work on time and look mostly human.

Of course, his early-rising butt was already almost to the office by the time he got my message, but he's oddly concerned about my habit of skipping breakfast. He's brought it up at least three times already.

"I don't know how else to explain to you that my stomach

doesn't want food first thing in the morning. My stomach, like the rest of my body and soul, wants to be asleep," I reply.

"Cut," Charlie calls, startling both of us out of our bickering. I didn't know calling cut was a thing they did here. Nor that Charlie expressed words in a non-grumbly fashion.

"If you are going to be at the stove for the rest of the time, I'm going to put another camera over there. Don't do anything interesting while we're not rolling," he offers by way of explanation. Margie was here to get us started today, but it's just been Charlie since then. Apparently, it's not abnormal to have as few as one videographer on any given FoF video. I'm still surprised they let Benny and me off the leash so soon, though.

He speaks, Benny mouths, looking at me with wide eyes.

I know! I mouth back, and we both try to suppress our laughter.

We keep quiet and stir our respective pots till the camera is ready, lest we be accused of doing anything interesting in the interim. But even once we're rolling, the remainder of filming is mostly the two of us standing at the stove, stirring the sauce, boiling the little potato dumplings, tasting the sauce, taking a tester nibble of gnocchi. We joke and bicker, and it's surprisingly . . . comfortable. Enjoyable, even.

But the fact remains that Benny is my competition. I have to stay focused on that if I want any chance of sticking around.

Then it's time for our first complete bites after we mix the gnocchi and sauce together with a sprinkling of parmesan over the top. Spearing one of the little potato pillows with my fork, I drag it through some extra sauce before popping it into my mouth. The flavors explode on my tongue, my taste buds experiencing something akin to euphoria as the fresh tomatoes and garlic and herbs and salt all meld around a light, fluffy center. I fight the urge to moan aloud, because oh. My. Pasta-loving stars.

I thought I loved pasta before. But then I met this gnocchi, which Benny says isn't even technically pasta, and all I know is that it tastes like my every good Italian restaurant and home-cooked comfort food memory rolled into one and amplified. I feel like I'm about to melt to the floor, literally light-headed from this rapturous food experience. The dish is savory and hearty and warms me from the inside out. My stomach troll is over the moon.

"That was the best bite of food I've ever had," I say when I'm able to speak again. If I had more presence of mind, I'd have realized that this would only inflate Benny's ego, but the words slipped out before I could catch them.

He laughs, indeed looking extremely pleased with himself. "Really? Well, there's way more where that came from." He takes a step closer, his voice going softer. "And imagine what I can do with a little time to make plans."

I nearly choke on my second bite. Doesn't he know that there's a camera still on us? I narrow my eyes at him, though he's probably beginning to think that's just how my face looks. He winks at me—freaking *winks* at me—before we have a few more bites and sign off, then Charlie declares filming complete.

With the camera off, Benny and I dig into the rest of the food, and I'm happy to be able to attack my plate like the ravenous monster I am without worrying as much about appearances. Including the appearance of my grumpy self next to the shameless flirt.

Early the next week, one of my biggest dreams comes true when I get to appear as a taste tester in a *World on a Plate* episode about Southern comfort food. Aiden volunteered me for it—which actually means that he volun-told me I'd be doing it—since I'm from Kentucky and therefore the resident fried chicken expert. Apparently. There are worse Southern stereotypes, to be sure.

"Here's your plate." Lily pushes a full platter of fried chicken and mac and cheese my way with gusto. I've never spoken to the beautiful Latina chef before today. She and Nia are collaborating on today's episode, and in person they're exactly what I expected: smart, kind, and gorgeous. They balance each other well, with Nia's easygoing sensibility and Lily's eccentric, somewhat spacey vibe.

I gingerly lift a drumstick with my fingers, inspecting it to figure out the best angle before diving in. There is no cute way to eat it, and that's just how it's gonna be. I have my mouth open wide and am sinking my teeth into the meat like some kind of wild animal, when there's a snort from off camera.

Scarcely pausing, I make direct eye contact with a chuckling Benny.

Oh good gravy.

I glare at him for a moment, then straighten back up and chew, trying to look like I'm carefully considering the flavors and all the other qualities that real foodies would care about, rather than letting my brain respond, "FOOD YUM, REESE LIKE." It *is* yummy, though, and I *do* like it.

"This is delicious," I say once I've swallowed, dabbing at the corners of my mouth with a napkin. "What kind of seasoning did you use?"

"Salt and pepper mostly but also a little paprika and garlic powder," Lily answers in her typical airy tone. "But the secret ingredient I played around with was . . . pickle juice."

She says this with a dramatic pause and the kind of inflection a magician would use to say "ta-da!" Lily is known for her affinity for adding unexpected twists and "secret ingredients" to her recipes, so this isn't really surprising. Still, I have to tamp down the instinct to gag. I *hate* pickles. And the concept of pickle juice is so disgusting to me, I can't think about it too much. I mean, the chicken is good, but it was better before she told me that.

Tasting the mac goes fine, as there are minimal frills and just thick, creamy, cheesy goodness. After I'm done with Lily's entrée, I get to sample the maple and brown sugar bread pudding that Nia prepared for dessert. I'm glad I'm getting full by this point, or else I'd be trying to eat the entire pan. I don't know if I've ever tasted anything so perfectly sweet and gooey.

I give the whole meal an emphatic seal of approval, throwing in a couple of Southern-isms for show before filming wraps up. Once Charlie's given the all clear and starts taking down his camera equipment, I relax my posture and lean against the counter with Nia and Lily to share the remaining food. Benny wanders over, less than casually eyeing what's left on our plates.

"Hello, ladies . . . ," he starts, and I fix him with a smirk. "May I?"

"Sure," Nia says, flashing her pretty gap-toothed smile. "You're Benny, right?"

We chat and eat for a few minutes more, Benny charming the pants off everyone present per usual.

"I might bring this pudding for the cookout. Are you all coming?" Nia asks.

Benny and I exchange glances, and I feel like we're the two kids in the class not invited to the Chuck E. Cheese birthday party. Clearing his throat, Benny says, "Uh . . . cookout?"

Nia's brow furrows, and Lily looks distracted by something over my shoulder.

"Hey, Aiden," she calls out. "Can the interns come to the cookout?"

I turn to see a confused expression on the boss's face. "Yes, of course. Didn't you two get the invite?"

Benny and I look cluelessly at each other again before shaking our heads.

"Huh. Maybe I sent them before you got here. Anyway, yes, all-staff summer cookout at six-thirty on Saturday. Seb's house in Queen Anne. BYO . . . juice or soda or whatever you like to drink."

I try not to roll my eyes at his shade, and I can tell Benny is holding in a laugh. Nia gives us another of her sympathetic smiles, adding quietly, "I'll forward you the email."

And just like that, it looks like I have weekend plans again.

Chapter Seven

I spend most of Saturday playing around with graphic design apps on my tablet. Margie casually mentioned wanting to create an *Amateur Hour* logo after we filmed our most recent video, and I jumped on it, asking her if I could present some ideas. She'd barely looked up from her computer as she gave me a "sure," and she might very well forget we had the conversation, but I'm excited enough at the prospect of doing real design work for Friends of Flavor—and, okay, showing off what I can do that Benny can't—that I've already started three different mock-ups.

That evening, Benny and I meet at the fountain between our dorms to head to the cookout. I'm not so keen on spending more time with him than necessary, but since I haven't trekked outside our few blocks of downtown yet—and the prospect of doing so alone makes me a nervous wreck—I agreed to his suggestion that we make the bus trip together. Seb's neighborhood, Queen

Anne, is a ritzy area on a hill that overlooks downtown and Puget Sound. As the city bus winds up, and up, and up steep streets, Benny gives me the scoop he's gotten from working with the other Friends. Apparently, Seb's husband makes bank as an exec at one of the big tech companies.

"They don't want any kids, but their dogs live in serious luxury," Benny says as we disembark at our stop near the top of the hill.

"Isn't that the dream," I sigh.

Benny uses his phone to navigate the rest of our path. As we get close, it isn't hard to pick out Seb's house. The music blasting out onto the street has to be breaking some kind of noise ordinance, plus there are Friends of Flavor–branded balloons tied to the mailbox.

Benny and I obey the COME ON IN! sign on the door, and I'm happy to be behind him as we enter the fray. There are more people here than I've ever seen around the offices, but I guess significant others were invited, along with the mysterious "suits" I always hear about and additional staff who work behind the scenes.

Benny glances over his shoulder at me as we cross through the kitchen, which is crowded with folks doing food prep. He gestures toward the backyard, and I nod at him with wide help-me eyes. It's way too crowded indoors for my comfort.

On the deck, Seb turns from his spot at the grill to greet us.

"So glad you both made it!" he says with a big, sparkling

smile. I cheese back at him like a dazzled superfan. Which I suppose I am.

Benny pokes me in the side, looking unimpressed by my reaction before he steps forward to give Seb a hug. "Hey, man, thanks for having us. Need help with anything?"

Seb looks around before picking up his spatula again. "Nah, I think we're good. Everyone's hanging out—Kath and Raj are down in the yard playing with the dogs, and I think Lily is taking pictures. Good night for it."

I let my eyes drift in the direction Seb is nodding in, and my jaw drops. The view from up here is *ridiculous.* We can see the entire Seattle skyline, with the Space Needle in the foreground and Columbia Center and surrounding skyscrapers in the distance, as well as the waters of Elliot Bay and the Olympic Peninsula beyond it, with ferries drifting in all directions. The sky has that golden evening glow it gets before a long summer sunset, making all of the glass and water shimmer.

It's breathtaking.

I now understand why people who can afford it choose to live up here.

"Not a bad view you've got," Benny muses behind me, and Seb chuckles. I tune out whatever else they say, letting my eyes take in the view without distraction.

Soon enough, Seb's husband, Harry, rounds everyone up to eat. At the other end of the sprawling deck, Aiden gives a short spiel thanking everyone for coming and for all their hard work so far this year, then directs us on how the buffet line will work. It's more detail than seems necessary for a group of people in the food industry, but such is Aiden's style.

The food, as expected, is phenomenal. Steaks, grilled veggies, half a dozen kinds of salad, Lily's new mac and cheese recipe, Nia's bread pudding, and more. Sticking with each other in the default awkward-together-instead-of-awkward-alone mode, Benny follows me down the line and we mutually decide a return trip will be necessary. We plant ourselves against one of the wide deck railings and use it as a makeshift table. Because, as Benny puts it, "We probably don't have the seniority to claim actual seats, right?"

As we enjoy the most gourmet cookout food I've ever had, a little group forms in our corner with Teagan and a couple of women from marketing along with some kitchen assistants I don't know. We eat and exchange small talk, with Teagan throwing the occasional eyebrow-waggling look between Benny and me when he isn't paying attention and me shooting eye-daggers at her in return. Both Benny and I visit the buffet a couple more times, as predicted.

A few different people have rotated in and out of our conversational orbit when an older man comes our way. He has a thick head of salt-and-pepper hair and is dressed more formally than most people here, in slacks and a tucked-in button-down with a tie. I peg him immediately as one of the suits—the nameless, faceless body of mainly old white guys who work at Friends of

Flavor's parent company and get the final say on all big decisions.

The guy confirms this when he holds out his hand to Benny and says, "Hello, I don't believe we've met. I'm Geoffrey Block, CEO of UltiMedia."

Whoa, so not just *one of* the suits. He's *The* Suit. I feel my posture straightening compulsively, all the little soldiers in my brain standing at attention—*smile calmly, not so big as to look silly. Eyes attentive, not deer-in-the-headlights. Is the neckline of my dress covering everything? What about the hemline? Handshake firm. How am I gonna introduce myself—*

"Hi there." Benny looks as casual and comfortable as ever. "Benny Beneventi, culinary intern. And this is Reese Camden, marketing intern."

Oh. Well, guess the introduction part is covered for me. I reach out my hand to Geoffrey Block, CEO, whom I've already decided must be thought of by his full name and title. I'm ready to at least say a "hello" or "nice to meet you," but the man's attention flickers over me, his smile tight as his eyes linger a second longer on . . . my legs?

"Reese, a pleasure. Nice dress."

Eek. One of his eyebrows raises just a touch, but before I even have time to register what the look means, it's gone and his focus is back on Benny, whose mouth is now set in a frown, eyebrows knit together with confusion. His gaze flits between the CEO and me a couple of times before settling on the former.

I don't know what my costar's look means, but I don't much

care, either. I'm trying to fit other pieces together in my head. So, hemline not satisfactory to the boss man? *Too* satisfactory? I shift from foot to foot in discomfort, wishing I could go back in time to roughly sixty seconds ago and make my escape before this encounter started.

"So, Mr. Beneventi—is that Italian? My ex-wife is Italian, but I won't hold it against you. Ha!"

His loud laugh is startling and so fake. It's what I imagine a Ken doll's laugh would sound like, made of the same plastic and performative masculinity. But I continue to stand there as Geoffrey Block, CEO, asks Benny about his background, what he likes to cook, what his goals for the future are. And what does he ask me?

A whole lot of nothing.

Even Benny—flirtatious goofball *Benny*—makes an effort to pull me into the conversation, with a "Reese and I made gnocchi this week," and, "Reese and I are both interested in staying with Friends of Flavor into the future, right, Reese?"

"Is that right?" the boss man says to the latter prompt before I can jump in. "The fall internship, then?"

Benny nods, still looking at me when I glance his way, but Geoffrey Block, CEO, doesn't seem to notice.

"You know, that could make things interesting. The dynamics here"—he points between the two of us—"two summer interns, one fall spot. Who stays, who goes? People love to watch a competition."

He winks at Benny and I feel my stomach turn over, my

dinner threatening to make a reappearance. I don't like the direction this is going in one bit. I look to Benny for his reaction, but he's hiding whatever he's feeling with a slightly stiffer version of his usual charming smile.

"Ha, I guess you could see it that way," he says ambiguously. "Did you see the last episode of *Good Chef/Bad Chef*? It got especially intense, huh?"

I'm grateful for the diversion and that Geoffrey Block, CEO, rolls right along with it. Benny continues to look my way with something like encouragement after each question the man asks, giving me an opening to answer first if I want. But my outright dismissal by this Very Important Dude, plus his musings about potentially capitalizing on the competition between Benny and me, has me so shaken that I can't find many words, and the ones I can are not especially kind. Not to mention the fact that in the rare moments when the older man's eyes return to me, they seem to go anywhere but my face.

Geoffrey Block, CEO, has just explained how he lives and works out of San Francisco but he's in town for the weekend and thought he'd make an appearance and isn't the food absolutely fantastic, when I clear my throat.

"Sorry, it was nice to meet you, but if you'll excuse me, I'm just gonna . . ."

I mumble some things that are definitely not words as I step away from Benny's side. He looks at me with a question in his eyes, but the other man barely even pauses his monologue as I make my escape.

I go to the other end of the deck and stand there, looking out at the incredible view again and letting the breeze cool my heated face and matching temper. Because what in the absolute hell? I have half a mind to go back there and deliver Mr. Geoffrey Block, CEO, a swift kick in the pants for that . . . whatever that was. Of all the people to treat me like a girl-shaped dress mannequin, I swear. But I would still very much like to keep my job, so I grip the deck railing and stand still, willing my irritation to subside.

Not too much later, I feel a hand brush my arm. It makes me jump.

"Sorry," Benny says when I whirl around to face him. His voice is soft and his expression more serious than I've ever seen it. "I was just going to see if you want to go down to the yard."

I blink a couple of times, coming back to the present. I nod before heading down the steps and onto Seb's perfectly maintained patch of grassy hillside. Katherine and Rajesh are, just as Seb described before dinner, jogging around and tossing tennis balls and chew toys to three fluffy, gorgeous golden retrievers. Several other people are milling about, and I see Lily perched on a branch in the lone tree. She alternates bringing a fancy Nikon to her eye and snapping a few shots of nearby buildings or the sky or water, then checking the screen to see the results. I'm inclined to get up there and join her rather than have to talk to anyone else tonight.

"You a dog fan?" Benny interrupts my observations.

"Love them," I answer, and follow him toward the playful goldens.

I don't consider until we're already right beside them that this means meeting Katherine for the first time. Rajesh, too, but *Katherine,* right when I'm all flustered and out of sorts. I freeze up on the spot.

They both greet Benny, whom they know by now, with casual ease, then turn to me, the strange girl whose strongest identifier so far is Kentucky Fried Chicken. I'm as incapable of finding words as I was with Geoffrey Block, CEO, but for an entirely different reason.

"Hey, I don't think we've met." The tiny, curly-haired queen of my heart stretches a hand out to me. "You must be the other intern I keep hearing about."

"R-Reese," I stammer, because apparently that's a thing I do now. I clear my throat and try again. "It's so great to meet you. I'm a huge fan, um, of your videos, obviously, but I've also been a reader of the Kat's Muse for a long time. It—I mean, you—well, my friends back home and I, we find it so inspiring."

That is the biggest understatement. I find myself in so many situations on a regular basis thinking, *What would Katherine do?*

Even in this moment, coming off an uncomfortable meeting with the highest higher-up of the company, I wonder what she would do if she was me. Or has she *been* me? Has she ever faced this kind of weirdness with Geoffrey Block, CEO? If I knew her any better, I might ask her. In my head, she's this big-sister figure who has all the answers and cheers me on. But in reality, she's a near stranger who has no reason to be more than politely indifferent to the new intern.

Her chin dips in acknowledgment as she releases my hand, her lips tipping up in a closed-mouth smile. "Thank you, that's sweet. Oh, this is Rajesh"—he gives me a two-fingered wave—"and I think we were just about to go up to the porch and hang out awhile. Raj?"

Rajesh nods and shoots me a toothy grin. "Sure, yeah. Good to meet you, Reese. See ya, Benny."

I'm confused by the abrupt getaway, but when I turn to see Benny hiding a smile as he scratches behind one of the dog's ears, it makes sense.

"I blew that, didn't I? I totally ran her off." I huff a disbelieving laugh and drop to my butt on the grass. The two dogs lacking Benny's attention come over and crowd my space, so I stretch out my arms to each side to accommodate two simultaneous belly rubs.

Benny sits beside me. The dog he's been petting curls up against his thigh, laying its head in his lap, and really, can they not right now? It's too much. Cute overload.

"Nah, I don't think you were over the top. My impression so far is Katherine's just humble and doesn't like talking about herself." He pauses, his eyes sliding to mine as his mouth edges into a smirk. "I can't tell, though. Do you have a bigger crush on her or Seb?"

I reach out and push his shoulder lightly, and one of the dogs lifts its head in dismay at the loss of my hand on his belly. I promptly resume rubbing, but not without another withering glance at the boy beside me.

He's right, of course. I might as well be the president of Katherine's nonexistent—for now, at least—fan club. But I like to think that if I hadn't just been thrown off-balance by a creepy company executive, I could have hidden it better. I let out a sigh, and as if he can read my thoughts, Benny speaks again, his voice both quieter and harder.

"That was weird back there with the Block guy, right?"

Hearing him acknowledge it aloud, some of my tension deflates. I release another long breath, this time flopping backward so I'm lying down in the grass.

"Weird is one word. Also rude, inappropriate, enraging," I say in a rush, bringing a hand to my forehead. "I couldn't tell how much you noticed."

"Of course I noticed," he says with a touch of defensiveness, crossing his arms over his chest. "He didn't compliment *my* clothes or look at me anywhere but my face. I mean, what the hell?"

It's oddly satisfying, hearing his validation and knowing I wasn't imagining things. I mean, I *knew.* But it's so hard not to second-guess yourself every time something like that happens, to wonder if you're overreacting or making something out of nothing. I give Benny a weak smile of acknowledgment, but my heart isn't in it. It feels like it's sitting in a pressure cooker back at the prep kitchens.

"I wish I could be as shocked as you are," I bite out. I let my fingers glide back and forth through the dogs' thick golden fur, trying to draw on the relaxed energy of these lovely creatures. "Unfortunately, it's upsetting but not all that surprising. As much as I know that sucks, that I should be able to expect better from grown-ass men, that it shouldn't have even crossed my mind whether this dress was appropriate when I was getting ready, I shouldn't be regretting my choice to wear it. I should be able to wear whatever I damn well please and yet . . . *ugh*."

I stand up and start pacing. One of the dogs also gets up and trails me, and it would be adorable if I wasn't so pissed off. The valve has been loosened, and I can't stop now. "You know, it's not like this is even an exceptionally revealing dress. I packed it thinking it'd be one of my work outfits for the summer, with a blazer or something. But then they went over the dress code on the first day, and I worried it would be too short. I mean, it's fingertip-length, but barely. I thought it'd be okay outside the office. It *is* okay, dammit. He's the one in the wrong."

Benny is quiet and when I look at him full-on again, his brow is wrinkled in confusion. "What dress code?"

I come to a halt, my own confusion mirroring his. "The . . . dress code at Friends of Flavor? Aiden talked about it my first day in the office when I sat down with him and Margie for an orientation."

"Huh. I didn't realize we had one."

I step closer, crossing my arms over my chest. "They—I mean, he— No one told you about the dress code?"

He shakes his head, looking almost apologetic. I look back

toward the sunset, narrowing my eyes. I mean, it could be nothing—Aiden could have just forgotten it amid all the other info he has to dump in an orientation. But something deep down—something that feels like the CEO's leering and his subsequent brush-off—prods at me, and I feel awfully inclined to believe the omission wasn't an accident.

"That's bullshit," I say under my breath, but apparently not quietly enough, as Benny straightens.

"Hey, I'm sure he meant to tell me. He probably just figured I wouldn't wear anything shorter than fingertip-length in the first place, so . . ."

Oh. Oh, bless his heart. He's trying to reorient us with a little humor.

"That's just it, though," I say, my voice strained with the anger I'm struggling to control. "The rules don't apply to you. The dress code's entire purpose is to police women's bodies."

"Care to elaborate?" Benny asks more softly, sincerity in his gaze.

I sigh. This—a work function with a guy I barely know whose main source of entertainment seems to be antagonizing me in the kitchen—likely isn't the time for such a discussion, to let the angry feminist within me come out. But on the other hand, maybe it's better to scare him off now, before he gets too comfortable with the less-authentic-but-easier-to-handle version of Reese.

"Ever since I was a little girl, I've been told how to be modest, to look 'professional,' to dress and carry myself in a way that will make people respect me. They always put it in nicer words, but the message is the same—that my body, my legs, my chest, my shoulders, my stomach, it all needs to be tucked in and hidden away. If it isn't, I'm not taken seriously. I'm giving everyone the wrong idea. I'm distracting boys from their education and work. It's . . . well, it's bullshit. And it's the reason why my instinctive response to that garbage back there"—I gesture to the deck—"is to wonder if it's my fault for wearing this dress. If someone is so overcome by those two extra inches of thigh I'm showing that they can't do their job, or converse with me like I'm a human being, that's *their* problem, you know? Why do I have to mold my appearance and behavior around their lack of respect or self-control, or whatever?"

My chest feels tight, my breathing is shallow. One of Seb's dogs still stands beside me, its hot breath warming my leg. I crouch to wrap my arms around its neck. I try to do a couple of slow inhale-through-nose-exhale-through-mouth breaths without being too obvious about it. But when I peer over at Benny, he's looking into the distance.

When he feels my eyes on him, he turns to meet my gaze. He looks . . . unnerved. And honestly, a little angry. I feel a pang of regret for bringing any of this up. I just couldn't help myself this one time, could I? Life of the party, Reese Camden. I'm opening my mouth to suggest we drop it when his voice stops me.

"I'm sorry," he says, nearly knocking the wind out of me.

"You're right, and that's really stupid and sucks that you have to think about those things. Is this . . . I mean, do you think you could tell anyone? About Block's comment?"

I'm struggling to follow anything after "I'm sorry." Have I ever, in my entire life, had a boy say they're sorry to me for any of this shit? If I have, I certainly can't remember it. I'm still blinking in surprise as the rest of Benny's words register.

"Um, no," I answer, shaking my head. "No, I can't. Or I won't. Because what would I say? That he told me my dress was nice? That seems so innocent when you say it back, you know?"

Benny's face scrunches up, clearly displeased with my answer. "But he was looking at you so . . . Gah, what an ass. I'd back you up if you wanted to tell anyone, Reese. That was gross."

I give him a sad, oh-you-sweet-summer-child half smile. "It was. But again, 'He said my dress was nice and looked at me weird'? Not the best claim for an *intern* to make against the *CEO* after meeting him once. This industry is hard enough to break into, especially as a woman. I'm not trying to make it any harder on myself. Besides, I've dealt with worse."

"What do you mean?" he asks, his head jerking my way.

I wave a hand, planning to just brush the question off, but something in his gaze has me reconsidering. There's a fire there, and I recognize it—it matches how I feel right now. And in a rare, surprising moment, I feel seen. And heard. Maybe even understood. That's the only reason I can give for why I tell him anything close to the truth next.

"Just some . . . ugly stuff happened early in high school, mostly rumors, but it made for a tough few years, where I didn't have a lot of people's respect or support. And the guy involved made it out scot-free."

I swallow past the lump in my throat. I haven't given him much, but it's more than I ever expected to tell another person who didn't know me prior to this "starting over" stage of my life. For one panicked second, I wonder, *Why, oh why, did I bring this up?* If Benny doesn't run screaming back up to the deck pretty soon, there's something wrong with the boy.

But then I feel his hand on my shoulder, giving it a soft squeeze before dropping back into his lap, and I turn to see his encouraging expression. He doesn't look like someone who is even considering running or screaming. So, definitely something wrong with him. But the feeling of mutual understanding persists, so I add one final comment on the subject before I let it rest.

"Anyway, I'm always trying to harden myself, to not let things like that get to me as much and not give people any more reasons to judge me, but it's a process."

Benny crosses his arms over his chest again, studying me with an intensity that almost makes me want to tuck and roll down the hill and into the bay, goodbye, cruel world. But he clears his throat and speaks before I can even pull my legs to my chest.

"That's . . . a lot. But I think I follow. Obviously I can be kinda oblivious about double standards—as pathetic as it sounds, I never had to think much about all this. I had this little Ma angel on my shoulder telling me how to treat women with respect and I was raised to know things like, 'If you laugh at that sexist joke your friend just told, she'll smack you,' right?" He sighs. "I want to do better, though. And I want to know more. I wish you never had to feel like any of this is your fault, because I think you're so great—" He cuts off, and I feel my breath catch.

He thinks what now?

"Uh, but I want you to tell me if there're ever ways I can help you or if I'm being one of the shitty dudes making things difficult. Or if there are any shitty dudes I can help you straighten out. Even if they're the CEO of a company."

Gracious, did it get warmer out here all of a sudden or is it just this objectively handsome, nice guy validating my feelings and offering his unwavering support? I swallow heavily. "Thanks, Benny. I didn't have any plans of talking your ear off tonight and wasn't even sure what I meant to say once I got going, but I . . . I'm glad you're here."

"Seriously, any time," he answers, his voice barely a whisper. But I hear it loud and clear.

Chapter Eight

By the time we're back in the office on Monday, I've decided that it'd be best if I avoid talking to Benny again.

He now knows way too much about my innermost feelings. I'm not sure what my juice box was spiked with on Saturday night, but I sure had to be high on something to talk as openly as I did with a guy I work with. A guy who was sweet and understanding, and whose dimpled, lopsided grin has been front and center in my mind for the better part of the last thirty-six hours.

There's no way this little fixation ends well for me. I wonder if there's some kind of witness protection program for when the perpetrator is you and the crime is aggressive oversharing. I'm treading dangerous waters in my self-imposed No Feelings Zone, having inched too close to Emotional Intimacy Island.

I do my best at a self-designed protection program, offering to take care of every errand for Margie just to stay on my feet and out of Benny's path. I get coffee for everyone and their mother, run some tablecloths to the dry cleaners, pick up a specially or-dered part for the KitchenAid mixer at a store on the other side of town. I am never as helpful as when I'm avoiding something.

He's texted me a couple of times—perfectly normal, chatty messages asking how I'm doing and telling me a funny Aiden story, but I haven't responded. Sure, I know we'll have to film another video together before long, but that's Future Reese's problem.

Unfortunately, a wrench is thrown into the works when Benny and I get pulled into another meeting with Margie and Aiden.

"Sounds like you made quite the impression on Mr. Block at the cookout, on top of what he's seen of your videos," Aiden announces, and while he likely intends for us to interpret "you" in the plural sense, he's looking only at Benny. "He and the rest of the suits love the tension inherent in the fact that you're both pursuing the fall culinary internship, and they'd love to play that up throughout the *Amateur Hour* series."

My stomach sinks, and I feel Benny shift uncomfortably a couch cushion away from me. He clears his throat and asks the obvious. "And . . . what exactly do they have in mind?"

Aiden runs a hand over his white-blond hair, which is smoothly gelled back without a strand out of place. "We're think-ing some smaller-scale competitions in each episode. Head-to-head showdowns with each of you preparing your own version of the same dish with blind taste tests to pick the winner, maybe some other 'challenges' around the kitchens as we come up with them. The same kind of banter and friendly sparring you already have, just amped up.

"It's still a work in progress, but think *The Amazing Race* or *The Bachelor*—a reality show competition format. But instead of money or a ring at the end, you're vying for the fall internship and a solo gig on *Amateur Hour*," he explains way too cheerily. It's not his future on the line.

A mild ache in my jaw clues me in that I've been clenching it, and I make a conscious effort to relax the relevant muscles. I lower my shoulders from where they sit just under my ears and smooth my hands over my jeans-covered thighs. Sure, they're changing the game up on us. My biggest insecurity in this competition—that I'm not as skilled at cooking as Benny—will now be front and center to entertain the masses. But I'll be doing myself no favors by falling apart in the middle of this meeting. Weird how sorting this out mentally doesn't seem to make my physical reactions fall in line.

Finally chancing a look at Benny, I'm relieved to see he doesn't appear totally at ease with the news. He's sitting forward, elbows on his knees and hands clasped tightly in front of him. He clearly hasn't given himself the relax-your-jaw command yet. I hope he doesn't get a headache.

"We won't be keeping score or anything, episode by episode," Margie offers, her tone a bit softer, almost conciliatory. "The competitions are mostly for entertainment value. But your overall performances and the skills demonstrated will be taken into consideration when it's time to make further employment decisions."

"Right," Aiden says shortly with a dismissive wave of his hand. "So, assuming we have both of your consent, we'll go ahead and get started with plans for the coming episodes!"

Our consent *is* basically assumed. Saying I'm not interested in openly competing for my future career prospects in front of a camera feels like an option in theory only. Aiden is so jazzed about the idea already, in part on behalf of Geoffrey Block, CEO, that I'm not sure his brain would be able to process "no" as an answer. And if I was to say no, to be the buzzkill or the difficult one, wouldn't I be all but wrecking my chances at the job?

So, after exchanging one of our now-familiar I-guess-we're-doing-this glances, Benny and I agree.

Later, back in marketing, Margie checks in with me, her voice hushed. It's clear she doesn't want to put me on the spot in front of our coworkers. "Are you sure you're good to go with this new direction, Reese?"

I turn from my spot at the TV-tray desk, pasting what I hope is a relaxed smile on my face. "Sure. It's a little nerve-racking, I guess, being pitted against Benny on camera. But I can handle it."

She doesn't look convinced, leaning against the file cabinet with her arms crossed, and I wonder for a second if I should be more open with her and own my vulnerability. I don't think she'd judge me, and she might actually be helpful. But the inkling of doubt, the worry that showing any weakness will ruin my credibility, is enough to stop me.

"Okay," Margie says. "Well, please feel free to reach out if that changes, or if there's anything more you need on my end. I want you to succeed."

My eyebrows raise and I nod, pretty much speechless as she walks away. She looked like she meant that. I want to believe she meant the most generous interpretation of her statement—that she wants me to succeed *over* Benny. Lord knows I could use a supporter higher up the FoF ladder.

Benny tries to talk to me about it, too, but I'm resistant, continuing to ignore his texts into the evening, even when he stoops to communicating in *Star Wars* GIFs. I would be lying if I said the image of R2-D2 with a closed caption that says [SAD BEEP-ING] didn't tempt me to give him something. If I was anxious about the growing pull I felt toward him before, that anxiety is quadrupled now. I can't let myself get any closer, any more attached than I started to feel at the cookout.

So I keep at my Extreme Erranding on Margie's behalf the next day. I'm getting a little heated from all this running around like a chicken with its head cut off, though, so when I settle in at my desk for a few minutes, I slip off my cardigan and hang it on the back of my chair.

It's only after I've taken a bathroom break and am back in the marketing office that I realize two things: I forgot to put my cardigan on before I left my desk, and it is no longer on the back of my chair. I might not have realized it for even longer, except that in its place is a piece of printer paper crookedly taped to the chair back with a message scrawled across it in what has to be my pink highlighter.

It reads:

THIS JACKET HAS BEEN ABDUCTED BY THE DRESS CODE JUSTICE FAIRY.

LordhaveMERCY.

All my plans for avoiding Benny fly out the window, replaced by a mix of irritation and something like amusement, though I'm trying to block the latter out. I snatch the note, then turn on my heel and stomp back out to the hallway to look for that exceptionally ridiculous boy.

Fortunately, it doesn't take much searching. I find him standing at a counter in Prep Kitchen 2 sharpening knives. I approach cautiously, trying to stay out of his peripheral vision to prevent either one of us getting stabbed.

"Benjamin Franklin Beneventi."

He turns his head at the sound of my stern voice, looking wholly unsurprised and not even flinching when I slap the note down on the counter. "Not my name." He gingerly sets down the knife he's holding before turning to face me. "But hi, how are you? I was starting to think you might be avoiding me."

So that's the game he's playing, huh? I feel my cheeks heat but force myself to keep looking at him. "I don't know what you're talking about. Where's my cardigan?"

Benny glances around the kitchen as if looking for the thing he has stolen within the last five minutes. His perusal of the room reminds me of the half-dozen other people in our vicinity, occupied with their own tasks but close enough to overhear this showdown. So, too close.

I reach out and grab the hem of Benny's T-shirt between two fingers, then turn and pull him along behind me as I look for someplace more private. I walk with purpose, as if I have a spot picked out already, which I totally don't. But when I come upon an unoccupied pantry, I pull Benny in after me.

Closing the door, I turn to face him. And find his face *reeeal* close to mine. The corners of his mouth are starting to tick up in a smile in spite of his efforts to hide it.

"Hey there."

I swallow the heady feeling I get at the sound of his voice this close, low and rumbly. There are only a couple of inches between our chests, no more than that between our faces, which are almost level. This would certainly be easier in, say, an open field.

I press my back flat against the door and clear my throat. "My cardigan. Give it back."

"I enjoyed our conversation on Saturday," he continues in that smooth bass as if I haven't said anything.

"What kind of kidnapper leaves a note identifying themselves as the kidnapper, anyway? What are you playing at?" I bite out with a frustration that is quickly fleeing my body.

Benny's eyes flit down to the floor almost sheepishly. "I don't enjoy what brought on our talk at the cookout, or hearing what you go through. But I was honored that you told me, and I like talking to you. I'd listen to you talk like that every day if you let me."

His words almost stop my breath, despite the weirdness of this situation he's facilitated and the way we're having two totally different conversations. I shake my head and squeeze my eyes shut, but they pop back open when I feel something brush past my hair. Benny stares at me intently, and I register that he's put one palm flat against the door beside my head.

He leans in closer, and I try my damnedest not to notice all the muscles in that arm flexing so close to me, but holy biceps, Batman, and oh my, how much closer can he get before he—

"Reese," he breathes, and I feel the word brush against my lips even though they still haven't made contact with his. I don't think I'm breathing at all. "We should talk about this competition thing."

At that, I let my breath out in a rush, sliding down the door and ducking out from under his arm. I walk as far away from him as I can, which isn't far because, well, pantry.

"What? We don't—it's not—no. We don't need to talk about anything. Give me back my sweater," I say as firmly as I can, hoping it hides the fact that I definitely thought he was going to kiss me for a minute there, and I definitely wasn't about to stop him. Which was foolish, obviously, so thank goodness he snapped me out of it.

Benny turns around with a smug, annoyingly perfect grin on his face. "All right. Would you rather talk about why you've been avoiding me since Saturday?"

"No!" I snap, then wonder whether it sounds like I'm admitting guilt. "I haven't been avoiding you. Are you even hearing me? Are you hearing *yourself*? We're here for one reason. I want my sweater back and you're going to give it."

"I would if I'd taken it," he answers, then starts sauntering toward me, folding his arms across his broad chest, which I need to stop noticing, gosh dang it. "I believe that was the work of the Dress Code Justice Fairy. With good reason, though, right? It's a stupid rule anyway."

He takes another step closer before I put up a hand to stop him. Then he plants his feet in a confident stance and keeps running that stupid, handsome mouth. "Your shoulders aren't distracting me from my work, Reese's Cup. But the fact that we've just been thrown this curveball where I have to compete for a job on camera in front of millions of people against a girl I'm starting to like a whole lot? That's been distracting me. And that the girl in question hasn't seemed to want anything to do with me ever since we had our first conversation about something real, and now I can't stop thinking about her, and her smile, and the sound of her voice—all of that is pretty distracting."

"Oh," is what slips out of my own mouth, ever so eloquently.

He can't? It is? I—what am I doing, for the love of— "Benny, first things first. You took my sweater and you've trapped me in a closet to force me to talk to you and that's all kind of manipulative, don't you think?"

Benny seems to consider this, his brow furrowing. "Technically, you trapped me in here." I'm about to protest, but he continues. "But I see your point. You can have the sweater regardless, and walk away right now if you want to, and I'll never let the fairy kidnap anything of yours again. But are you sure you don't want to talk about the showdown stuff? I'm not trying to pressure you, but personally, I . . . I'm kind of freaking out."

He reaches up to rub the back of his neck, face downcast as he takes a few steps in a tiny circle. He looks endearingly vulnerable, and I feel myself softening against my better judgment.

"It freaks me out too," I admit, not sure if I'm referring to the job so much as the fact that he just straight-up said *he likes me,* but I am choosing to only outwardly engage with the former. "I just don't see what we can do about it at this point."

"We can still turn them down if we want to. I mean, if both of us say we'd rather not do this one-on-one competition thing and just keep filming the kinds of videos we already are, they probably wouldn't turn us down, right?"

I raise an eyebrow. "Uh, I don't think we have that kind of leverage yet. It's what the suits want, so I think it's pretty much a done deal."

Benny nods, but he's eyeing me thoughtfully and pulling on his bottom lip with his teeth. "It's just—well, you always talk about not feeling too comfortable making things without a recipe. So maybe if there's anything I can do to, uh, well, help out, without making it obvious that I'm helping out, I totally w—"

My jaw drops at the patronizing turn this conversation has taken. "Beneventi, I know you are *not* offering to go easy on me or, worse, *let* me win these showdowns."

Benny starts shaking his head rapidly, but his denial is belied by his reddening cheeks. "No, that's not what I mean. I just—"

"*Good.* And don't even think about trying it. I'll know. I don't need your help to succeed, okay? Not today, and not at any point for the rest of this summer, no matter what else happens."

"Got it," he says with a gulp, eyes crossing as he stares at the finger I have in his face.

"Good. When I beat you, I want to know it was fair and square."

I let my hand fall and his face relaxes into a small grin as he leans into me. "'When' you beat me, huh?"

I nod, feeling more motivated to go through with the new format than I've been since Aiden and Margie introduced it. "You heard me."

His grin grows, his eyes warming as they roam my face. I suppress a shiver, trying hard to stay defiant and ragey despite the fact that he is distinctly neither.

"So what about the other thing?" he asks, head cocked.

I try to step back, forgetting that I'm unable to go far. "What other thing?"

"The thing where I like you."

I suck in a sharp breath. So much for not having to acknowledge that part.

"You don't even know me," I shoot back.

Benny shrugs. "Not a whole lot, no. But I'm starting to, little by little, and I like what I do know. Why don't we go out sometime, and we can get to know each other better?"

I'm shaking my head before he's even finished the question. "No thanks. Are we done here?"

"You won't even consider it?" He touches my arm as I start to turn toward the door. "What do you have to lose?"

Clearly he doesn't realize that's the worst way he could've framed it. "A lot, actually. Namely that fall internship we're about to be competing for in front of the world?"

"Yeah, but that doesn't have anything to do with what we do outside of work, right?" he says, indignant. "I wanted to ask you out before they called us in for that meeting, and it hasn't changed anything for me in that regard. We can both still work, still compete just as hard. It won't make a difference if we're friendly with each other or, well . . . more."

I shake my head, rubbing my temples. *More.* "That's not—no. Maybe it doesn't make a difference to you, but I can't be distracted. And I'm not about to look like the silly teenage girl with a silly teenage crush on her coworker. This job is all I care about right now and I want to be taken seriously. I don't need anything to take away from that."

"I'm distracting, huh?" Benny says with a little smirk, taking a tiny step forward, but only to reach for something on the shelf beside us. "You've *bean* thinking about me, too?"

He's holding a bag of dried pinto beans. Good gracious.

"Food puns are not going to help you." A total lie. Food puns are one of my favorite things, right up there with sweet tea and days I don't have to set an alarm clock. But he already knows too many of my weaknesses.

"Come on, Reese's Cup." He puts the beans down and goes for something else. "You won't regret it. I'm a *fungi*."

Now he's holding a tiny pot in which someone is growing mushrooms. Jesus H. Did he stock these shelves himself? Did I walk right into his master plan? I cover my face with my hands.

"Spice up your life!" He grabs a jar of thyme, which is more herb than spice, but I doubt that matters to the boy right now.

"Really, though, we can keep doing our thing at work. I'm certainly not going to stop pursuing the fall internship, and I know you're not either. We just won't tell anyone about our, er, personal lives. We'll keep it on the down low." He crouches and I wonder momentarily if he's adding charades to this whole bit, but he's reaching for the bottom shelf. "I wouldn't want anyone to get . . . *Jell-Ous*."

A box of mother-effing gelatin. "This is absurd," I say, although my resolve is weakening to the consistency of the mix he holds in his hands. "What if I just don't like you like that, Benny? Is that a good enough reason?"

He steps back, his face falling. "Oh. Well, yeah." His voice softens. He reaches up to readjust his cap, which I've determined is his nervous habit, and lets his hand linger to scratch the back of his neck. "But I thought—or, well, I hoped—"

"I didn't say I don't." I cut him off before I've thought twice about it. Just seeing him wilt like that melted my cold heart even more, dammit. I sigh. "Just . . . what if."

He looks back up at me with the widest, most hopeful eyes, and I know I'm screwed if I don't get out of this pantry stat. Benny Beneventi is truly wearing me down with shockingly little effort. I don't understand this overwhelming urge to agree to a date with him despite knowing that it's a terrible idea. Somewhere between the arms and the empathy and the terrible pun-laden lines, he's gotten to me.

"One evening. Just a few hours and you never have to see me again outside of work if you don't want to." His eyes roam around the pantry, clearly scanning for his next food victim. I tap my foot as I wait. "*Lettuce* have a chance."

I narrow my eyes at the leafy bundle he's holding. "That's arugula and you know it."

"I'll get on my knees and beg if I have to. I'm not kidding."

Looking into his earnest face, I believe him. And then he bends one knee and starts to drop to the floor. I grab his arm. "Don't do that. You don't know what's been on this floor."

He straightens back up, grinning like a kid on Christmas. "Is that a yes?"

I look to the ceiling and let out one more long, hard exhale, summoning every ounce of the good sense my mama raised me with to overrule my dumb, impulsive heart. "Benny, I can't. Not now."

Looking back down, I meet his dejected puppy eyes for only a second before I turn for the door, and this time, he doesn't stop me. "I've gotta get back to work, okay? And if you want this job as bad as I do, you probably should too."

Stepping out into the hallway, I let the door fall shut on Benny, and on all the possibilities I can't let myself consider.

Chapter Nine

If I thought my rejection was going to change anything about our working relationship or deter Benny from being his typical Benny self, I quickly learn I was mistaken. That evening, only a few hours after I left him in the pantry, he sends me a YouTube montage of Sylvester Stallone in the Rocky movies training for his fights, with the caption, "Me preparing for our showdowns."

He's a resilient little booger.

It's only a few minutes before we start filming our first competition-style video on Thursday, and I'm reaching back to tie my apron around my waist when I feel myself getting tugged back by the strings.

"What the—"

"Gooood morning, Reese's Cup." Benny's voice is at my ear.

I whirl around and look him straight in the face as I redo the knot at my back. "Benji."

"Ready to get culinarily destroyed?" he asks with a cocky

smile. Annoying as it is, I much prefer this attitude to that of the Benny of yesterday who offered to go easy on me. It almost feels like our conversation in the pantry never happened. Which is a relief, of course.

I shake my head, narrowing my eyes and crossing my arms again in my best attempt at looking intimidating in my pale pink apron and today's shirt, which is printed with tiny French bulldogs. "Not a chance."

He matches my stance and glare, but there's still a teasing glint in his eyes. "Game on, Camden."

For our first showdown video, Aiden is brought in as a host to explain the new format of the show, what Benny and I are "competing" for, and how the challenges will go down. It's clear someone somewhere is looking out for me when Aiden tells us that, for our first challenge, Benny and I must each make our own variety of homemade ice cream. I've made ice cream a million times in Mamaw's kitchen, big batches that my brothers and cousins and me devoured sitting on Mamaw and Papaw's porch in the summertime. It's one of the things I feel most comfortable making on my own.

We have access to whatever we want from the FoF fridges and pantries for flavoring or toppings, so I go with a fancy Swiss chocolate for the base with plans to infuse it with pureed mint. It's a glorified mint chocolate chip, but it feels like I'm taking a huge risk. Benny gets quite the kick out of teasing me about putting leaves in my ice cream, even though I show him repeatedly that the mint is not in leaf form by the time I'm mixing it with the chocolate.

Filming goes into a second day since we have to let our batters chill overnight, and the trash talk does not slow down. I don't respond to most of his texts between Thursday night and Friday, because I'm too keyed up about this first battle. On Friday, each of us let our batters run through the ice cream makers and then chill them for a few minutes in the blast freezer so they harden quickly, then we sample our own and each other's before bringing in the judges.

My mint chocolate is delicious—and not at all leafy. Benny has made a mixed-berries-and-cream concoction that is, I hate to admit upon tasting it, next level. Nia, Seb, and Lily are brought in as the blind taste testers, and while they stress that both ice creams are excellent, two out of three prefer Benny's.

He takes an obnoxious bow as the whole group—including me, grudgingly—gives him a round of applause. I try not to let my annoyance show until filming wraps up and most people disperse from the kitchen, at which point I take it out on a sticky spot on the counter where some batter spilled.

"I think you got it all." Benny's voice is so close behind me that I nearly jump out of my shoes. "Keep scrubbing that hard and you'll wear a hole through the counter."

"Keep minding your own business if you don't want me to wear a hole through your head, mister."

He laughs as he leans against the counter beside me, one

muscular forearm making its way into my line of sight. "I'm not even sure what that means, but you're cute when you're grumpy. Relax, Reese's Pieces. It's still early in the season and we're only oh-and-one. Not that anyone's keeping score."

I grit my teeth but say no more, and soon enough he gets the picture and makes himself scarce. He's joking around, but I'm already all too aware of the score, picturing it in bold letters and neon lights:

Benny—1, Reese—0.

I spend most of the weekend hunkered down over my sketch pad and tablet, hoping to have some *Amateur Hour* logo designs and a few other illustrations, in the style of what I used to do for my food column in the school paper, to show Margie by Monday. After much pestering and reassurances that it will be strictly platonic, I agree to join Benny on Saturday night for what he's advertised as a "quick" dinner at Dick's Drive-In, but we end up talking and laughing over burgers and milkshakes for a couple of hours. I'm annoyed at myself for having a good time, and for forgetting about work for a while, despite my best intentions.

But come Monday, it's back to business. I email Margie first thing when I get to my desk, even though I haven't seen her around the office yet, asking whether we can meet to talk about my designs. I haven't decided if it'll seem like I'm trying too hard if I show my boss this work I wasn't explicitly asked to do, but she's got to see what I'm capable of. Her response comes within five minutes.

R—
Sure, let's go for coffee this afternoon, 2pm. Bring your designs.
Thx,
M

My eyebrows lift in surprise. A coffee outing is more than I expected, but I'm happy to accept. And nervous as hell. I spend most of the day half-heartedly tending to the social media likes and replies while worrying my bottom lip between my teeth and braiding and unbraiding my hair over and over again. I know I look like a mess by the time I gather my laptop and my bag and meet Margie by her desk, but seeing the exceptionally frizzy state of her own braid helps put me at ease.

She leads the way to a coffee shop I haven't been to a few blocks from the office and offers to buy me a drink when we get there. I can't decide whether it would be worse manners to turn her down or to let her buy me something; somehow Mama's teaching never prepared me for this situation. I end up asking for a glass of water—still an order, but it doesn't cost anything.

Either I've found the best of both worlds or made myself look like even more of a head case.

When Margie sits at the window-side table I've selected, she wastes no time, jumping right in before she's even set her coffee mug down. "So, what have you got for me?"

"Oh!" I squeak in surprise, even though this was the whole point of our outing. I scramble to pull my computer out and open it up between us on the table, tapping in my passcode to reveal the handful of windows I have at the ready. "I can start with the *Amateur Hour* logo designs. You mentioned wanting to have something to put on the UltiMedia home page, so I put together a few options that I hope look consistent with the other series' logos but also represent the, uh, *vibe* of our show. I have mock-ups ready of what they could look like as banners at the bottom of our video thumbnails, title screens for the beginning of each episode, things like that. So to start, I have these three. . . ."

I click around until the three designs are pulled up on the same screen, turning the laptop so it faces Margie as she blows steam off her mug. Her eyes narrow as she leans in to study the designs, and I do everything in my power not to bite my bottom lip clean off while I await her reaction. Her face is unreadable. After a minute or two, she looks back up at me.

"These are excellent," she says, and while there's only a hint of a grin in her expression, I feel like she's giving me a standing ovation. "I like the one in the middle best, with the colors and nods to key elements of the *Amateur Hour* brand, but I'll put it out to the team and see if there are better arguments for the others. Send me all the mock-ups you have for those, if you will. What's next?"

Oh. *Oh.* Was that . . . it? Was it really that easy? She likes them and wants to use one of them, just like that? Trying to hide my utter shock, I blink a couple of times and nod, turning the computer back my way.

"O-okay, well, I'm so happy to hear that. Thank you. I'll absolutely send them your way, and let me know if you need anything more from me on, uh, that front. The next thing I wanted to show you is kind of out of the blue, not something you've asked me to work on, so I totally understand if these aren't anything you can use, but I was just pulling from some of my experience—you might have seen the samples in my portfolio from my food column in my high school paper, and, um—"

"Reese," Margie says coolly, and my eyes snap up to meet hers. "There's no need to be so nervous. You're doing a great job. I'm happy to look at whatever ideas you want to show me."

I take a sip of my free water and swallow heavily. "Right. Got it. No nerves! Thank you. So, I did some illustrations."

Turning the laptop around again, I explain each drawing as I click through them. I've drawn a couple of the most recent dishes and also ones from the most popular episodes of Lily's, Katherine's, and Nia's series—baba ghanoush and samosas from *World on a Plate,* Easy Peasy Split Pea Soup and Julia Child's Play Boeuf Bourguignon from *Fuss-Free Foodie,* and a baked Alaska and cannoli cheesecake from *Piece of Cake.*

I've also done some minimalist illustrations of each of the Friends, highlighting their respective settings and personal style with mostly solid colors and basic shapes. Since Rajesh's show takes him to a lot of different restaurants around the country, I've drawn him with wavy black hair and brown skin, standing under a generic restaurant sign and wearing a graphic T-shirt and the green backpack he always carries on his travels. Seb and Aiden are side by side in the FoF studio, in their white and red aprons, respectively, and looking like the little culinary angel and devil on your shoulder. And I've depicted Katherine standing in one of the prep kitchens with her hands on her hips and her wild auburn hair piled in a bun atop her head. She's surrounded by plates of miscellaneous food and the yellow notepad she jots her recipes down on, using the most basic steps and terms, and then displays on camera at the end of each episode.

Margie spends a longer time looking these over, her face still giving little away. The longer the silence stretches after my explanation of each drawing, the more nervous I get. Finally, when I feel like I'm seconds away from snapping the laptop shut, maybe even throwing it into Puget Sound for dramatic effect, she nods. Then nods some more while a real, teeth-showing smile spreads across her face. I practically melt into my chair with relief.

"Wow," she says, her gaze moving back to me. "You've got something very special here, Reese. I'm so glad you took the time to create these and show them to me. They are absolutely the kind of thing we could use to punch up some of our social media content. We could have illustrated ads for upcoming episodes, or downloadable illustrations for desktop or mobile wallpaper, maybe eventually some prints for purchase . . ."

She goes on, listing all the possibilities she sees "off the top of her head" for my designs, while my own head spins. I wonder for a moment if I'm dreaming this, as it's better than I imagined the conversation would go. But if it was a dream, my hands probably wouldn't be shaking in my lap like someone slipped a shot of espresso into my tea this morning. I keep nodding, even when I don't fully know what Margie's talking about because what the hell, take my drawings and put them on the side of a bus, tattoo them on Aiden's face, I don't care. They're *my* real-life designs that are maybe, possibly, most likely getting used by the real-life Friends of Flavor!

"Now, there is another thing I was hoping we could cover today while it's just the two of us, away from the office," Margie says, flicking her braid over her shoulder, then leaning in and folding her hands on the table. I sit up straighter and try to school my expression into Serious Businesswoman Reese Camden, not Blissed-Out Fangirl Reese Camden. "And it's especially relevant given what you've shown me today. Reese, I know you may worry that Benny has the leg up when it comes to the fall internship, given that he's already a culinary intern. But I don't want you to count yourself out too soon.

"Between you and me, I'm not especially keen on the whole fight-to-the-death model for *Amateur Hour,* but it's not the be-all and end-all. Keep figuring out your strengths"—she taps my laptop—"and play to them. I believe you have a lot to offer this company, and want you to believe that yourself. I'm rooting for you. All right?"

Well, I certainly didn't think I could be any more floored than I already was by her reaction to my designs, but here I am— more than floored. Grounded? Trampled? It's all I can do to nod and thank her, and try to take Margie's words—her belief in me—to heart.

And she sure follows through, sending my designs around the office and up the FoF food chain to wherever these decisions are made. Later that week, they're already using the brand-new *Amateur Hour* logo that I created. All the existing episodes are updated with the design in a new title screen and banner at the bottom of each video thumbnail, and my logo gets listed alongside all the other series logos on the UltiMedia home page.

The design they go with was Margie's initial favorite, as well as mine. The capital *A* in *Amateur* is wearing a backward ball cap like Benny, a macaron stands in for the *o* in *Hour,* and cartoon versions of Benny and me stand back-to-back between the two words. I almost made cartoon Reese slightly taller than cartoon Benny as a petty power move but held off. The positive reception for my work makes me feel powerful enough, and even though it didn't play out on video, I give myself a point on the mental scoreboard.

Benny—1, Reese—1.

My partner in, well, whatever you'd call what we're doing these days, seems a bit shaken when I see him for the first time after my designs are put to use. I'm standing at the front desk talking to Teagan when Benny comes back from lunch. He saunters over to join us, eyeing me almost suspiciously.

"Reese's Pieces. Way to undersell your casual drawing habit to me," he says, giving me an assessing once-over. "That's some secret weapon to whip out without warning."

I widen my eyes, feigning innocence. "Oh, was I supposed to give written notice? 'Dear Benny, I'm about to make an effort at my job'?"

Teagan covers a giggle with her hand. "I mean, he's not wrong to be worried. You delivered Margie a whole-ass branding package, while he's been cleaning kitchens and waiting for Aiden to tell him when to start cooking again."

I bite my lip, trying to hide the gratification I get at Benny feeling any of the self-consciousness I'm so accustomed to.

He sticks his tongue out at Teagan like a little kid. "Yeah, and remind me, who won the first showdown?"

"We've only filmed one, so don't get too comfy," I say with an eye roll. "Nice sportsmanship, though. Good to see how quickly you've abandoned all efforts to make me like you."

The last part slips out before I consider our small audience, and I hear a soft, delighted gasp from Teagan. Benny straightens up, his face brightening and one eyebrow raised in teasing challenge.

"Is that what you think? Oh, sweet, lovely, stealthily talented

Reese. I'm only demonstrating how well I can separate work from the personal. That's why you didn't want to go out with me, isn't it?" He steps closer to me and I back up, flattening myself against the front of Teagan's desk and regretting that she's witnessing any of this. "I haven't abandoned any efforts when it comes to you. I'm just playing the long game."

He backs away, eyes twinkling with mischief. "See you in the kitchen, yeah?"

Before Teagan can suppress her laughter enough to pester me about any of what just happened, I start toward marketing, calling over my shoulder, "Nothing to see here! Back to work!"

The next time I see Benny, we're filming our next cooking showdown video in which we have to prepare omelets. Toward the end, he shocks the hell out of me by making a point of giving a shout-out to his "more artistically gifted costar," directing the audience's attention to our show's new logo and all the places it can be found, and making sure they know it was designed by me.

As much as I'm still trying to keep my distance, that one gets him a hug once the cameras quit rolling and PK 2 empties out.

"Is this a sympathy hug because your omelet won the taste test?" he murmurs grumpily into my hair, wrapping his arms around my waist and holding on for longer than I initially planned when I made this impulsive move.

I shake him off and step back, hoping he didn't notice my full-body shiver from his warm breath and strong hands. Lordy, can my body chill out?

"No, it's a thank-you hug for paying me such a nice compliment at the end." With a teasing smile, I reach up and give his cheek a pat. "Don't you worry. I don't have any sympathy for you."

"Good. When I win your affections," Benny says, his displeasure at losing fading into a mischievous smile as he deliberately echoes my words from last week, "I want to know it's fair and square."

Chapter Ten

Over the next week, Benny and I get a bit of a respite as the episodes we've already filmed are released and other FoF shows occupy the filming schedule. Benny does his normal thing, assisting around the kitchens, while I'm in my marketing nook. True to Margie's word, I continue to not be responsible for monitoring responses to *Amateur Hour* videos, but word around the office is that we're a major hit, especially with the new, more competitive format. Benny informs me that there is at least one Twitter account dedicated to memes about us.

He and I mostly see each other when we walk home from work and sometimes for dinner, either pieced together in one of our dorm kitchens or sourced from our growing list of Seattle's cheapest dining establishments. I'm doing my best to stick to my guns—to keep up our normal amount of jokey banter, occasionally roast him for his over-the-top lines when he tries them, and to seem as generally unaffected by him as I can.

But it's more of a struggle by the day. He's just so *nice,* so consistent and clear in his intentions, in the fact that he enjoys my company and wants to know me better. The feeling is mutual, but I'm still too afraid of everything I have to lose if I give in to it. So I continue to roll my eyes at his flirtiest efforts, hoping it hides how, little by little, I'm melting into the Puddle of Goo Formerly Known as Reese.

Still riding the high of the logo and the break from *Amateur Hour* filming, I'm feeling good when it's time to make our next episode. So good that I'm not even especially bothered by my lack of any damn clue as to how to make soft pretzels. I think that whoever planned this "challenge" thought that Benny and I would get creative with gourmet toppings or special flavors, but they didn't count on basic pretzel dough being its own challenge for me.

I was able to come up with something somewhat doughlike and semi-pretzel-shaped, but it ain't pretty. My ugly dough babies are baking in one of the ovens right now, and Benny's just put his in—after fishing them out of some boiling water concoction; since when do you boil baked goods?—so Charlie pauses filming and we start to relax.

Until Aiden marches onto the scene. "Reese, can I speak with you for a moment?"

My brows lift in surprise, but I nod.

"I already know you're winning this one, but at least make sure those don't catch fire, please," I say to Benny as I follow Aiden into the hallway.

"I'm gonna need you to be a little nicer on camera," Aiden announces without preamble, before we've even come to a stop.

My head jerks back involuntarily. "Um. Be nicer?"

"Mm-hmm." He nods like this isn't strange or awkward or in earshot of most of the office. "Had a conference call with the suits. Feedback is you're too b—er, mean. Intense. People think you aren't cheery or perky enough, or nice enough to Benny, and it's off-putting. They like your look, but they want you to smile more, try to appear a little upbeat, more energized. Perky. Like Benny, but feminine."

I make a noise of pure disbelief, but try to cover it with a cough. Off-putting? *Smile more?* Perky? And I am 90 percent sure he was about to say "bitchy" before he stopped himself.

"I told them you could manage," Aiden says, giving my shoulder a go-get-'em-champ pat. But he can't help but ask, "Am I right?"

I nod wordlessly, because what else am I supposed to do when confronted with this kind of feedback? Ask for specific dialogue recommendations? Other directions so that I meet expectations? Clarify whether ever-serious Katherine has been given such directions before, or quiet, subdued Seb?

But I don't have the chance, as Aiden marches into the kitchen and I follow in a daze.

Benny leans in and catches my gaze. "Everything okay, blondie?"

I shake my head and give him a withering look for the

not-so-endearing endearment. Then I check myself—be nicer, happier—and try to turn my expression into something at least neutral, if not pleasant, smiling and offering a less-than-believable, "Fine!"

I'm embarrassed to have been given a talking-to, even though I think it was for a stupid reason, and I worry that it's a sign of worse thoughts the suits have about me. That they wish I was more like my costar in every way—i.e. male—but this was the only criticism they could acceptably say aloud. This is definitely a point in the Benny column. Which, with my omelet win and Benny's imminent pretzel victory, brings us to **Benny—3, Reese—2.**

My oven beeps with the arbitrary time I set, bringing the conversation to a halt as Charlie sets the cameras up to start filming again. I bring my non-pretzels out to cool, but my mind is still reeling even as I try extra hard to paste on a smile. I feel my pulse pounding, the beginnings of a headache coming on. I thought I was keeping up so well—learning more around the kitchen every day and holding my own on *Amateur Hour.* It was the furthest thing from my mind, whether I looked happy enough while doing it. Because I *was* happy. *Am* happy.

I think.

It's hard to tell what my real feelings are anymore, as I focus intently on the arrangement of my every facial expression and gesture, the tone of my voice, the brightness of my smile.

Benny's laugh brings me back to the moment as he gives me some deserved but still good-natured ribbing. I've ended up with what are essentially dinner rolls that tried to dress as pretzels for Halloween. Benny's, meanwhile, are mall-food-court-level perfection. Apparently the boiling part—plus baking soda—is what gives pretzels their tough, dark brown exterior. Add that to the ever-growing list of things I didn't know that I didn't know about cooking.

I try to seem like a good sport about the loss, since this really isn't what's upsetting me today. By the time we've wrapped up, I've let out enough nervous chuckles that I probably sound like a broken Tickle Me Elmo. Benny can clearly tell something's up, and he pulls me aside before I can run and hide in my marketing corner for the rest of the day.

"Hey, no hard feelings about the pretzels, okay? Your weird-shaped dinner rolls were bomb. Ten out of ten would serve at Thanksgiving."

That gets a genuine, if small, laugh out of me. "It's fine—I had no chance on this one."

"Everything else okay, then?" His expression is soft, his eyes concerned and searching mine.

I cross my arms over my chest, discreetly tucking my clammy palms against my sides. "Yep, all good. Just, uh, been a long day."

My voice comes out less steady than I'd prefer and I'm fighting a chin wobble with everything in me. Benny frowns, stepping a bit closer and softening his voice even further.

"You're not a very good liar, Reese's Cup. You know you can talk to me, right?"

Squeezing my eyes shut for a moment, I summon all my strength to lock the feelings down. Then I give Benny my most serene, no-really-everything's-fine look, because you know what? Things could be a lot worse. I can buck up and smile more if that's what they want, and pretend to be the fun, easygoing girl that I'm not. I can do my best to avoid Aiden, until I don't feel so much like biting his head off, and eventually my bruised ego will heal.

"I appreciate that," I answer, because it's true. "But I don't need to today."

"Well, the offer stands." He looks sincere, but I can see the hint of a sardonic smile playing at the corners of his mouth. "The offer to talk about your problems. Or to share our hopes and dreams, or hang out platonically or not so platonically, or really just about whatever you need, any time. You know where to find me."

I turn to make my retreat toward marketing but also to keep Benny from seeing the color rising in my face. "Duly noted, Beneventi."

When I allow myself a final peek over my shoulder just before turning the corner, it's to see his dimpled full smile. And in return, I go full goo-puddle, all my worries and admonishments from the big bad boss be damned. Goodness, I'm in deep.

The following morning, I get up early for the only two people who can get me to do so voluntarily. Well, it's mostly my own fault. I've been shaken up by the recent events at work, and also by the fact that I can't stop thinking about Benny's open-ended offer to be there for whatever I want or need. I'm finding myself more tempted to take him up on all of it—from talking about my problems to the non-platonic hangout—but I just don't know if it's the right move.

So I womaned up and told Nat and Clara that I needed to talk. They were on board, of course, but they're road-tripping and moving Clara into her summer leadership camp in North Carolina and likely won't have phone service once they get into the mountains. Thus, a seven a.m. prework call for Reese.

I came to one of Seattle's plentiful coffee shops for the occasion, both to get better Wi-Fi than the crappy stuff in my dorm and to fuel up with caffeine. I open my laptop and plug my headphones in, blowing on my London fog before taking a too-hot sip anyway.

My friends are going to call me, so while I wait, I check my phone and see a couple of texts from Benny. True to his word to Margie and Aiden, he has been sharing the occasional picture of me on his personal Instagram to give me some semblance of a social media presence. He always sends me the pictures to approve before he posts them, and last night after I fell asleep, he sent one of me laughing at something in PK 2 while putting my apron on. I don't remember him taking it, but it's not a bad shot. And the fact that he wants to post it is pretty cute.

And hey, maybe this will help with my Perky Problem. *Look, I can smile and laugh! I'm a happy, cheerful person!* I grimace at the thought even as I grant permission with a thumbs-up text to Benny. Just in time for the call to come through. I answer on my computer, and Natalie's slightly blurry face fills the screen.

"REESE, CAN YOU HEAR ME?" she yells, causing me to nearly spill my latte and yank the headphones out of my ears.

"Yes, grandma. Please use your inside voice," I scold her, but I'm stifling a laugh. It's way too good to see her face and hear her unnecessarily loud voice.

"Sorry," she says at normal volume. "I've never FaceTimed in the car before, so I wasn't sure if all the road noise would be too much. Enough chitchat, tell us all the latest on your megacool job and celeb status and ball cap boo *now*!"

"Hey, Reese," I hear Clara say in her calmer tones, and Nat rotates the phone so I have a view of both her riding shotgun and Clara at the wheel. The latter, always more responsible than Nat or me, does not take her eyes from the road.

"Hi, Clar, and lovely to see you, too, Nat. Nice weather we're having lately, isn't it?"

"C'mon, cough up the goods, Camden. We don't have all day."

"We have about three more hours," Clara says, and Nat gives her a stink eye that she can't see.

I laugh at the familiar dynamic that I've been missing. "Okay, okay. So have you been keeping up with *Amateur Hour?*"

Natalie scoffs. "Of course we've been keeping up with our adorable best friend kicking booty *and* with her costar making constant heart eyes at her."

"He does not make heart eyes at m— You know what, not the point. Well, things at work have gotten a bit more, uh, complicated since I last gave you the rundown."

While we text regularly, I've been bad about giving detailed updates on everything lately, so I start in now. I go all the way back to meeting Geoffrey Block, CEO, at the cookout to the introduction of the head-to-head competitions for the fall internship and end with Aiden's talk with me yesterday about the suits' feedback. Nat and Clara listen and occasionally ask questions, and I start to realize I should have cracked open the emotional fire hydrant a little sooner. Letting it all out this way feels good, even before my friends give me their thoughts.

And they sure have thoughts.

"Aiden, you pasty, misogynistic asshat," Nat fumes.

"You know that's absurd, though, don't you, Reese?" Clara's response is characteristically more contained. "You're very personable on camera. You smile just as much as any of the other Friends do on their shows."

I shrug. "I thought as much too, but clearly something about me isn't working. I don't know, I just worry that even if I make a push to be the most dazzling ray of sunshine they've ever seen, there will always be something else about me that's lacking. That the people up top already like Benny so much that next to him, I'll never quite measure up."

Nat pouts at me. "I want to fly out there and crack some suit-wearing skulls for making you feel that way. You're perfect already."

"I know it sucks to get feedback like that," Clara says. "But unfortunately, you can't control what other people are gonna think of you. So you have to focus on the things that *are* in your power. Like your amazing designs that your boss is in love with."

"And how good you've gotten at fixing your hair and makeup for filming," Nat adds.

"And your impressive cooking skills."

"And giving the cute boy who is super into you a big ol' smooch."

That gets Natalie an eye roll. "And how exactly will that help me get the fall internship?"

She waves a dismissive hand. "Unrelated. Just another thing within your power that I think you should consider. Any day now, that boy is gonna ask you on a date, mark my words."

I grimace. "Weeelll . . ."

Nat and Clara both gasp, and Nat nearly drops the phone as she bounces in her seat. "Reese Camden, do you mean . . . ? How? When? And you didn't tell us?"

I sit back in my chair with a sigh. "Yeah, so that's the other complicated bit."

I relay the story of Benny's food pun warfare and my rejection, as well as some of the ways he continues to express his interest—the ones Clara and Natalie haven't seen on *Amateur Hour,* anyway.

"Excellent pun repertoire," Clara says.

"Oh gosh, this is the cutest. I can't, this is so cute. And please clarify, why didn't you tear the ball cap off his head and stage an instant pantry make-out sesh?" Nat looks at me like she's disgusted by my actions, or lack thereof.

"Good gravy, what is it with you and the ball cap?" I ask.

She shakes her head. "You know I've always had an athlete thing. Answer the question."

It's true. Nat dated at least one member of every boys' sports team at our school at some point, never for very long and always dumping them for reasons like "too alpha," "didn't shower after practice," or "Republican."

"I don't know," I say. "I barely knew him at that point. They'd just decided we'd be competing for the fall internship on camera, and it didn't seem worth the extra complication. But the more I've gotten to know him, the more I like him. And that scares me, because the more I like him, the harder it'll be for me to want him to lose out on the job so I can win. And of course I'm afraid that I won't get it in the end anyway. And no matter how much I like him, I might resent him if he gets it, and honestly, what's the point in setting ourselves up for that?

"And the last thing I need, with people already scrutinizing everything about me, is for anyone to find out that there's any-thing more than a working relationship between us. Then I'm the lovesick girl, not a serious chef in training. I'm not going to chuck all my plans out the window for the first guy who comes around and treats me halfway decent."

Natalie and Clara both make *hmm* sounds. I sort of regret telling them about Benny in the first place; they're invested now, so they won't let go easily.

"Not to bring everything back to a TKM post," Nat begins. "But remember that TKM post Katherine wrote about romance novels?"

I blink, trying to jog my memory. "Vaguely?"

She clears her throat, and I feel like I'm in for a lecture. "Well, our girl Katherine is a proud romance reader and believes that it is, in fact, the most feminist genre in fiction. People think it's all about finding love and that women can't be happy without a romantic partner. But Katherine and I agree that most romance is actually, at its heart, about women asking for and getting what they want, whether it's out of a partner, career, life in general. It's all about claiming your own happiness and not judging what it is that makes you or anyone else happy, and what's more empower-ing than that?"

I purse my lips, trying and failing at deciphering her implica-tions. "I'm gonna need you to spell it out for me. The message you're getting at."

"What I think she means is," Clara cuts in, "those books, in most cases, tell women that they can have it all. And *you can,* Reese. I know you think a relationship ruined everything for you last time, but you were younger and dumber and more easily fooled by a guy who really wasn't worth it. If you think Benny can make you happy, then give him the chance. Give *yourself* the chance."

"But the job . . . ," I groan, running a hand down my face.

"Honestly, I think competing with each other is kinda hot," Natalie says. "All that trash talk, trying to one-up each other? It's like some seriously drawn-out foreplay."

I choke on my drink.

Clara's voice is steady and patient as she continues through my coughing fit. "Take care of the things you can control, but don't worry about hypothetical future conflicts or resentments when they don't exist yet and maybe never will. Liking a guy doesn't make you any less capable of doing your job. You can be a career-minded badass and have your own great love story— they're not mutually exclusive."

"Yeah, Clar!" Natalie pumps a fist, and I shudder again at the volume pumping straight into my eardrums. "And if you need any more convincing, might I remind you of all of our pro-Benny points?"

I'm about to tell her no, that isn't really necessary, Clara's speech got the message across, but Nat is already counting things off on her fingers.

"One, the face—I mean, the smile, the dimples, the eyes, all of it. Two, the emotional intelligence. We love a man who is in touch with his feelings and opens up to you."

"Three, the height," Clara adds, surprising Natalie as much as me, judging by the look Nat gives her. "What? I like that y'all are even, or Reese might even be a tiny bit taller, but he doesn't seem threatened by it."

"Hmm, good point," Nat says. "Four, not to be mostly physical, but the body . . ."

I laugh as my friends continue to wax poetic about Benny, based on what they know about him from the videos and me. Admittedly, what they're saying is getting to me. Should I give a date with Benny a chance? Could we balance a romantic relationship with this completely bonkers work situation we're in? Would the risks be worth it to spend more time together, no matter what came of it in the end?

The conversation moves on naturally as I continue to mull things over, and Nat fills me in about the latest contact she's had with her randomly assigned roommate, who seems to be a shy introvert, bless her heart. We talk about what's on the schedule for Clara the next few days, which is a bunch of seminars and team-building activities, and all the podcasts Nat has downloaded for her solo drive back to Kentucky. When they have to pull off the interstate to refuel both car and stomachs, we start to say our goodbyes.

"Now, Reesey, I want you to give this nice young man a chance," Nat slips in before I have a chance to hang up.

Clara, having safely parked the car, leans in to face the camera. "Yes, promise us you'll think about what we said."

"No, I don't want you to think about it anymore." Nat shakes her head. "I want you to agree to go out on a date with him. Do you need me to draft a text for you?"

I shake my head. "No, I don't need that."

She frowns. "Are you sure? Because sometimes you come across a little snippy in text form and I just—"

"No, I don't need you to draft anything," I cut her off, pausing for dramatic effect as I take the last sip from my mug. "Because I'm going to tell him in person."

Their celebratory squeals echo in my head as I pack up my things, set off for the Friends of Flavor offices, and start my day. Buoyed by their excitement, I consider how to carry out my mission as I tend to the various likes and comments on FoF social media.

By lunchtime, I've got a plan. I grab a piece of paper from the copy machine outside marketing and scribble down a note. This isn't totally in line with what I told Nat I'd do, but I figure a written transaction is safer. Less awkward for both of us if he's changed his mind about said non-platonic hangout or, I don't know, found a less neurotic girl to date.

I swing by one of the pantries and find the other prop I need for my gesture—a small, wax-covered wheel of cheese. Securing the note to it with a piece of tape, I head for the cubby where Benny keeps his things, surreptitiously keeping an eye out for the boy in question. I make it there without spotting him, thankfully, and am starting to wedge the package in a spot beside his backpack where he won't be able to miss it when his voice behind me nearly scares the life out of me.

"Ah shit, is the dress-code justice fairy coming for me now?"

I whirl around to face Benny. "I swear, I should put a bell on you."

His lips edge up on one side and he crosses his arms over his chest. Today's shirt, I can't help but notice, is especially tight in the sleeve area. It's honestly rude.

"Whatever you're into, Reese's Cup. That for me?"

He nods at the offering I haven't quite let go of, the note now crinkled in my death grip. Guess we're doing this. I thrust the cheese toward him, unable to look away from the wall behind him as I do. He takes it and when his head tips down to read the note, I watch the smirk fall from his face.

B,

Let's go on that date. When's gouda for you?

R

"Reese . . ." Benny looks up and meets my eyes, a series of expressions flashing across his face. Blankness bordering on confusion shifts to surprise, then, finally, to absolute eye-twinkling, toothy-smiled elation. "I didn't know you were so cheesy."

A relieved laugh escapes me, and I echo his words from the pantry a few weeks back. "Is that a yes?"

He shoves my shoulder playfully. "Like you even have to ask."

Chapter Eleven

I stand in front of the mirror the next evening, minutes before I said I'd meet Benny by the fountain. I don't look especially flushed nor abnormally pale. No goose bumps or beads of sweat. All in all, nothing to suggest that I've legitimately come down with a fever.

This morning when I woke up and remembered what I had done the day before, fever was my first guess as to what must have come over me. Why else would I have sought out Benny, despite all my reservations, and used a food pun to ask him on a date? Second guess was that I'd been possessed by demons, but it's hard to plan an exorcism with such late notice. So here I am, slipping my feet into my fancy sandals and setting out to meet my possible knight in shining ball cap.

And, against my best judgment, feeling excited about it.

Turning the corner from the stairwell into the lobby, I catch a glimpse of Benny through the glass front doors before he can see me. He's also changed clothes since we walked home from work together a couple hours ago, so I won't look overdone. He's wearing fitted khakis and a light blue button-down with the sleeves rolled up. The T-shirts he usually wears draw attention to his biceps, but it's clear that I've been overlooking some seriously nice forearms. Am I into forearms? I didn't know that about myself. He has sandals on, too, and a brown ball cap, which keep him from looking too formal. The word "dreamy" floats through my mind and out again before I can linger on it or wonder when my relationship-adjacent vocabulary became so 1950s.

Goodness, I'm just going on a *date,* the first in almost four years and with a guy I've been trying hard not to like, but I'm so nervous you'd think I was expecting a marriage proposal. I was happy when we'd agreed to meet up later in the evening, after each doing our own thing for dinner, thinking the extra time to myself would help me chill out. Clearly that didn't work as planned. Benny must see me in his peripheral vision as I step outside, because he turns my way, his eyes widening a touch before his face breaks into a big smile.

"You look gorgeous," he says matter-of-factly, and my stomach does a backflip as I briefly glance down at my simple yellow sundress, its skirt swishing just above my knees. I lean into his open arms for a hug and notice that he smells amazing, like cinnamon or nutmeg, a spicy sweetness. Because of course he does.

"You clean up pretty nice yourself," I allow myself to say, still fighting the grin I'm feeling on the inside.

"I don't know about all that." He waves a hand in a *pssh* gesture. "Shall we?"

He tentatively rests his hand on my back as we head down the sidewalk, and the touch is surprising but not unwelcome. I remind the part of me that wants to freak out that this is Benny, who has shown me nothing but kindness so far, even if he's a little much at times. Trust until given reason not to.

"I wish I could tell you I have a car to drive us in, but my brother Enzo has mine for the summer. I'm going to make him feel really bad about it now that I—well, now that I need it more than I thought I might."

I smile at that, and the fact that he seems to be implying something like "now that I'm taking out a girl I like." He pulls out his phone with a look of apology and goes to call a rideshare.

"No worries," I assure him. "I don't mind helping pay for the ride, either."

"Nope, not tonight. I don't know if you've heard, but I'm a big internet star now. Raking in some serious dough."

I give a small laugh and roll my eyes, but my shoulders tense up at the reminder of his rising star, of my fear that I'm barely keeping up, of what that could mean when the summer ends. I try to halt that train of thought. I went to him with the intent of finally giving this date thing a try, and I need to do just that. *Try.* And that probably means giving the worries a rest for a few hours.

Our driver arrives and Benny crawls into the back seat after me and confirms that we're going to a place called Golden Gardens. Sounds like a retirement community to me, but I'm going to trust that my date knows what he's doing.

My date. Be still my totally-off-its-rocker heart.

We ride most of the way in comfortable silence, each of us looking out our window. I don't know about Benny, but I haven't seen much of Seattle yet, outside of the journey from the airport to the dorm to Friends of Flavor and to Seb's house. Once we get out of downtown, the scenery changes substantially. There are still hills, but instead of skyscrapers, they're covered in a mix of evergreen trees, Craftsman-style homes, and freestanding restaurants and shops. We cross a bridge over Lake Union, where there are people on everything from yachts to paddleboards floating past the rows of houseboats along the banks. The urban fades into suburban, and before long, into a long stretch of marinas along Puget Sound. Sailboats on sailboats on sailboats, belonging to people who very likely earn more in a day than I will all summer.

Then, suddenly, we're at a drop-off point at the end of a parking lot, and the driver slows to a stop. Benny thanks him before exiting the car and offering a hand to help me out. I have a couple of seconds to decide that his hand feels nice on mine before it's gone again.

"Not too shabby, eh?"

I follow his gaze to the sandy beach. Lazy waves lap at the shore, and off in the distance, huge, snowcapped mountains glow in the evening sun. There is a distinct lack of elderly people playing shuffleboard.

My jaw drops. "I'm definitely not in Kentucky anymore."

Benny laughs, looking back out at the mountains and sliding his hands in his pockets. "If I have my bearings right, those should be the Olympics, out on the Olympic Peninsula."

He starts walking toward the beach at quite the clip, and I nearly have to jog to catch up. "Is there a reason we're running?"

He lets out a single loud laugh but slows his pace. "Sorry. I just want to make sure we have a lot of time out here before sunset, which should be around nine-oh-eight."

Benny rattles this off without checking his phone or anything, his words coming even faster than his steps were. He was like this all day, come to think of it—talking a mile a minute while we did some organizational tasks around the office assigned by Aiden and Margie. I thought he was just on edge because menial filing jobs aren't his thing, but the way the anxious-puppy energy has persisted, I'm not so sure.

"Wow. How do you fit this stuff in there with all those recipes?" I tap the top of his head and he elbows me in the side.

We walk until we get to a sidewalk that borders the sand and follow that. The beach is busier than I'd expect for a weeknight, but it doesn't feel crowded. There are people playing volleyball, kids chasing each other and throwing Frisbees, dogs sniffing for anything dropped by the many picnickers. A few people dip their toes in the water, but no one's really swimming. Benny, Pacific Northwest trivia pro this evening, tells me that Puget Sound is frigid for most of the year. It's a pleasantly warm evening for now, but I wouldn't mind having a jacket. Maybe we'll find our way to one of the pits with bonfires burning farther down the beach.

I'm starting to wonder if we're ever going to walk on the actual beach when it occurs to me that I can take matters into my own hands. I split off from Benny and step down into the sand and out of my sandals. He does the same and I stand there wiggling my toes while he rolls the bottoms of his khakis a couple of times. When he straightens up with a smile, we keep going, down to the waterline.

"I don't know if you want to—"

"*Shoot*, that's cold!" I yelp, hopping back toward dry ground the second the water meets my skin.

"I tried to warn you," Benny says ruefully.

"It's a beach! How could I not get my feet wet?"

He looks amused. "That must be a Southern thing. Like presweetened tea."

I give him a small shove and he skips backward, laughing. He gestures to a long piece of driftwood that looks just shy of being purposefully placed. But I take a seat anyway, stretching my legs out and burying my chilly toes in the sun-warmed sand. Benny plops down beside me and stretches his arms over his head.

"Are you about to accidentally-on-purpose drape one of those arms over my shoulders?" I ask, surprising myself with my flirty tone.

"Wasn't the plan, but would it work if I did?"

"Maybe."

"Noted."

He brings his arms back down to rest at his sides and I feel him watching me as I look at the gently rolling waves. A seagull drifts down and lands a few feet in front of us, pecking delicately at something in the sand.

"You know, I always thought seagulls were just all one kind of bird, but there are over a hundred species native to Puget Sound alone," Benny says.

I can't keep my head from tilting back, my eyes from rolling upward, or the next words from coming out of my mouth. "You know, I enjoy these fun facts. I do. But is there a reason you're, uh, sharing so many this evening?"

"Ah." Benny chuckles softly, his chin dropping toward his chest. "Too much, huh?"

"Maybe a little. I mean, I'd never been to the West Coast or seen the Pacific before this summer, so it's cool, but I would've thought it'd all be less . . . fascinating to someone who's, like, been to Italy and France and lives on the coast, too."

He's still looking down at his hands, folded between his knees, when he speaks next. "Can I be honest here?"

"Please." I match his soft voice.

"I think you think I'm a lot cooler than I actually am," he says, reaching up to readjust his cap. "I've put up a pretty good front as long as you've known me, I guess, but finally being out here with you? I'm nervous as hell."

I don't know what I was expecting him to say, really, but "I'm nervous" was not on my admittedly rather rusty radar. So after another moment I do what any smooth, mature woman would do, and ignore that part entirely.

"I don't think you're that cool."

Benny looks back up at me, and I'm relieved to see he's laughing. His normal big, easy laugh. "Good. You're perceptive."

I give him a smirk before facing forward again.

"I'm the baby of the family, you know," he continues.

I nod. He told me that when we had lunch the first time, when I told myself that I would never ever be in the exact position I'm in at the moment, on a date with the guy I'm trying to see as *just* my competition. I see now that it was always gonna be hard to keep Benny as *just* anything.

"And my family is full of big personalities. I mean, *big*. Loud, sarcastic, emotional, proud, loving. They do it all big." He makes a wide arc with his hands. "And I think I've always found it easy to trail along behind them, keep in the background, go along with whatever they did. I tried the same sports as my brothers growing up. I always had the same teachers, and they'd always mess up and call me Manny or Leo or Enzo before landing on Benny."

I'm watching his face now, and his expression settles into a grimace as he looks back toward the water. "I started working at the restaurant as soon as I was old enough, just like they did. But each of them, they're still there. Manny's engaged, Leo's got another part-time gig, Enzo's in school, but ultimately, they all plan to stay in San Francisco and work at and eventually run Beneventi's. And the last couple of years, it's kinda hit me that I might not want the same."

Something about the way he says it makes me think that he's never done so out loud before. His voice gets a little rougher, as if he's pulling each word from deep within himself and pushing it out by force. I stay quiet.

"I applied for this summer internship without telling anyone, and I told my parents only a few weeks before I was supposed to leave. They were pissed. My brothers froze me out for a couple days, mostly just out of bitterness that I'd gone behind their backs. So they all got over it, assuming they would just hire an extra set of hands for the time I was gone and that I'll be back in the fall and everything can go back to how it was. At some point, I've gotta tell them that I'm not coming home."

Whoa. Not coming home . . . because he definitely plans to stay at Friends of Flavor? The reminder that he wants the fall internship at least as bad as I do—or worse, that he might already be counting on getting it—makes my hackles raise and stomach churn. I'm trying to take his separation-of-work-and-personal spiel to heart, trying to believe what Nat and Clara said about how I can have it all, but comments like that don't make it easy. It's hard not to feel like the fall internship is this cloud hanging over us at all times—something we can't avoid in just about any personal conversation about our goals and dreams.

But what he's telling me feels so personal, so difficult for him, that I don't think he even realizes how it sounds to me. And I don't want to drag him down further with my worries when he's trying to express his own. Not to mention putting the cart before the horse—I mean, this is only date number one. The stakes just feel higher for us than they might if this was gonna be a normal relationship between coworkers. One of us will be staying at Friends of Flavor after this summer, and one of us won't.

For now, I try to stay engaged with Benny's story. I brace myself on my hands as I lean back and stretch my legs farther in front of me. "Does that stress you out?"

He shrugs, mimicking my pose without seeming to think about it. "Yeah, but it also feels inevitable. They *will* find out sooner or later, so I'll have to find the words." He lifts and readjusts his cap again. "But I guess I'm telling you all this because . . . well, because I don't have my shit together. I can talk a big game but I've never done anything out of my family's shadow, just as Benny, the individual. But that's the only Benny you know. And I'm worried that when all the smoke and mirrors and cheesy lines are gone, you won't like what's left."

My eyebrows lift in surprise and I study his face. His expression is more vulnerable than I've ever seen, and the confession turns my focus from Benny the coworker and competitor to Benny the surprisingly sensitive guy. I have the sudden, totally stupid thought that I want to kiss him. Even more than I did while we were in the pantry, when I also kind of wanted to slap him.

But I know myself, and I know that probably shouldn't happen tonight. Not when I'm still trying to work out all my mixed-up feelings. Slow and steady.

"I like this version of you more than the one with the bad come-ons," I answer honestly, and his mouth tilts up on one side. "If you want me to like you for who you are, you just have to keep showing me who that person is."

Benny nods and I can see his heavy swallow. He's like one giant, boy-shaped ball of nerves right now, and I feel compelled to give him a little bit of myself in return.

"I think I know how you feel, living in others' shadows. I mean, it's different, but I have these two best friends at home, Natalie and Clara, and they are the strongest, smartest, most impressive people I know. Clara was the first person in our grade to come out as gay. In *middle school*. You know how awful kids are in middle school to begin with, right? And she made the decision to tell people at thirteen years old. Her family was supportive, thank goodness. But they were basically run out of their super-conservative church for the 'scandal'—the very church my family still attends, but without me ever since."

I sigh, my frustration building anew as I remember what my best friend went through—what she continues to go through each day in different ways, making a statement she never set out to make just by being who she is.

"I'm still figuring out where I stand with the man upstairs himself, but that was when I first figured out that Christians weren't always what I thought them to be. Natalie almost punched another girl in the cafeteria when she came up to our table to tell Clara she was going to hell. There were a lot of others who went the 'hate the sin, love the sinner' route, but do you really love the person if you hate a key part of their existence? But Clar went on to start a GSA chapter at our high school that had, like, fifty members by the time we graduated. And she would travel around to other schools and give talks and help them start their own clubs. She had a whole slew of colleges fighting for her to enroll there."

I trail off, shifting to sit cross-legged and running my palms over the little lap-shaped tent created by my dress. I peek at Benny from the corner of my eye, raising a brow as if to say, *Am I boring you to tears yet?* But he gives me a smile, one where I can just start to see the suggestion of a dimple, and it's all the encouragement I need.

"And then there's Nat, who's a firecracker." I huff out a laugh, shaking my head as a slew of sassy Natalie-isms float through my head. "Her family runs a horse farm for the out-of-town owner. She's been getting up before the crack of dawn to muck stalls for as long as I've known her. She's gotten to know all the other farmhands, a lot of them immigrants, and treats them like family, babysitting their kids and helping them learn English in her downtime.

"But, like you, she had no interest in sticking around after high school." I give Benny another glance and he nods in understanding. "She's a theater kid, and loves school and learning to boot, and her family does *not* understand. They'd never come to her plays even when she was the lead—which was most of the time. I swear, they try to make her feel like the biggest snob in the world for wanting an education, of all things, and haven't expressed any pride in all the cool stuff she does or that she's the first in the family to go to college. And thank goodness she has a bunch of scholarships to an artsy school in the Northeast, because her parents refuse to help her out now that she's leaving."

I stop for a breather. I feel oddly vulnerable, telling these stories that aren't even mine per se. But Natalie, Clara, and me, our lives have become so intertwined, we're a three-piece braid. Our stories overlap and twist around one another's and run together till it doesn't make much difference whose hurts or happinesses are whose. It's only now, as we're splitting off from each other for the first time in years, that I've even had occasion to consider our relationship from a distance, let alone share it with another person.

But the connection I'm starting to feel with Benny is the strongest I've had with anyone outside my two best friends. I want to know him and, even more surprisingly, I'm beginning to want him to know me.

I take another long breath before continuing. "They've both

been through so much and are so resilient and hugely impressive, and beside them I feel so . . . ordinary. Not to mention privileged. Like my problems aren't problems and my accomplishments, well . . . they're lacking. I could've stayed in that church when Clara was shut out and no one would have batted an eye. My parents encouraged me to apply to any schools I wanted, made sure I felt like money was no object. The biggest struggle in my life so far has stemmed from stupid high school drama that was maybe even partly my own fault, but Nat and Clara stuck by me and supported me like there was nothing more important to them. They even introduced me to Friends of Flavor a few years ago. They pushed so hard for me to apply for this internship, and I think a big part of why I wanted it so bad was to make them proud or, like, try to live up to the kind of person they think I am. The kind of people *they* are. I'm not envious of the fact that they've struggled, by any means; I'm just in awe of them and don't feel worthy of such amazing friends. I don't think they have any idea how much I want to deserve them."

I feel Benny staring at my profile, and my cheeks heat. I've never told anyone what I've just told him, and I feel . . . exposed. But also refreshed, in a way that I didn't expect. A weight I didn't even realize I was carrying is, if not lifted, then lessened, like it's been shifted into a comfy backpack that takes away some of the strain.

"You know, I don't know your friends, and I don't know all

the things you've been through," Benny says in a low voice. I look at him and find his gaze filled with warmth and admiration. "But I feel pretty confident in saying that they're already proud of you. *You're* smart, *you're* strong, and though it's not the most important part by a long shot, you're beautiful."

"There's that smooth talker again," I say with a laugh that I mean to sound light and teasing, but probably doesn't hide the fact that I'm freaking out on the inside over his compliments, so simply stated but so monumental to me all the same. And that look he's still giving me—who needs a beach bonfire to heat things up? Not him, apparently.

"I mean it. I'm pretty confident you already deserve your friends." He glances down at the sand with a small half smile. A breeze blows and, despite my date's hotness, I realize how chilly I'm getting.

"You want to walk?" I suggest, mostly to get my blood pumping but also because I don't want Benny to feel like he has to keep praising me all night. He nods and we set off side by side down the beach.

"Hey, can I take your picture here? You know, making an appearance on the Instagram."

I laugh, skipping down the beach to stand in front of the water and stretch my arms out wide. He snaps a couple of photos and gives me a thumbs-up, calling out, "Perfect, Reese's Cup."

Smirking, I return to walk beside him, leaning in closer to try to get some of his warmth.

"You cold?" he asks, and I nod. "Should I . . . ?"

I feel his arm shift behind me and I answer, "Um, yeah. Sure."

His hand comes to my shoulder and pulls me closer. He rubs up and down my upper arm a few times to generate some heat, and it's like I can feel the touch down to my toes. When I shiver this time, it isn't temperature related.

This guy.

"How much time do you spend in the gym, boy?" I'm nothing if not tactful.

A startled laugh escapes him. "Um, every other day typically. More if I need to de-stress or something on an off-day. It relaxes me."

"Naps relax me," I murmur.

"I like those, too."

"Do you wear a hat to the gym?"

Another laugh. "No, actually."

"So you *can* take it off?" I reach up and poke his cap. "I was starting to suspect it was a Darth Vader situation."

"A Darth Vader situation?"

"You know, like you were in a lightsaber battle that almost killed you and now this hat is your life support slash armor that you have to wear to stay alive. And it gives you a deep, husky voice."

Benny brings his hand up and pulls my head toward him, pretending to mess up my hair. I laugh and break away, but I'm pleased when he tucks me back against his side.

"Reese," he says into his free hand cupped over his mouth, in a deep, staticky attempt at a Vader voice. *"You . . . are . . . a . . . nerrrrd."*

I let out a particularly embarrassing snort. "And you're not especially good at impersonations, Benvenidos."

He bends over laughing at that one. "It's actually bienvenidos, if you were going for Spanish, Reese's Cup, and benvenuto in Italian."

I roll my eyes. "Yeah, okay, and you're *actually* the nerd here."

We continue walking, talking, and laughing for a while, and even when the sun starts to set, I don't feel cold. I think I could stay out here all night if sleep wasn't a thing. I'm comfortable with Benny, and more than that, *happy.* But between the darkening sky and our yawns increasing in frequency, heading home seems imminent. As we walk back to the park entrance, my phone buzzes in my pocket. Benny is distracted calling us a car, so I take the opportunity to check it.

There's a new email from Aiden and a new calendar notification, both linked to my work account and labeled *FoF Bainbridge Island Weekend.*

It might as well be a bucket of cold water dumped over my head. As I open the email and skim for pertinent information, my heart beats faster. It looks like they've planned a trip this weekend—as in, two days from now—to a cabin owned by one of the suits, where we'll be filming special episodes of a few different FoF series. We'll stay overnight Friday and Saturday and partake in various "rustic" culinary activities, such as fishing and cooking over a campfire.

Beneath the details about where and when to meet Friday, there are sections in which Aiden has laid out what particular people should bring and/or plan for. I scroll until I see **Benny/Reese** in bold letters, followed by, "Expect to film an ep of AH with special guests. Bring your A game and positive attitudes."

A lump forms in my throat. Why does that feel like a specific callout, and in an all-staff email? Have I really been that much of a Debbie Downer? Now I have less than forty-eight hours to prepare for a double sleepover with all of my coworkers and both my bosses during which I need to be on my "A game" the whole time. The sudden pressure makes me feel like I might throw up.

"Ride's here," Benny calls from the curb, where he's standing. My feet propel me toward him, but my mind is on a different path, my anxieties flooding back in anew. It's been easy enough for the last little while on this beach to be us—Benny and Reese, the people, not the Friends of Flavor interns or stars of *Amateur Hour*. But once we leave, we're back to the FoF offices . . . and then what?

I crawl into the sedan and Benny follows, shutting the door behind us and confirming where we're headed. I'm suddenly incapable of conversing with the ease that I have been. My responses get shorter and shorter until Benny must sense I'm not feeling chatty anymore, and we both look out the windows like we did on the way there.

Maybe this weekend won't be so bad. I just can't let Aiden or anyone else see me at anything less than my best. The fall internship is the next step to my dream, and the stars are aligning. I'm never going to get this exact opportunity again.

We're almost back to campus, and I'm so tense I feel like a rubber band on the verge of snapping, when Benny looks at his phone. He must not have seen the notifications when he was calling the car, but now he taps the screen a few times and his eyes linger on it. His brow furrows as he reads, and he lets out a soft, "Oh."

We come to a stop at the curb in front of the dorms. Benny pockets his phone and thanks the driver before getting out of the car, reaching back to offer me his hand as I follow. I start to pull my hand from his once I'm standing, but he laces our fingers together and begins walking.

"It's this weekend trip that's got you freaking out, isn't it?"

Wow. The nerve of him, to read me so easily and be exactly right.

"I'm not freaking out," I protest.

He bumps my shoulder with his, then uses our linked hands to pull me back to his side. "C'mon, Reese's Cup. This has been the best date of my life. I can't speak for you, but it seems like you had an okay time, too. You're crushing it at work as both a graphic design superstar and chef in the making. We get a free sorta vacay this weekend. What's there to worry over?"

I narrow my eyes at him as we approach my dorm. I know

he's not that dense—that he hasn't forgotten everything that hangs over us work-wise—so he's clearly doing his best to put me at ease. And best date of his *life*? That has my heart speeding up for a different reason entirely.

"I just . . . feel a lot of pressure when I'm around people from work. Like I have to be the most competent, collected version of me at all times. That's a lot to keep up for a whole weekend in an unfamiliar place," I say. The partial truth, at least.

He pulls me to a stop outside the dorm and turns so we face each other. His gaze is warm and, admittedly, comforting. "I've seen you outside of work a decent amount now, so I feel like I can confidently tell you that even when you're not trying, you're still the coolest girl in the room. If you're just being *you*, you're doing enough. Promise." He pauses, and I try to quickly blink away the emotions threatening to leak out of my eyes. "And I'll be right there with you. Don't know if that makes it better or worse, of course. Hopefully better."

I laugh at the teasing note in his voice, and am surprised to notice the calm that's slowly washed over me at his words. Without really thinking about it, I step into him and put my arms around his waist, letting my chin rest on his shoulder. He wraps his solid, warm arms around me, pulling me closer to his chest.

"Definitely better," I answer softly.

When I'm back in my room, though, getting ready for bed, the worries certainly aren't gone. The pressure is still there, the end-of-summer decision still looming, my mental scoreboard with its flashing lights ever present. But all those worries are fighting for brain space with thoughts of Benny, our conversations, and how good he makes me feel. And like in any fight, I know that eventually one side will have to win.

Chapter Twelve

"Not bad for a summer home, huh?"

I hear Aiden, but I'm too distracted by our surroundings to acknowledge him. We've just unloaded from the SUVs that picked up the Friends of Flavor crew halfway through the workday to beat commuter traffic, took us to the ferry, and delivered us on the other side of Bainbridge Island to this behemoth they call a "cabin."

Surely they had to chop down half a forest to build this thing. It's twice the size of the fancy Smoky Mountain lodge where my family went on winter break one year on my papaw's dime after he had an especially good day on the casino boat. This is less of a cabin and more of a palace that happens to be built out of logs and surrounded by evergreens and blue sky.

Inside, my eyes roam over the vaulted ceiling, the sweeping staircase to a cozy-looking loft that's larger than my family home, the plush furniture covered in plaid flannel throws, the giant kitchen with stainless steel appliances. They couldn't have picked a better spot for the videos they've planned, as far as I can tell.

Benny nudges me with his elbow, bringing my attention to Teagan, who's standing in front of everyone with a sheet of paper in hand and reading out room assignments.

"Lily, Katherine, you'll be upstairs on the right, the bedroom with a bearskin rug," she calls out. Lily makes a horrified face.

Teagan keeps going down the list, naming enough rooms to fit everyone who came, which, while not the whole office, is still a lot of people. I zone out, wondering which of the suits owns this place. Is it Geoffrey Block, CEO? Does he have twenty-five children? How many rooms in the house are dubbed "man caves"? At least three, surely. When does he find the time to come here between all the very important business he does?

"Reese!" Teagan chirps, shaking me out of my snarky thoughts. "Benny! We don't have enough bedrooms for you both, so you can decide between yourselves who gets the last room on the ground floor at the end of the hall and who gets one of the couches in the basement. Hope that's okay."

The cheeky wink she sends me and the note of mischief in her voice make me suspect she's trying to hint at something. If my life was a romance novel, this would be the point where, uh-oh, there's only one bed and Benny and I will have to share it, and, oh no, sexy times inevitably ensue. I feel my cheeks flush, even though I know this is a work trip and that, despite our meddling receptionist's actions, no one is actually trying to make the two teenage interns share a room.

"You can have the bed. I'll take the couch," Benny says coolly. The rest of the group is gathering luggage and moving toward their assigned digs. Honestly, Benny looks way too good to have come off a morning of cleaning kitchens, and it's pissing me off a little. I look into his pretty eyes and narrow my own.

"Don't be a martyr."

"I'm not!" He throws his hands up. "The couch sounds nice. The whole basement to myself, I mean, c'mon. They're spoiling me."

I smirk, not convinced. "That's one way of looking at it. Are you sure? I really don't mind either way."

"Positive," he says, then gently taps his fist on my shoulder as he starts backing away, and raises one eyebrow suggestively. "Long as you come visit me."

I just shake my head, fighting my smile and feeling my blush return. This boy.

After locating my room, I spend a few minutes settling in. I shoot a text off to Natalie and Clara, who have requested updates on what they refer to as my romantic weekend getaway with Benny. The thought of telling them that there's only one bed left between the two of us makes me laugh. Best to not put any more ideas in their heads.

Before long, Aiden calls us all back and informs us that we—the six Friends plus Benny and me—will be filmed going fishing for a special episode of *Cross-Country Cookery.* A local chef who fishes as a hobby will be joining as our instructor.

Less than an hour later, we're all decked out in hilariously ugly, chest-high rubber waders and most of us are waist-deep in the chilly sound, with some taking to the activity better than others.

"*Ohhh* God, this is so gross," Benny groans, holding a worm between two fingers and trying to psych himself up to put it on his hook.

"Benny," I call out, "no one's gonna revoke your man card if you don't use the live bait."

A few yards away, Nia and Katherine snicker, making my life complete. I'm actually having fun out here, hanging out with all the Friends at the same time.

"But the artificial ones are neon and sparkly. There's no way the fish believe they're edible," Benny argues, his expression still one of disgust as he wades back over to his spot beside me with his fishing rod and its freshly baited hook swinging awkwardly. I've already given him two warnings about impaling one of us by accident if he doesn't learn to wield the rod properly.

"Tell that to the two I've already caught!" Aiden yells cockily.

He's being annoying about the fact that he is the only one of us who has caught anything so far, but I can't help being a little impressed. Not that I'd ever tell him that.

Benny settles back into position, and our kindly instructor resumes talking about the migratory fish that come through here. Over the next couple of hours, it feels like we've learned all we could possibly need to know about fishing techniques in general and Bainbridge Island in particular.

As far as carrying out said techniques, we all have room for improvement. Benny doesn't catch anything. By what feels like total chance, I catch one teeny-tiny baby trout. Benny makes a big show of saying how it's cheating since I'm from the country and do this all the time, at which point I whack him with my (hook-free) rod and remind him that I grew up in a landlocked suburb and he's being a sore, fishless loser.

But it's all in good fun, as confirmed when Benny asks me to take a picture with him while we're wrapping up and then poses with his arm as tightly around my waist as is possible with our massive rubbery overalls.

Back at the cabin, we strip out of the borrowed gear and start to split off when Aiden springs another surprise on us.

"Interns!" he calls from the driveway, and Benny and I turn from the cabin's front door, which we were about to walk through. "Can you be back in the kitchen in fifteen? Dinner's on you tonight."

I shove down the growl that wants to come out. *Really?* It's been a long day already, we've been on camera a bunch, and I was hoping to be off the clock now. Benny looks none too pleased either, but we both know we're getting orders disguised as a question, so we murmur our assent.

The others are generous and let Benny and me have first dibs on showers—we've all gotten varying degrees of sweaty and muddy today. I get ready as quickly as possible, securing my hair into a still-wet bun and already calling this video a loss on the personal appearance front.

Back in the kitchen, Benny, of course, looks refreshed and somehow even better than this morning. It's infuriating.

Aiden explains that this will be a crossover segment of *Amateur Hour* and *Cross-Country Cookery*. Normally Phil, the Bainbridge Island chef and fisherman who's been with us for the afternoon, would teach Rajesh how to cook his signature dish, but today Benny and I have been tasked with preparing our own versions of a meal using the fish the whole group caught. Raj and Phil will be on hand for guidance and sous-chef duties.

The funny thing is that we didn't actually catch that many fish, and certainly not enough to feed the whole house. So most folks' dinner is going to be the dozen or so pizzas Aiden will order after filming, while whatever Benny and I make will go to a select few judges.

"So, I've literally never cooked a fish in my life," I say as soon as we've split up to discuss our plans, Benny with Phil and me with Raj.

Raj laughs. "It's not so tough. I'll even clean and ready 'em into little fillets for you, how about that?"

"Perfect. Can I convince you to be my sous in all our episodes from now on?"

"Get back to me with salary and benefits and we'll talk," he calls over his shoulder as he grabs a cutting board and heads to the sink.

We have a fridge and pantry full of vegetables, spices, and other ingredients at our disposal. Running through the options in my head of meals Mamaw has taught me that I could pull from, it hits me that I know exactly what to do with the fish.

Pretend it's chicken.

It isn't the most sophisticated tactic, and I'm not even sure it'll work. But I can fry me some tasty chicken, and I imagine it can't be too terribly different to fry fish. And if there's any rule of thumb in my grandparents' kitchen, it's that anything can taste good if it's made with enough butter and salt.

After another hour or so of chaos around the kitchen with the four of us chopping, mixing, battering, stirring, and playing it up for the camera all the while, Benny and I set the plates out for our judges, who end up being Katherine, Seb, and—as a wild card, since she hardly ever appears in videos—Teagan.

I feel like it's comically obvious whose meal is whose. Benny's fish is beautifully seared, with a lemon-rosemary glaze and sitting on a bed of wild rice with grilled asparagus on the side. It's becoming clearer to me all the time that the boy understated his abilities that first day, telling me he could only do pasta and pastries. Anyone who can whip something like that up without a recipe at their side is a pro in my book.

On the other hand, my dish is straight out of a heart surgeon's worst nightmares. Piles of fried fish still shimmery with grease and heavily salted and peppered, next to mashed potatoes with an extra pat of butter on top, as if the multiple sticks that went into their preparation weren't enough. It's stick-to-your-ribs, clog-your-arteries goodness. Or at least the bit I sampled tasted good to me. I cross my fingers under the counter, hoping at least two of the judges agree.

Benny, Raj, Phil, and I watch as our three coworkers on the other side of the counter take a few bites from each plate, chewing and nodding and murmuring among themselves. Then they give their decisions.

"This all tastes awesome, you guys!" Teagan says, aiming a couple of claps in each of our directions. "But I have to say, I just love a good fried fish. So dish two really did it for me."

I bite my lips between my teeth to try to keep my reaction from slipping out. *Me, me, that's me! My first time cooking fish in the history of ever!*

"Both plates were delicious, truly. I'm really impressed," Seb begins diplomatically. "And I love fried fish, too. But I don't know, today I was feeling something lighter. The lemon glaze was crisp and fresh—it tastes like summer to me. I'm going to have to go with dish one. But really, they were both amazing."

It's down to Katherine. My heart rate picks up as she begins speaking. "I loved both preparations of the fish. Really a tie for me on that front," she says, pursing her lips and twisting a loose reddish-brown curl around her finger. "But these are the best mashed potatoes I've ever had in my life. So I'm choosing dish two."

I let out an inhuman shriek, then clap a hand over my mouth in instant embarrassment. Everyone's eyes dart to me, and I see Charlie trying not to laugh behind the camera. After a second of silence, I squeak, "I won!"

Everyone laughs then, with some quiet applause for me. Rajesh gives me a high five, then Phil shakes my hand and offers his congratulations. Benny reaches a hand out like he's going to shake mine, then pulls me in for a surprise hug at the last minute. He claps me on the back in a goofy, friendly way, but leans in to say for my ears only, "You're cute when you defeat me."

I laugh and start to push him away, but it must be the excitement of winning that makes me joke in an especially flirtatious tone, "I'm always cute."

"Well, yeah," he deadpans, like I've stated the most obvious thing in the world, and I have to turn my face away from the heat rays his eyes are shooting at me.

Distractedly, I add today to the score in my head: **Benny—3, Reese—3**. Even footing once again.

We wrap up the video with Raj thanking Phil for joining us, and we all chime in on the signature "Have a flavorful day!" The pizzas arrived on the back patio a little while ago, so those of us who were filming go get our share while the ones who already ate come in to clean up the kitchen.

As we fill our plates with pizza, Aiden tells Benny and me that we won't be in any more of the content filmed this weekend, so we're free to hang out and relax when they don't need our help behind the scenes.

Benny receives this news as happily as I do, leaning in with a mischievous smile as we post up on a bench side by side. "We're off the hook, Reese's Cup! Much like the many fish we didn't catch today."

I laugh, elbowing him as I chew a bite of pepperoni. "I wonder if they appreciate their freedom this much."

When he speaks again, it's quieter, like he doesn't want the other FoF staff milling around the patio to hear. "Hey, since we know we're not on camera any more this weekend . . ." He pauses, and I raise an eyebrow. "What would you say to a temporary cease-fire? You and me, let's forget about all these competitions and the job and just, I don't know, enjoy this place? And, um, each other? Not that I'm implying—I mean, I just want to hang out. Not saying we have to—oh God, rewind. Delete the last twenty seconds. Let me start that over."

He hangs his head and I can't stop the loud laugh that bursts out of me, causing several heads to turn our way and conversations to pause for a second. Once they've resumed, I pat Benny's knee, which rests scarcely an inch from mine. "Stop it, I know what you mean. I think, anyway." I offer him my hand to shake. "I'm in. Cease-fire, truce, whatever. We're not competing for anything the rest of this weekend."

He takes my hand in his, giving it a shake, then holding on a bit longer, tighter. When he brings his gaze back up to mine, the warmth and affection in his eyes makes my breath catch.

"Good," he says. And it really feels like it is.

Chapter Thirteen

I hit the hay early and sleep like the dead that night, exhausted by the day, the week, the whole summer so far. When I wake up—earlier than I normally would on a weekend—there's a single text from Benny on my phone.

> **Benny:** Hey sleeping beauty, come down to the basement when you get up. Dress for . . . outdoor activity

I laugh, then get up and try to make myself look halfway decent in my "outdoor activity" attire of leggings, a T-shirt, and my most comfortable tennis shoes. The house is quiet enough that I guess most people still aren't up, and I venture down the first stairwell I find to an expansive finished basement. I weave around pool tables—plural—an air hockey table, and a few old-school arcade games, calling out, "Benny?"

"Over here, Reese's Pieces."

I follow his voice and find him sitting on one of three couches that frame an entertainment center. He's pulling hiking boots on and is dressed for the day in jeans and a red-and-black plaid flannel over a white T-shirt. He stands when he's finished and I look him up and down, crossing my arms to try to mask how flustered he's gotten me.

"You look like the Brawny paper towel man," I spit out, as if it's a bad thing. On Benny, it is very much not. "What are you up to?"

"Get with the program, girl, this is my great-outdoors uniform. We're going hiking."

I raise an eyebrow, mildly amused that he wants to go hiking bright and early on a Saturday morning—everything about Benny says city boy, but good for him for trying something new. "We?"

He adjusts his black baseball cap. "Well, I am. And I'm inviting you to join if you want. Pretty please with Reese's Puffs on top? I texted Aiden and he, well, he asked me not to text him before nine a.m. ever again. But he also confirmed we're free to do our own thing for the morning. I looked at the cabin's info packet and there are a few trails that start right outside. Eh?"

I pretend to mull it over a couple more moments before relenting. "Lead the way."

His smile is wide as he gestures for me to follow him up the stairs, out the door and toward one of the trails he read about. This one begins by a tree marked with a single stripe of white paint. We're supposed to follow these markers until we reach a loop trail in a state park that'll take us down to the water and back.

We walk the first few minutes in relative silence, me behind Benny, definitely not stealing glances at his butt. Mama would be washing my *mind* out with soap if she had any clue. My attraction to this guy is at a level that I've never felt for anyone. Not just physical, either. It's in how he talks to me and listens to me and makes me laugh; it's how I want to be around him more and more, all the time basically.

And he's been giving me space to figure out what I want. He's made it clear that he's interested, and I get the sense that he's waiting on the same interest from me before he tries taking it any further.

It's my move. Am I finally ready to make it?

"How you doin' back there, Backwoods Barbie?" he calls from a few feet ahead.

I gasp. "Did the California boy just make a Dolly Parton reference?"

He shrugs his wide shoulders before looking over one and tossing a wink my way. "I contain multitudes."

I mime my heart beating out of my chest. "Keep 'em coming, Campground Ken. I'm doing great."

He slows his pace to walk alongside me. "Have to say, this is an improvement over the last time I went hiking."

I laugh. "Do tell."

"It was a school trip. The teachers thought it'd be good for a bunch of city kids to see the great outdoors, I guess. And your boy thought it'd be a great idea to pretend to be outdoorsy for the girl he had a crush on. She was the camping-every-weekend, rock-climbing, kayaking type. A real promising match in young, deluded Benny's head.

"So I bought these boots—the very same ones I'm wearing now—for way too much money, plus a new backpack stuffed with a bunch of new gear I didn't need, since we'd be spending one night in the woods and not a month in the Alaskan bush. And you know what?"

He pauses, so I bite down on a laugh and say, "What?"

"She was actually impressed. For all of two seconds when we first got off the bus, and then her new *boyfriend*, the cross-country team's star runner *Derek*, came and whisked her away, and the two of them ran the freaking trail to our campground. Show-offs. And what did I get out of it?"

I can't stop my laughter now. "A hit to your pride?"

"And blisters, Reese's Cup! On my feet from the not-broken-in boots, of course, but also on my shoulders because my backpack was so damn heavy. It was miserable. And when I got home, my brothers would not stop roasting me for being so dumb. Literal insult to injury. But if there's any silver lining, it's probably that I kept wearing the boots just to prove they weren't a totally useless purchase, and now they're hella comfy. So joke's on you, Allie Templeton!"

"The one that got away," I say dramatically. Then, after a pause, for reasons I can't defend with anything other than "green-eyed jealousy monster," I add, "Surely you didn't need to try that hard, though, right? I imagine there were plenty of girls into the Beneventi boys."

Benny chuckles, reaching back to readjust his cap. "Into my brothers, maybe. But once again, you give me more credit than I deserve. That was probably the height of my 'game' in high school and you see how successful it was. I was always the friend, not the boyfriend, which was okay. Better than being neither, y'know."

We continue on in silence for a few moments while I consider this. I'm hard-pressed to picture any girl being Benny's friend and not being interested in more.

"What about you? Lots of sad boys back in Kentucky, pining away for the pretty blonde who moved across the country?" he teases, but his voice is quieter and the smile he gives me is tight, framed with tense lines instead of the dimple I love. There's that vulnerability again, the one I see more glimpses of all the time.

"Hardly," I say, laughing, and it sounds darker than I meant it to. And then, compelled by the fresh mountain air, a touch of insanity, or maybe just this trust I've built with Benny, I continue on a sigh, "I've not had the best experiences with guys."

Reese Camden, queen of the understatement! Benny, bless him, tries to give me an out when I hesitate.

"Reese, you don't have to tell me your story just because I told you about how I got such nice footwear."

I laugh, but now that I've started, I feel committed. "No, it's fine. I think—I *want* to tell you."

It's true, oddly enough. I've never had to tell anyone before—back home, anyone who mattered had been present for it all. But if there's going to be anything more with Benny and me, he needs to know where I'm coming from. Not only that, but I feel like confiding in him as my friend. Someone who understands me, who never seems to judge me and cares about me as I am. It feels right letting him in on this side of me.

"So, it was my freshman year. I was pretty happy, normal, I had plenty of friends. I was the worst flute player the marching band had ever seen, but I had fun doing it. Then a couple months into school, I was at a party where I met this senior guy, John. He was cute and really popular—on the soccer team, homecoming king, a leader in his church youth group. And for whatever reason, he started hanging around me."

I pause as Benny touches my arm and leads me around a muddy patch. Even distracted by my story, the contact doesn't go unappreciated, my disappointment spiking as soon as he lets go. I clear my throat and continue. "Everybody knew John as the Nice Guy. And he was—sweet and charming, he took me on dates he planned, and when he asked me to be his girlfriend I said yes.

"Once we were 'official,' though, things started to feel more . . . intense." I feel Benny's head turn toward me, but I don't think I can do the eye contact thing till I get through this. "He laid out his boundaries immediately—we could kiss and that was it. Anything else would be too tempting, and he was waiting for marriage. Now, I was fourteen years old, mind you, and had yet to so much as hold hands with a guy before John. It seemed pretty hard-core to have this talk, like, day one, but I thought maybe that's just how relationships are."

It appears we've reached the state park trail now—the path is well maintained and there are other hikers up ahead. We walk over a little wooden bridge that crosses a creek and wave to the couple passing by. I wait until they're out of earshot before I go on.

"Well, it turned out the talk was much more for his sake than mine. Right away, it seemed like the lines were getting pushed. He'd kiss me at the end of a date, then *he'd* be the one to start moving things further, and I was attracted to him and having fun, so I didn't stop anything. But eventually, he'd stop himself and immediately start feeling bad.

"I would go home confused, and we'd have a talk the next day where he'd tell me whatever we'd done couldn't happen again. But it would, and whenever we did something he regretted, he started to blame me. *I* was the one who stayed in his car too long when he was dropping me off at night. *I* had looked so pretty at school that day. *I* was wearing something that gave him im-pure thoughts. *I* hugged him first, and he couldn't help but want more."

Benny lets out a disbelieving laugh, and I glance over to see him shaking his head. "You know that's bullshit, right?"

I swallow, watching our feet hitting the dirt, step by step.

"Absolutely—*now*. Back then it was confusing, and I wasn't sure what to think, but more than anything, I was tired of feeling so bad. I was too stressed about what I'd do wrong next, when the switch would flip and he'd be upset with me. So I ended it."

"Hell yeah, you did," Benny nearly yells.

I chuckle, swatting his arm as another pair of hikers passes us and waves.

"So, he didn't much like that. He got angry, and he told everyone who would listen that I was the worst thing a girl at our school could be—a slut. Not in so many words, Nice Guy that he was, but the prevailing story became that I'd wanted to move faster than he did—which is laughable—and was trying to pressure him into sex. And ever so nobly, he'd dumped me. It was clearly ridiculous if you knew anything about me, but he had just about everybody whose opinion mattered in his pocket, even a good few who I'd thought were my friends. I was a skanky freshman who didn't know how lucky I was to be with John in the first place and was only after one thing. I got attacked so much online that when deleting comments and blocking people wasn't enough, I left social media completely."

I pause to catch my breath, more winded from the story than from our walk, or so I'd like to think. Benny stops beside me, resting one hand on his hip and running the other over the top of his cap. He looks distraught. I decide that's preferable to looking, I don't know, disgusted by my presence?

"God, Reese, I can't believe . . . That's terrible. Jeez. I'm so sorry."

I shake my head between breaths. "Yeah, it wasn't much fun."

"Were Natalie and Clara around for all this? What did they think?"

"Oh, completely. They were lifesavers." I exhale and start walking again. "It was the worst time in my life so far, but they stuck beside me. I quit marching band, I stopped going to parties and school functions. I felt awful about myself, and still confused, but also mad as hell. Because I learned through all of it that as a girl, I couldn't win. He walked away smelling like a rose. I didn't sleep with him, or even try to, but I was still labeled a tramp. If he'd wanted to go all the way and I hadn't, though, I would've been a prude. You're damned if you do, damned if you don't.

"It's why I'm so weird about being online and looking professional in front of our coworkers. There's a constant meter in my head going, 'How is this gonna look to everyone? What factors are working against me today? How can I give myself the best odds of being treated as fairly as a guy would be?' And it is seriously exhausting. I can make myself as likable as possible, and it's still never going to satisfy everyone."

The trail dips lower and flattens out. I hear waves crashing quietly and know we're getting close to the shore. One of my shoelaces has come untied, so I take a few steps to the side to fix it. Benny stops alongside me.

"Part of the reason I love Katherine's blog, let alone FoF, so much," I say from my crouch, "is that Nat and Clara introduced me to both when I was going through all that. And it was like, wow, the world is so much bigger than my small town. And here's a woman who doesn't take shit from anybody and commands respect and is living her dream. I think that's when the dream of coming out here and doing this job—even though I didn't know about the internship at the time—started to take shape in my head. So, four years later . . . here I am."

I straighten back up and let out a long breath, then bring my hands to my nervous stomach, then back up to rub my eyes, which have miraculously refrained from leaking. Probably, I've been sweating out any potential tears. After a few moments of tense silence, I hazard a look at Benny.

For the first time since I've known him, he looks sincerely angry. His brow is furrowed, his mouth set in a hard line, and he's glaring into the trees around us as if he doesn't want me to see the ferocity in his eyes.

"Sorry," I say instinctively. "I know that was a lot. I just—"

"Hey," he cuts in almost sternly, his gaze darting to me and instantly softening. "I feel like after all that, the last thing you should say is sorry. All right?"

I nod and now I'm the one who has to look away, the pinpricks at the backs of my eyes signaling that I might not have sweated out all the tears yet. Benny has somehow found something to say that feels like just what I needed to hear.

I feel him step closer, not quite touching me, but his arm is hovering as if he wants to wrap it around me. "If anything, I feel like apologizing. That's so— God, I hate it for you." He pauses, giving me a hesitant look. "Was that . . . I mean, have you dated anyone since him?"

I shake my head and Benny sighs.

" 'Good' doesn't feel like the right thing for me to say exactly, because I hate that he's your only relationship experience. But good that no one else has hurt you like that. Guys are so full of shit."

I look at him with watery eyes. "You're not shitty, though."

A smile starts at the edges of his lips. "Aw, Reese's Cup. That's the sweetest thing you've ever said to me."

I laugh then, letting a couple of tears spill onto my cheeks. Benny's face gets serious again as he brings his free hand up to wipe the tears away, then leaves it resting against my jaw.

"Seriously, Reese. I'm so sorry that happened and that you continue to deal with it. I wish I could take it all away and make the world an easier place for you by the sheer force of how pissed off I am at everyone who hurt you."

I blink in surprise, but I know what he's feeling. And it is so very validating to have another person see my side after all this time. Not just any person, either—this boy who I like a whole, whole lot.

"Thank you, Benny," I whisper as I pull back. "For trying to understand. It means everything."

One side of his mouth pulls up in a sweet smile, his eyes filled with affection. "Thanks for trusting me enough to share. And hey, I think we've about made it to a good view. Wanna go see what's out there?"

He points in the direction of a flat path, and I nod in agreement. It takes us only a couple dozen steps before we break through a patch of trees and step onto a long, rocky shoreline.

Benny is a few feet ahead of me with his arms raised, his fingers laced together and resting on the back of his head. The wind off the water hits me hard, drying any remaining moisture on my face and leaving me feeling refreshed. I walk up beside him and put my own hands on my hips to take it all in. The waters of Puget Sound lap at the shore before us, and beyond them is a stretch of gorgeous mountains. The sun is still rising in a perfectly clear sky, casting everything in a golden glow. The only sounds are the gentle waves and my breaths mixed with Benny's, both of which are starting to slow down again.

As I look out over the unbelievable scenery, barely off the high of telling this guy my story and feeling like he truly heard me, my heart is so full. It's more than I've let myself feel all at once in what seems like years—warm, and hopeful, and cared for.

And then Benny turns to me and says, "I want you to know that I'm on your team. Doesn't matter what happens with us, or with the job, whatever you need, I'm here. I'm your guy. That okay?"

I see the vulnerability in his gaze and with it, the strength and sincerity. Combined with the fact that he still looks like Mr. July in a Hot Lumberjacks Calendar, it makes me want him more than I've ever wanted anyone. Before I can overthink it or talk myself down, I turn to face him. He looks at me, a brow lifting as I step closer. His arms drop to his sides and one corner of his mouth hooks upward, his gaze still questioning. When our faces are just a few inches apart, I lift my arms and wrap them around his neck. I pause for just a moment, looking for confirmation that he wants this too, and the feeling of his hands resting gently on my waist gives me the answer I need.

I lean in and press my lips to his. It's soft at first but with no uncertainty. Benny responds instantly, like he's been waiting for this at least as long as I have. His hands move from my waist to my back, tightening around me and pulling my body closer to his.

My thoughts are a blur of *yes, good, right* as I tilt my head, deepening the kiss. Every inch of me is tingling and I know that I want more of this and for a long, long time. But before too long, before I feel ready for it to end, Benny pulls away. He brings his hands up to frame my face, his lips edging up on one side and his eyes moving between mine with a look of warm intensity.

"Better than okay," I answer his question belatedly. He looks confused by my words for a moment; then his head tips back with a laugh.

"Is this really happening?" The disbelief in his voice makes me blush immediately.

I nod, and when I answer it's with more than just this kiss, this singular moment in mind. "If you want it to."

Benny breathes out a chuckle and lets his forehead rest on mine. "I've only wanted this since I heard you rant about sweet tea."

Now I'm the one laughing. I step away, but not without finding his hand and linking our fingers together, pulling him a few feet toward the water to sit down on a rock alongside me.

"Really? That's what did it for you?"

He leans back on his elbows. "That, and everything else I've learned about you since. Why, what did it for you?"

Oh my stars. He can't just casually drop these things on me. I purse my lips and turn my face away, trying to keep from looking as affected by his words as I am.

"Mmm, probably your gnocchi."

Benny laughs and bumps my arm with his. "Appreciate the honesty. I have a very specific set of skills and I'm prepared to use them as much as I have to."

"I think this'll work quite nicely." I return his smile, then lean over to kiss him again. It's like now that I've started, I can't stop. He straightens up to wrap his arms around me again and good *gravy*. His kisses are sweeter than the sweetest tea, hotter than Kentucky summer sunshine. They make me want to forget everything that's held me back in the past and fall headfirst into this, into him.

A while later, it's once again Benny who pulls back, though it looks like it pains him to do so. He rubs his hands over his face like he's trying to bring himself back to the present.

"Wow, all right. As much as I'd love to cut ties with the civilized world and change my permanent address to this rock ledge right here with you, and believe me I would"—I smirk as he pulls his phone out of his pocket, glancing at the screen for just a moment before sliding it back—"I think Nia and Lily are making brunch, so everyone's gonna be up and at 'em soon. And neither us showing up late nor the smug, my-dreams-just-came-true look on my face would help us keep people from suspecting anything romantic is going on here. Which I'm guessing, at least for now, is what we still want? To keep it quiet?"

I bring my forehead to his shoulder, concealing my red face. "Agreed, Bento box, but in that case, I'm gonna need you to stop making me blush so hard."

His laugh echoes through the trees as he scoots away and pushes to his feet, offering his hand to pull me up. "Bento box. That might be my favorite one yet. Can you imagine if my parents had gone with Lorenzo, Manuel, Leonardo, and Bento Box Beneventi?"

I help him reposition his hat, which has gone slightly askew, considering the fanciness of his brothers' full names and what that suggests for Benny's. We keep our hands linked together as we start back down the trail and I can't stop the goofy smile it puts on my face. "Now that we've kissed, do I get to know your first name?"

"Aha! The real reason for your actions today—exposed! That took no time at all." He points an accusatory finger at me.

"You're avoiding the question," I singsong.

Benny seems to consider his next words. "I don't know, I think I might hold on to this secret a while longer. It's the last bit of mystery around me to keep you interested."

I push him and he narrowly misses a tree branch.

When we make it back, delicious scents are already emanating from the cabin. We unlink hands and head inside to find that Lily and Nia have prepared an impressive spread of Belgian waffles, a few breakfast casserole dishes with some kind of eggy, potato-y goodness, and a big platter of bacon. Nia is being filmed making crepes to order, presumably for an episode of *Piece of Cake,* with an array of fillings on offer. Benny and I slip in just in time to join the line, and I get a crepe with Nutella and strawberries before we join some of the other Friends at the long dining tables on the back deck.

The food is amazing, but this morning with Benny, along with the secret looks he keeps throwing my way as we eat and the occasional squeezes of my hand under the table? Those are so much better.

Chapter Fourteen

That night, we all sit around the campfire built by Katherine earlier for the episode of *Fuss-Free Foodie* she filmed about her favorite "easy campfire meals." Because of course she has this badass wilderness woman side, too.

Benny and I spent most of the day bumming around, playing cards and board games and trying to stay out of the way of those who were filming. Eventually we were tasked with keeping the fire alive after Katherine's filming was done so we could all use it for s'mores later. Somehow, despite having maybe half of a survival skill between us, Benny and I have managed. And now that everyone has their s'mores and the night is dying down, we can rest again.

I lick marshmallow off my fingers as Benny muses over possible Instagram captions for the picture we took in our waders yesterday. With the many thousands of followers he's gained since we started making videos, he puts a comical amount of pressure on himself to have good captions.

"See, it kinda looks like the end of my line is connected to you. So what about 'caught me a winner'?"

I give him a withering look. "You caught nothing, city boy."

Benny pouts. "I thought that was pretty cute."

"It is," I say, then lower my voice to a whisper as I add, "You are. But we're being subtle, remember?"

One side of his mouth quirks up and he gives me a wink before looking back at his phone. Gracious, do I want to kiss those dimples again.

"All right, all right. I got it—'Coming soon: Fish of Flavor.' Eh?" He raises his eyebrows and I laugh.

"Fine by me, you punny fella."

Before long, the flames in the firepit are embers, and little by little, people head off to bed. I decide to turn in before Benny and give his shoulder an affectionate but discreet squeeze before going inside, leaving him chatting with Seb and Raj.

Once I'm in my room, teeth brushed and pajamas on, I climb into bed and mess around on my phone a bit. Impulsively, I go to Benny's Instagram page from the Friends of Flavor account, which I'm logged in to, and take a screenshot of his latest post to send to Natalie and Clara. Under the picture, I text my own caption.

Reese: #instaofficial

Reese: or should I say oFISHal

Natalie: !!!!!!!!!!!

Clara: wait so does this mean real life official too

Clara: ???

Natalie: YOU CAN'T DROP THESE BOMBS WITH NO DETAILS

Reese: Would y'all give a woman time to type pls

Reese: Ummm I think real life official too? As in, we kissed today

Natalie: !!!!!!!!!!!!!!!!!!

Clara: !!!

Reese: . . . a lot. But we haven't done the "what are we" talk. And we're keeping it a secret

Reese: Except for this convo I guess lol

Reese: So shh

Natalie: Oh my god I'm having heart palpitations

Natalie: Lord help

Natalie: SOS girl down

Reese: Thank you for handling this so coolly. Really helping me continue to not freak out about it yet

Clara: happy for you, R. he seems great. and super hot ofc

Natalie: I just want you to feel my undying love and support

Natalie: Undying, even if I myself literally die right here from my heart attack

Clara: I thought it was palpitations

Natalie: Excuse me Clar I'm not a doctor

Reese: Nat = dying, Nat's love = not. Got it

Reese: And I love you both too;)

When I close out of my texts and go back to close Instagram, I hesitate. I don't know if I'm feeling too hyped up on lovey vibes or what, but I make the stupid, stupid decision of clicking open the comments on Benny's picture.

So cute so cute sooo cute!!

You guys are obvi together, just tell us

Bennnyyyy she's not good enough for you cmon. I'm single

Reese looks like she's gained weight. Must be all those desserts in the kitchen lol

Reese ur so pretty! Benny u should lock it down:P

anyone else think she seems kinda slutty like always all over him

Cute couple. My husband and I love to fish together.

I don't see you working out, she seems like such a
snob

if ur lookin for a partner i'm a CATCH

Cropping this so she's out of it lolz

My cousin went to school w that girl and said she's a
skank

I drop the phone like it's burned my hand. I'm an idiot. Never
ever in all my days has anything so good appeared in social media
comments that it was worth reading all the bad.

My hands are shaking, and I roll over so I'm lying on my
stomach and then ball my hands into fists and pull them to my
chest. I lay my head facedown into the pillow and try to take
deep breaths.

The scaries are coming on.

Those thoughts I try to beat away, the worries that have
plagued me for years about who I am and how the world sees me.
I like Benny, I do, and I think I can I trust him. But have I really
thought this through? If it goes south between us, I cannot go
back to where I was almost four years ago. I *will* not. I've never
let myself be this open and get this close to a guy, and within the
first twenty-four hours of it actually becoming something, I'm
spiraling.

It was probably a mistake, opening up to him and then basically throwing myself at him right after. He responded like any

decent person would; that doesn't mean I should try to kiss every decent person's face off.

I hate how much my whole life feels dictated by trying to recover from a stupid freshman-year mistake. How I still care so much about managing what everyone thinks of me, despite being able to talk for days about how impossible it is to please everyone.

Needless to say, I don't fall asleep for a while.

I'm cagey and distant the next morning. I grab some cereal from the fend-for-yourself breakfast buffet, then retreat to a lone chair at the far edge of the deck with my sketch pad, working on a drawing of the view from the cabin. It's mostly an excuse to make me look busy and deflect the attentions of a certain ball-capped charmer.

After everyone's had breakfast, we pack up our things and straighten up the house, preparing to head back to the city. Benny keeps trying to catch me alone and start a conversation, but I keep finding reasons to brush him off. After we've finished up and piled into the SUVs, I end up in the third row between Benny and Rajesh. Charlie and a couple of camera techs I don't know take up the remaining seats in the middle row and the passenger seat.

On the way back to the ferry, Raj regales us with a story

about the time he and Lily entered a local charity's chili cook-off for an episode that never aired because neither of their chilis even broke the top five. Aiden thought it was too embarrassing for FoF and told editing to scrap the footage.

As Benny laughs along with the others, he presses his leg against mine and I feel some of the tension in my body ease. It's as though I physically sense that I'm safe and well, but my mind isn't convinced, yet.

As soon as we pull onto the lower deck of the massive ferryboat and park, we all pile out and head upstairs to the passenger decks, where there are seats, food, and, best of all, *views*. We split up, all of us responsible only for getting back to the cars before we dock. Benny has every reason to be a little irritated with me by now for not talking to him, and I hate pushing him away after the amazing weekend we've had. But I don't know how to make myself stop. We're sitting in a couple of seats in the front row by the panoramic windows facing downtown Seattle. When I feel him shift like he's going to leave, I grip the hem of his shirt and pull him back.

He looks at me with confusion. "I was going to get some coffee. You want anything?"

Oh. He's not upset? I probably should have given him more credit.

"I could go for some tea."

He gives me one of those devastating smiles and takes my hand, pulling me up to follow him to the café. He squeezes my hand once I'm standing, a soft reassurance, before dropping it as we walk. We get our drinks, and I doctor mine up with the necessary amount of sugar while Benny pays.

"Hey," he says, resting a hand on my arm as I start to walk back to our seats. "Come with me?"

I raise an eyebrow skeptically but give him a small nod. He takes us down the hall and around a corner and then up another stairwell. On the uppermost deck, we walk through the less crowded seating area, waving to the few Friends we see on the way. But Benny doesn't stop; he holds the door open and leads me outside.

The wind immediately sends my hair flying in all directions as we walk up to the railing and look out over the water and the cityscape ahead of us. The ferry moves deceptively fast, I realize now that I feel the outside air. It's hard to keep my eyes open, hold my hair back from whipping me in the face, *and* hold my cup of tea. But I also can't look away—it's beautiful, the skyline reflected off the water and the sunshine off them both.

Benny sidles closer to me, his arm brushing mine. "Seems like something's been on your mind today," he says quietly. "Not having regrets, are you?"

He asks the question in a teasing tone, but when I peek his way, there's worry in his expression. And in that moment, I want so badly to not let him down. I want to be a good . . . whatever I am to him, a girl who's fun and easygoing and doesn't let the little things get to her. Because a few Instagram comments—those are little things, right? I want to let myself enjoy the feeling of being with Benny as long as I have it. I'm probably overreacting to the online stuff. But even if I'm not, it isn't his problem. I can handle it.

I think.

"Not at all," I whisper back with a smile, bumping my shoulder against his. "Just tired, I think. Nothing some properly sweetened tea can't fix."

A shiver runs through me and Benny cocks his head to see the goose bumps on my foolishly bare arms. I was comfortable in short sleeves earlier, but with the wind, I'm wishing I'd brought my jacket from the car.

"Hey, take this," he says, removing his flannel before I can protest.

I tear my eyes from the buff chest and arms that are all the more noticeable in just a T-shirt and shake my head. "No, you'll be cold. I'm fine."

"Reese's Cup." He gives me that lopsided smile I can't resist "You're shaking. Unless we go inside, I won't be happy until you let me play the chivalrous dude, just this once."

I roll my eyes at him, but I don't want to go back in, either. I accept the shirt and pull it on. *Gah,* it's toasty warm and soft and wonderful. It smells like that sweet-spicy Benny-ness and does nothing at all to stop the pull I feel toward him. My heart is saying, *Go time, screw taking it slow, you've had weeks, forget the competition, it's still the weekend cease-fire, he's dreamy, go go go while you have the chance.* And for once, my head isn't putting up any solid counterarguments.

He looks like he's thinking the exact same thing. His gaze drops to my lips and his head shifts almost imperceptibly closer. But my reason prevails in time for me to tilt my head toward the indoor seating, where any number of people we work with could be watching through the windows.

"Not here," I whisper.

Benny's lips twist into a smirk as his eyes scan the deck. His gaze pauses on something before coming back to me and he murmurs, "This way."

"Someone's feeling bossy today," I mutter, but once again, I follow. I'm such a sucker. We walk around the corner and down the deck to a small alcove. There are only a couple other passengers on this side of the deck, and they're at the opposite end, looking in no hurry to come back this way.

Essentially, it's as discreet as we could expect to find in daylight on top of a public ferry.

Benny wastes no time setting his coffee and my tea down by our feet, nudging me so my back is against the wall, and stepping in to press his lips to mine. Between his gentle care for our beverages and his obvious desire for me, it's the hottest thing I've ever experienced. One of his hands grips my waist while the other slides into my hair until he's cupping the back of my head, guiding me to just the right angle so he can kiss me more thoroughly.

I let out a soft gasp as he moves even closer, his body molding against mine. My hands start in fists that grip his T-shirt, but at some point they travel up to the back of his neck, one going farther, under the brim of his hat. The idea hits me then, and I keep nudging up, up, until I snatch the hat off his head. Opening my eyes, I pull back with a smile, and—oh. *Oh.*

"Goodness gracious, Benny, why on *earth* would you hide this beautiful head of hair all the time?"

He looks down sheepishly, sending a couple of dark curls tumbling over his forehead. The top of his head is covered in a thick layer of them, shiny and perfectly tousled in spite of his best efforts to crush them in a structured fabric dome day in and day out. The sides are cut short, which makes it harder to tell that he's hiding anything this gorgeous under those caps of his.

"Maybe I thought it'd be too much for you to handle. I didn't even own a hat before this summer," he jokes with a sideways smirk.

I bring my hands up and thread them both through his curls slowly before grabbing hold and pulling his head back to mine. Brushing his lips with mine, I say, "On second thought, you might've been onto something."

He laughs into our kiss, but then pulls back, seemingly just to look at me. There's so much affection in his eyes, my heart feels like it could beat clear out of my chest.

"I like you, Beneventi," I say, without even thinking about it, the words coming out in a breathy voice I can't believe is my own. "I'm glad you want to be my teammate."

His head falls back so he's gazing at the cloudy sky as he pulls me close and squeezes me tight, answering on a sigh, "Camden, the feeling is mutual."

Before too long—and definitely before I'm ready for it—the announcement that the ferry will be docking soon comes through the speakers. Car passengers are supposed to return to their vehicles. I pull Benny in for one last, lingering kiss, then we try to help each other look marginally less disheveled before we head inside.

Hopefully everyone will assume it's just the wind that's turned our hair this messy and our lips and cheeks this red. Wind does that, right?

Lucky for us, we don't run into any of the FoF crew until we're back at the car. Raj told Charlie he was switching to Katherine's car, so it's just Benny and me in the back row. In a pleasant surprise for the two of us, the driver says that FoF has paid him through the rest of the day, so he can take home anyone who didn't leave a car at the office. That only applies to Benny and me, and our dorms are close enough that he'll hardly be going out of his way, so we gladly accept the offer.

The men in the front continue chatting as we disembark from the ferry and start winding through downtown. While they're otherwise occupied, I lean in closer to Benny.

I pull his arm toward me, wrapping my own arms around it as if his bulky bicep is both my space heater and my life raft. I don't know what's coming for us, but today, I want him as close as possible while I have him. He seems to soften at my touch, scooting over so our thighs are pressed together and resting one hand on my knee.

I'm more relaxed than I've been this entire trip. Trust. Comfort. That's what this is.

So much comfort, in fact, that it's hard to keep my eyelids from drooping.

When the stoplight we're at turns green, the sharp left turn of the car has me sinking harder against Benny's shoulder. He tips his head down a tiny bit lower, his breath warm against my ear as he whispers, "Norberto."

My eyes pop back open and my nose scrunches. "Huh?"

He yawns into his next words. "My first name."

I stiffen in his arms, a laugh bubbling up from my chest. "I— I'm sorry. *What* did you just say?"

I feel him shaking as he laughs softly. "You heard me, Reese's Pieces."

"I just . . . I can't believe my ears, *Norberto*. You could've given me a few hundred guesses at least," I whisper-laugh. "Well, shoot fire, no wonder you go by Benny!"

He pretends to push me off the seat, adding as I continue to giggle, "Your support means the world."

But he's still laughing too. Eventually, the chuckles subside and I feel both of our breathing slow. I vaguely register us stopping to let out Charlie and another camera guy at the FoF office, but I can't rouse myself enough to say goodbye. I wake again to

Benny telling me that we're at the dorms. As we head toward our separate buildings, I sigh contentedly thinking about all that the weekend has brought.

A fried-fish victory. A temporary cease-fire. A boy named Norberto.

It's like my first taste of what life could be like if I get everything I want out of this summer. And with one taste, I already crave so much more.

Chapter Fifteen

For the first few days after Bainbridge, I stay in my bubble of Benny-induced giddiness. They have a lot of footage to sort through from the weekend on top of some new episodes of *Good Chef/Bad Chef* to shoot, so Margie and Aiden have us on the ordinary intern grind. But less attention on us also means more opportunities for Benny and me to hang out under the guise of working, and to generally pretend that our weekend cease-fire still stands. We spend nearly all of our days together, both at work and in our free time, and somehow, I still find myself wishing I could see him *more*.

I refrain from telling him as much, though. My kissing him on a regular basis has already done too much for his ego.

On Friday morning, Benny and I are sent on a mega–coffee run to combat some of the sluggish vibes that have been hitting the office hard throughout this busy week. The nearest Starbucks we try has a line almost out the door, so we walk to one a few blocks farther from the office, in the hopes that the travel time will be made up for by less time standing in line.

"I just find it so wild that when Katherine started at FoF, the percentage of men to women employed by UltiMedia was seventy-thirty," I say, finishing up my recap of the latest post on the Kat's Muse as we speed walk our way through the morning commuter bustle.

"I thought she said it was more like seventy-eight–twenty-two," he replies.

"Oh really? You're probably right. I just remembered the seventy and—wait." I stop in my tracks, physically and verbally.

Benny comes to a stop a few feet past me, his shoulders tensing. I slowly step closer, nudging him nearer to the building next to us so we're not standing in the middle of the sidewalk. His eyes dart everywhere but to mine, his expression as guilty as that of a kid with his hand caught in the cookie jar.

"Benedict Cumberbatch. Have you been reading TKM?"

He huffs out a breath. "You know, you've used several versions of Benedict already."

I give him an unimpressed look, crossing my arms over my chest. "You're one to talk."

"Yeah, but there are only, like, two real Reese's candies. There are tons of words with Ben in them."

"Quit trying to distract me, boy, and answer the question."

He takes a deep breath as though gearing up to reveal something deeply personal, or shameful. "I've, uh, done some reading, yes."

216

If I liked this guy any more, my heart might fall to pieces. I try to keep my tone casual. "Oh yeah? How much?"

He looks at me guiltily.

I raise an eyebrow.

His mouth tilts up on one side.

I purse my lips.

"Most of her posts from the last five years," he mumbles, picking at a ragged fingernail.

My heart beats a little faster. "Learn anything interesting?"

"A lot." He nods, still not lifting his head. "The patriarchy is some bullshit."

I'm trying not to smile like an idiot, but I can't keep my lips together as I step closer and put a finger under his chin, tipping his face toward mine. "Why are you acting like you don't want me to know you've been reading my favorite blog of all time?"

Benny shrugs, but I'm not letting him look away. "I don't know. I guess I wanted to brush up on all this stuff since this site has been so important to you, but I didn't want it to look like I was just studying so my girlfriend will like me, rather than reading it because I'm interested, which I am. Interested in TKM. And, um, also in you. Two separate things."

The superficial side of my brain stutters over one word he casually dropped in there. "Your girlfriend, huh?"

His eyes close. "Oh God. I didn't—I mean, you don't have to—"

"I'm good with 'girlfriend.' Just confirming I heard you right," I tease, stopping him before he hurts himself jumping over these conversational hurdles. He opens his eyes again, gaze warming as I move my hand to his cheek. "You're a good guy, Benny."

"Okay, but the bar is basically on the ground. I could be a lot better."

I study his sincere expression, thinking of when I first saw him and how I judged him to be just like all the others. But I couldn't have been more off. He's so attentive, seeming to pick up every crumb of my thoughts or interests or time he can get and using it to do something sweet or learn about something new because I care about it. And now I see that it extends beyond me. It feels like I've stumbled upon a gosh darn unicorn. I don't know what to do with someone this purely good, but I'm trying my best to take it in and reciprocate.

"Benjamin Button—"

"Weird but okay," he mutters.

"—you have never been hotter than you are at this moment. Keep doing what you're doing, okay? You're a good guy, you have fine reading taste, and I really, really like you." He looks up at me, his smile growing as I add, "And you know you can always holler if you want to talk women's issues."

His expression turns mischievous. "Oh, I'll be hollering. Like, the wage gap? The hell is up with that?"

Overcome, I'm about to pull him in and kiss his face right there on the sidewalk of a busy downtown street, but I'm stopped by a hand on my arm and a gasped, "Oh my God!"

That's a real good combo for sending me into cardiac arrest, but my response in this case is to jerk my arm away and turn to face my assailant, ready to . . . what, slash them with Margie's company credit card? I've backed straight into Benny, who puts his hands on my shoulders protectively.

Shocking absolutely no one, I'm sure, this is an overreaction to the embarrassed woman standing beside us, who looks maybe a decade older than we are and is at least a few inches shorter.

"Oh my God," she repeats, bringing a hand up to one of her reddening cheeks. "I'm so sorry, I didn't mean to freak you out. But you're Reese! And Benny! From Friends of Flavor, right?"

My brain is taking a moment to catch on, wondering, *How can she know that? Real people have seen our videos?* Fortunately, my less socially awkward half steps in, taking his hands off my shoulders and holding one out to her.

"Hey, yeah, that's us. And you are?" Benny asks, bouncing back from his momentary sheepishness to ooze charm once again.

The cute grown woman blushes for real now, giving this teenage boy her hand. "Oh, my name's Anna. I'm such a big fan of your videos. I can't believe I ran into you! Could we maybe take a picture? A bunch of my coworkers watch, too. They won't believe this."

Benny glances at me with raised eyebrows and I can tell he is loving this. "Reese's Cup?"

Anna giggles as she pulls a cell phone from her giant purse. "Gah, yes! All the nicknames—you guys are the cutest!"

I laugh awkwardly as Benny continues to grin. We lean together and Anna squeezes between us, snapping a couple of rapid-fire selfies. Hopefully I look less shell-shocked than I feel.

She thanks us and compliments our videos again before rushing off wherever she was headed, and Benny and I start walking toward coffee again. His hand brushes against my back for a moment. "You all right there?"

I shake my head, all thoughts of Benny and TKM now overtaken by my first real encounter with a . . . well, I guess with a *fan*. "That was so weird, right? Someone recognizing us?"

He shrugs and I can hear the smile in his voice. "Not the first time it's happened to me."

"Oh hush, Mr. Big Shot." I swat his arm, but he doesn't react. "Wait. You're serious? When? I'm with you, like, all the time!"

I look at him in disbelief and he smirks, holding his hands out in a placating gesture. "Not all the time. It happened once at the gym, once at the grocery store, another on my way to work in the morning. I think that's it, though."

I gape at him. "What? How come this is the first time it's happened to me, then? What am I, chopped liver?"

We're at the Starbucks now and as Benny reaches over me to open the door, he makes a big show of flexing. "Maybe there's something about me that's just, I don't know, more *memorable*."

Taking our spot at the end of the fortunately short line, I roll my eyes. "Right. Thank you for that, sir."

He snickers and leans in to whisper in my ear, "More likely, people are less intimidated by me than by the hottest blonde to ever grace their computer screens."

"Oh, good save," I deadpan. "Keep it up, Norberto."

He drags a hand over his face. "Never should've told you. What was that you were saying just a few minutes ago, about how you 'really, really' like me? I've been reading your favorite blog, remember?"

That gets a laugh out of me. "Oh lordy. Maybe there are some things I shouldn't have told you, either."

Benny gives me a wink, then his expression turns more serious. "Oh, that reminds me, there was something I wanted to tell you about today. You know, before we got derailed by how amazing I am and how legions of fans follow my every move." I elbow him, and he laughs before continuing. "So, I talked to my parents yesterday."

"Oh yeah?" I turn as we move up in line, giving him my full attention. Clearly he wanted to tell me that for a reason. "How'd it go?"

"Surprisingly well, actually. They've been watching some of our videos and seem impressed. But mostly it was good because they are seriously nuts about the couple of servers they hired for the summer."

I raise an eyebrow, not sure I understand. "Interesting."

Benny nods. "Yeah, so, that made me feel a lot better. I mean, I still haven't told them I'm planning on staying in Seattle past the summer, but knowing they have some new people they're excited about, that they might not need me as much, that was good to hear. Makes it easier to think about leaving them."

"Oh yeah, of course," I say with a nod. I get it, and I'm glad for him that he's feeling some relief. I know how much he worries about the tension with his parents. But whenever something about the fall comes up, I feel my nerves building. I can't help my mind from going straight to the question of the internship and what it means for us. I clear my throat, realizing I probably haven't said enough. "That's great, Benny, seriously. What do you think—I mean, what might you do, hypothetically, in the case that you didn't get the fall internship?"

I regret the question as soon as I pose it, and chancing a look at him, find his brow furrowed. "Well, of course I don't know if I'll get it. I don't mean to sound like I'm counting on it." He lowers his voice even though I don't think anyone in the place cares to listen to our conversation. "Honestly, Reese, anything could happen with the fall spot. And if you get it, I'll be happy for you. I'm planning on staying around regardless, though. I want to try for culinary school at some point, so if FoF doesn't happen, I'll just do that sooner. This one job doesn't have to be my whole future."

I nod, and when Benny nudges me, I look back up to see him giving me his most heart-melting smile. "You still gonna hang out with me when you're a big-time college student?"

"Of course," I answer with a smirk just before we reach the counter. Benny takes care of our order—as much black coffee as our arms can feasibly transport—then as we wait, he changes the subject to the latest Aiden drama from the *Good Chef/Bad Chef* set, where Benny's been helping out some this week. I half listen, and laugh at the right times, as we gather our caffeinated bounty and start back toward the office, but I'm increasingly distracted.

The cease-fire bubble has been popped, at least for me. If the run-in with the fan hadn't done the trick, all of Benny's talk about this fall sure did.

I want to be as unperturbed by this competition as he seems to be. I feel guilty that I still think of it as a competition when Benny doesn't seem like he's tallying scores at all times in his head. I care about him so much, and I want him to succeed.

But I can't put aside what I want for myself, either, and this job feels like it *is* my whole future—everything I've wanted, dreamed of, planned for, waiting on the other side if I can just get my foot through the door with that fall internship. I wanted to build a career at Friends of Flavor before I ever knew Benny, and if he decided he was over me tomorrow, I'd still want this job.

And even as he says how happy he'd be for my success, he's not going to be stepping back and letting me have it. I don't want that and I've told him as much. So why would I even think about doing the same? I shouldn't. I should continue to work as hard as I am, do my best, and hope that it's enough. Keep pushing and keeping score.

I haven't added any points to the tally since Bainbridge, but this coffee run has brought it back to the forefront of my mind.

The fact that Benny's had all kinds of fan run-ins and this was my first feels significant. Is it just because he's active on social media? Or is he more popular with viewers in general, because of who he is? I can't help but lean toward the latter. And surely viewer opinion matters to Aiden, Margie, and the suits. I add a point in Benny's favor on my mental scoreboard.

Benny—4, Reese—3.

The ding of the elevator breaks my train of thought, and the only remaining passenger besides Benny and me gets off at a floor a few below ours. When the doors close again, Benny leans over and lands a kiss on my cheek.

"What was that for?" I ask, trying to shove the intrusive thoughts out with a smile.

He sighs, leaning back against the elevator wall with his share of the coffees propped against his stomach, his serene smile suggesting he doesn't have a care in the world. "Just basking in my good fortune, Reese's Cup."

And even as my heart swells, my stomach sinks.

Chapter Sixteen

The following Monday, I find myself questioning every choice that has led me to the point of standing in front of a crowd in rubber overalls. Aiden's most ridiculous idea for *Amateur Hour* has come to fruition, and Benny and I are being trained by the Pike Place Market fishmongers in the tricks of their trade. Like everything else in our show, they make a competition out of it, seeing which one of us does a better job of throwing and catching and, most importantly, not dropping the fish purchased by customers. It all goes well enough until I throw a massive salmon that Benny catches with his face.

Wising up to our total ineptitude, the fishmongers let the two of us only handle the smaller fish from then on. I kind of figure that Benny's injury and the way he completes the rest of filming with an ice pack strapped to his face will garner him more of the sympathy vote, but the crowd never forgives him for fumbling that fish. Somehow, I manage to not make the same grave error, and when the time comes for jury-by-cheering, the significantly louder screams are for me. *Point Reese!*

Benny—4, Reese—4.

Back in business, baby.

When the video goes up the next evening, it instantly becomes our most popular episode to date. The replay of the fish hitting Benny is a work of art. I laugh until I cry, both watching it in my dorm alone and with Benny at work the next day when he's supposed to be cleaning up PK 2 after an episode of *World on a Plate*.

"That'll teach me to ever mess with you," he grumbles. He gets a mischievous glint in his eyes and leans farther into me as if about to do something totally not in line with our relationship-under-wraps plan, but we're interrupted—thank goodness—while he's still a couple of feet away.

"Oh good, you're both here," Aiden's clipped voice rings out. Margie is at his side, but Aiden launches into their purpose without letting her get a word in edgewise. "We're sending you to UltiCon. It's UltiMedia's big convention highlighting all their shows and creators, and it's become pretty huge over the past few years. We want to capitalize on your viral video at Pike Place and keep getting your faces and the *Amateur Hour* brand out there. For whatever reason, you two are working for audiences, and we can't let the moment pass."

It's such an odd combination of compliment, passive aggression and shameless money- and attention-grabbing. So, quite on brand for Aiden.

A bit more gently, Margie offers, "We've continued to be impressed by the response to you two and your show as a whole, even before this latest episode. We think that your videos have made Friends of Flavor more accessible to younger audiences and also those with less culinary-specific interests than our typical viewers. Your appeal is widespread and powerful, and we want to celebrate it."

That sounds a little nicer than "capitalize on it." My brain catches up to what they're saying. "When do we leave?" I ask. "And what will we do there?"

"You'll go with the rest of the Friends on Friday," Aiden says. "There's a meet and greet that evening, and on Saturday, you'll be doing a large group cooking demo slash Q&A with the Friends. Besides that, enjoy the conference. Mingle, meet fans, make connections. We're going to trade off doing social media takeovers on the Friends official accounts, and, Benny, update your personal page throughout like the rest of the Friends will be doing. Any other questions? I'll have Teagan book your travel and forward you the info."

Benny and I look at each other, wordlessly understanding that, as per usual, whether or not we have questions doesn't matter much. We're going, and that's that.

"Nah, we're good," Benny says. "Let us know if there's anything else we need to do."

"Of course." They both head toward the door and Margie leaves, but Aiden turns back just before he walks out of the kitchen and points to Benny. "Actually, Ben, come with me to my office. We've gotten some media requests with regard to the fish video, and I want to see which ones you might be interested in."

Benny looks startled, though whether it's from our boss telling him he has "media requests" or calling him "Ben," I couldn't say. Probably both. "Oh. Uh, I need to finish cleaning up the kitchen first. But it'll only take a few minutes," he offers.

Aiden scrunches his nose, casting a quick, unimpressed look in my direction. "Leave it. Reese can handle it. It's probably more up her alley anyway."

I suck in a sharp breath before I can stop myself. *Pardon?*

Benny, less used to these things than I am, pushes back. "What's that supposed to mean?"

Aiden, already turning away, falters. "What? I just mean, uh, she's— Reese seems tidy. Come on, we've got work to do."

My sweet, well-meaning boyfriend looks at me with a stormy expression. His eyes tell me that we are indeed thinking the same thing—that our boss fully implied I'm more suited to cleaning the kitchen because I'm a girl. And I wasn't even supposed to be cleaning it in the first place—I just popped in to laugh over the video with Benny before going back to marketing. But is this really the hill either of us wants to die on?

Go, I mouth, shooing him with my hands. With obvious reluctance, he follows Aiden out of the kitchen. My head is spinning, and I don't know which part is most upsetting—Aiden's sexist comment or that apparently Benny and Benny alone is a media darling now. Looks like I might've miscalculated who really came out on top in our last video.

Our earlier conversation comes back to me—how the fall internship isn't everything to him, unlike the way it feels to me. But now my thoughts are colored with a stronger sense that Benny is the bosses' clear favorite for the job, and the public's. *He's* the one Aiden pulls away for special requests from the adoring media. I'm the lowly, replaceable kitchen wench who stays behind to finish his cleaning. It stings more than I want it to.

But really, the kitchen won't clean itself, so I wipe up the floury counters, scrape burned-on bits of cheese from a baking sheet, and load the rest of Lily's used dishes into the dishwasher. All the while, I'm fighting the bitter voices in my head wanting me to get mad at Benny.

It isn't his fault he's a likable guy. Or that we may or may not work for raging misogynists. He even tried to speak up for me, or at least to challenge one jackass statement. He probably would've pushed harder if I hadn't stopped him.

I can deal with this. I can separate my feelings for my boyfriend from my worries about work. Of which there are many. Like the fact that, once again, we're leaving town this weekend, with only a couple days' notice. I just need to stay focused, to not give people any legitimate reasons to think less of me or to otherwise cause any messes.

Shouldn't be a problem, right? I hear I'm quite tidy.

Chapter Seventeen

Early Friday morning, Benny meets me outside my dorm with his suitcase in hand. He takes my suitcase and puts both of them in the back of the ride-share he ordered to take us to the airport.

Acknowledging that he is with Morning Reese, Benny doesn't try to chat much, just holds my hand in the back seat and runs his thumb absently over my fingers. It's so nice, I almost wish we could just tell everyone we're together so he could keep doing this at the airport, on the flight, till the day I die, whatever.

But once we pull up at the departures curb, he lets go of my hand and grabs both of our bags again, thanking the driver on my behalf. I drift like a zombie through check-in, and by the time we've waited in all the lines and are past security, I'm awake enough to speak.

"You're cute and I like you" is the first thing I say when I walk up behind him at the security exit. He's checking the big departures screen for which gate we're at.

His mouth turns up in that lopsided smile, proving my point. "Well, good morning. You're beautiful and I *really* like you."

"Don't try and one-up me at this hour, Benicio del Toro."

"Ooh, deep cut. Have you been Googling names with 'Ben' in them in your downtime?"

"No." *Yes.*

He smirks. "Come on, let's get you on the plane so you can finish your REM cycle."

Katherine and Aiden are at the gate already when we arrive, and the rest of the Friends and a few other staff trickle in soon after. No one is especially talkative, save for when a couple of different people come up and ask for pictures. Pictures! At the airport! And not just with the standard Friends of Flavor chefs, as I first assume they will. They want to talk to and pose with Benny and me, too.

I haven't been in this position since that random lady on the sidewalk, but none of the others seem surprised one bit. They look totally at ease with these "fans," almost like they expected this.

Because they did, I realize. Because we're on our way to a conference meant for fans of UltiMedia franchises like ours, where there will be actual, formal meet and greets.

Why didn't anyone tell me to dress up a little? I'm the only one of the Friends of Flavor crew who looks sloppy—as I always do while flying—in leggings, an oversize T-shirt, and worn-in tennis shoes, my hair thrown up in a messy bun and not a spot of makeup on my face. I am the basic white girl ruining all the cute shots.

But I do my best to make up for it with my sparkling personality, for which I have to dig deep before nine a.m. Soon it's time to board and I can relax again, settling in my seat next to Benny and then spending most of the couple of hours to L.A. sleeping with my head resting on his shoulder.

We caravan to the hotel, which is just a few minutes' walk from the convention center. Aiden checks us in, then passes out room keys and UltiCon badges.

When we're released, I am happy to flop onto my king-size bed in my very own room and stare at the ceiling for a while. I don't much know what to expect from the next few days. How many people are going to be here, and of those, how many care anything about me? Since I mostly avoid the comments—that one moment of weakness excepted—I don't know what the reactions to *Amateur Hour,* or to me specifically, are, beyond what Benny and Aiden and others at work have told me in passing. It worries me a tad, finding out for myself, coming face to face with real viewers.

But there's no backing out now, so I shower and dress in some of the better clothes I brought and slip my feet into a pair of wedges. I fix my hair so it falls in loose waves and do my makeup enough that I'll look like a living human in pictures.

Before I know it, it's time to head to my first-ever meet and greet. I'm putting the lanyard with my badge over my head when there's a knock on the door. I see Benny through the peephole and open it.

"Hey, you." I smile, still pulling strands of hair out from under the lanyard as I let him in.

"Wow." He eyes me from head to toe and back up again. "You look way too good to be with a scrub like me."

I laugh, patting the light stubble on his cheek. He's in one of his typical tight T-shirts and jeans, plus, of course . . .

"You could lose the hat, you know. Show off that beautiful mane of yours to the public."

He rolls his eyes, but he's smiling as he pats his backward cap. "It's my signature look—people will be expecting the hat."

"You're nothing if not a man of the people."

We stand there smiling like the smitten fools we are for a few moments.

"You're tall," Benny says, nodding down at my shoes, which, now that I think about it, do put me a few inches over him.

"Too tall?" I ask self-consciously before I can stop myself.

People are weird about height. It seems to me like the last nonnegotiable, appearance-related deal breaker that a ton of folks can't get past—the insecurity they feel about their height, whether they're taller or shorter.

Kinda messed up, when you think about it. Which, as a tall-ish girl, I often do.

"What? No," Benny says, waving away the suggestion. "You look amazing in those. I'm enjoying the view from down here."

I laugh, but I could also melt clear through the floor and the six below it, down to the lobby. The concierge would have to sweep me off his desk. It'd be real gross.

Instead, I put my hands on Benny's shoulders and lean in to kiss him. His hands come around my waist and pull me closer, and oh my stars, are we sure we need to be present at this meet and greet? Because I could stick around here for another while.

Benny breaks it off, though, pushing my hips back to set me away from him.

"Remind me again why we aren't doing that twenty-four hours a day?" he says breathlessly, his eyes roaming over my body even as he pulls his hands back in fists as if to keep them from doing the same.

"Well, sleep, for one thing," I answer.

"Who needs it?" His eyes meet mine again and he grins, those dimples making my knees weak. "But I guess we should go meet everyone else before they think the two teenagers have been up here doing unspeakable things to each other from the moment they gave us rooms in a hotel."

I feel the blush in my cheeks and shove him lightly, then take his hand and pull him out the door behind me. But not before stealing one more quick kiss.

There is no way I could have anticipated the madness that is the meet and greet. The conference organizers don't bring us into the exhibition hall until right at the session's start time, so there's no sit-there-and-wait-for-people-to-trickle-in period. No, the doors open and we walk in—Aiden, Katherine, Nia, Seb, Lily, Rajesh, and me, with Benny bringing up the rear—to a large room packed wall to wall with cheering people, all here to meet us. Even the experienced Friends seem surprised at the high turn-out, but they wave like we're a mixed-gender One Direction circa 2013, so I do the same.

But since we're not at boy band levels of fame and impor-tance, the meet-and-greet format is somewhat loose. There's a long pseudo wall of UltiCon banners that we stand in front of, with a few yards between each of us so people can move down the line and get their pictures taken by UltiCon staff as they go. There are several high-top tables set up with Sharpies for us to sign anything fans have brought with them, like old Friends of Flavor cookbooks or, you know, cardboard cutouts of Benny's face. The organizers explained to us how it would all work before we got here and said that the line should move "organically," but seeing the mass of people packed in, I predict it may be as organic as a ten-car pileup.

I am at least pleased to be stationed between Seb and Benny, probably the two coworkers who put me most at ease. Still, when the rope is dropped at the head of the line to kick off the meet and greet, my stomach drops a bit, too.

The interactions start off pretty tame. A group of teenage girls is the first to come through.

"Oh my God, Reese!" a cute redhead squeaks, throwing her arms around my shoulders.

"Oh," is the startled response that comes out of my mouth. The first girl releases me and her friends each give me less aggressive hugs in turn.

"We love *Amateur Hour*," the one with a cat-ear headband says, then lowers her voice. "What's it like working with Benny?"

The other two waggle their eyebrows suggestively as if we're gossiping about boys at a sleepover. Except usually when I do that with Nat and Clara, it's about how much we don't like one guy or another.

I let out a laugh that hopefully sounds breezy and not flustered at this being my very first meet-and-greet question ever. "It's great, most of the time. He's a trip, but we're good friends."

They look a little disappointed at my failure to, what, divulge to total strangers that kissing Benny's face has become my favorite pastime? I sign each of their UltiCon programs, we take a selfie, and they've cheered up by the time they move on to the boy in question.

Before long, the vibe changes.

"You're even more beautiful in person," says a man who's at least my dad's age. The plastic smile I've had on since the event started falters, and possible responses flash through my mind. *That's inappropriate,* for example, or, *I don't know what you expect me to say to that.*

What comes out, though, is a meek "Thank you."

Sometimes, I feel like having good manners is a curse. The man stands beside me for a picture, his hand resting dangerously low on my back, and I stiffen instinctively. The desire to step away is so strong, it almost pains me to keep still. Each fingertip pressed against the fabric of my skirt feels like a flag staking claim, saying that as long as I can't overcome the awkwardness of saying no, the "yes, touch me anywhere you want" is implied.

Without my thinking about it, my eyes flit to Benny, who's engrossed in talking with a family. I look toward the camera again, a large part of me wondering what I was hoping for—for him to see the guy's hand, how close he's standing, and swoop in and rescue me? Go all alpha-male-territorial on a random Friends of Flavor fan?

No, I don't want that. Or at least, I don't want to want it. I don't want to feel like I need a guy to protect me from another guy. But I know I would feel safer, more at ease, if Benny or Seb or even Aiden was over here to run interference, and that sucks.

The guy moves on, and I know the whole interaction took less than a couple of minutes, but it felt so much longer. I don't relax at all after that. The next couple of hours are a blur of handshakes and hugs and fist bumps and constantly trying to manage my actions and reactions. How close I let people get to me. How friendly I can be without inviting unwanted flirting, or worse.

A group of college-aged guys come through, and maybe in

any other context, I'd find some of them cute. But their roaming hands and insinuating comments and questions are definitely not cute.

"You ever on the FoF subreddit?" one in a HAVE A FLAVORFUL DAY! T-shirt asks.

"Uh, no, not really," I say, signing his friend's homemade poster of the FoF logo.

I look up in time to see the guy who asked the question share an amused glance with another in a backward cap like Benny's. "Some fans on there found some old spring break pictures of you and posted 'em. Gotta be honest, it looks like being around all that food lately has agreed with you."

His lascivious gaze travels a slow path up and down my body, and I feel my jaw drop. He . . . They . . . *What in the actual hell?* So many irate responses tumble through my head, I don't even know where to start. My face feels like it's on fire. Who thinks it's okay to say things like that to a complete stranger? Do they realize that I'm an actual person, that I may not want their opinions on my looks, good or bad? Except, I realize, they probably don't care.

I could slap those smug smiles off their entitled white-boy faces. But what good would it do? The comments and the looks are already out there. I feel like I need a shower. Would it make anything better to give them a good telling-off? Would I make things awkward for two seconds until they leave or, worse, Aiden notices and gets on me for being rude to fans?

Before I can decide or so much as utter a sound, the guy with the poster says, "C'mon, let's get a picture."

They crowd in, two on my right and three on my left. Hands come around either side of my waist in a firm grip, more territory-marking flags. And I don't stop them. I give a tight, teeth-only smile as the camera snaps, and then they're moving on, backslaps all around for a job well done, a cloud of too-strong cologne in their wake.

I curse myself silently for being so passive. But it's like each time I let something slide, more of my righteous anger, my will to push back slides away with it.

A while later, when a man unbuttons his shirt for me to sign his bare chest, I do it. When another lifts a pen and reaches for my wrist, I'm too confused to pull away before he's written his phone number *on my skin*. It's becoming physical, the feeling of weakness each of these encounters gives me. My shoulders grow more hunched as time passes, my body more tired, my voice softer.

There are, of course, innocent comments, like girls who tell me they love my hair or clothes, or the many, many people who enjoy my accent. But not once during the whole meet and greet does anyone talk to me about cooking. Not that I'm an expert, Lord knows, but that's our whole shtick.

A family—two parents and two young daughters—comes through and the girls look up at me with gap-toothed smiles as I sign their conference programs.

"You're my favorite Friend," the littler one says.

"I want to be on *Amateur Hour* when I'm bigger," her sister adds, mispronouncing "amateur" something awful, but it only makes her cuter.

I crouch down to their level and offer a wobbly smile. "Y'all are too sweet."

They lean in while their parents take our picture, and while my smile is a bit more genuine with the cuties beside me than it has been with others today, it's still hiding my true feelings. Because what I really want to say is that I hope all their dreams come true, but maybe not any that put them in this exact position I'm in. I want to cover these sweet, tiny humans in some magical Bubble Wrap that protects them from strangers who would make them question their worth. I want to make sure their parents teach them the line between being polite and letting others disrespect their boundaries so that when the time comes that someone tries to cross a line, they're braver than I am and speak up.

Instead, I thank them and smile and wave as they move down the line.

I peek over at Benny occasionally, and his fan encounters seem to have some consistency. People of all genders and from ages sixteen to sixty have been throwing themselves at my boyfriend. I feel for him at first, knowing how not-fun it is when that happens. But Benny handles it like a champ. His smile doesn't look any less genuine, picture after picture. I wonder what he thinks about all the attention—if he ever has the kind of thoughts that I have about personal safety and boundaries, or if it just seems like harmless fun. The ease and confidence in his expression and movements make me think it's the latter.

All in all, meeting so many fans is overwhelming, an emotional and sensory overload. As the massive line of people is coming to an end, a lady in a KATHERINE FOR PRESIDENT T-shirt approaches.

"Ah, Reese!" she says with a giddy smile. "Could I hug you?"

Not many folks have asked that today. So when they do, it feels like an amazingly kind gesture instead of, say, basic human decency.

"Absolutely," I say warmly. Her embrace feels eerily like my mama's—soft and supportive. I'm shocked to feel tears pricking at my eyes as I pull back. I blink rapidly and focus on signing the picture frame she brought. Nice as this woman seems, I don't want to look like an affection-starved maniac. I've had enough human contact today to last me a few decades, probably. But it's different feeling a hug so familiar, one that's so much like home.

"You are just so bright and strong," she tells me as I hand the frame back to her. My brows raise at such a nice compliment, one I don't especially feel like I've earned. But she continues, "It's great to see such a confident woman who doesn't let all the haters get her down."

She's not the first one who's said something along those lines today. Others have commented on the Reddit situation those guys talked about, or how they think it's stupid how mad some commenters get when I tease Benny. I guess it's easy to seem confident when I don't have much clue what goes on in the comments on my own videos. It sounds like there's a lot that I'm missing—for good reason, of course—but catching whiffs of it makes me all the more tempted to have a look for myself.

After what feels like both three days and three minutes, we make it through the end of the line. The quiet in the room, which is now occupied only by my coworkers and a few UltiCon personnel, is almost disorienting.

We're thanked for our time and we thank the UltiCon staff in return for the invitation, then we're set free for the night. Some of us talked on the walk over about sticking around after our session and exploring the convention a bit. But we didn't plan for how exhausting this was going to be.

When Rajesh suggests we ditch and get dinner instead, most everyone agrees, but I make excuses to head back to the hotel. I am so drained. There's an uneasiness in my stomach after everything, and I don't think I can pretend to be fine in front of everyone for one more minute, let alone an hour or two.

Benny tries to join me to make sure I'm okay—I claimed it was stomach cramps, thinking that would deter him—but I insist he go eat and catch up with me later.

Back in my hotel room, I change into the ratty old T-shirt and shorts I sleep in. I spend a few minutes at the sink scrubbing at the phone number on my wrist with soap and water, but when my skin is red and raw and the ink still faintly visible, I give up and settle into bed. I try to work on an illustration of the Christmas-in-July cookies Nia made—Margie wants to use my drawing as a promo for the *Piece of Cake* episode going up next week—but my hands are unsteady. Every line I draw comes out like an angry slash. Not wanting my cutesy cookie picture to turn into a horror movie poster, I decide to pack it in for now. Then, knowing it's probably the worst thing I could do but feeling helpless to stop myself, I open up my phone and pull up a random episode of *Amateur Hour.* It's the one where we made gnocchi, before we'd formally shifted into competition mode.

I scroll down to the comments.

why are they letting this bitch ruin so many videos these days

Benny: 1. Funny 2. Talented 3. Good-looking. Girl intern: 1. Boring. 2. Ugly. 3. Can't even cook. Wtf fof???

she srsly can't go 5 mins w/o making some stupid comment about the patriarchy

I watch this channel for the food not for an idiot pushing her views on everyone

Why doesn't she go back to her hick town and leave fof to real chefs

My heart is already racing. Where the devil is all this coming from? Nasty, senseless comments about how I'm single-handedly ruining the whole channel, when I'd been in all of two videos at that point. Nearly of their own accord, my fingers scroll back up the screen and hit Play so I can rewatch the video and try to see what I could have done or said that was so awful.

But it's just as I remember, a pretty light, funny compilation of the two of us bantering and cooking. The closest I notice to anything controversial is when I make a casual joke about my insistence on moving the heavy cans of tomatoes myself, saying that we don't want our food to taste like wasted chivalry. Benny laughs.

But that's all there is.

I click through to our other episodes, and they all have similar comments. There's some positive stuff, too, and some creepy stuff. But to my admittedly biased eyes, it feels like a Reese hate-fest, with commenters going on and on about how stupid and useless I am, how I clearly make Benny miserable and he doesn't deserve this treatment, how I'm sending Friends of Flavor down the drain.

I rewatch each video with the volume high enough to overcome the sound of my blood rushing in my ears. There's more of the same tame content and disproportionate rage in the comment sections. There are also plenty of comments about how slutty I seem, how Benny is a great guy, and how I'm not good enough for him. A few times, people claim to know me or know someone who knows me, referencing what a terrible person I was in high school, saying I don't deserve to have the platform I do now. It seems believable enough that they could be from my school.

Clicking on a link in one of the comments takes me to the Friends of Flavor subreddit, where I'm shocked to find whole threads dedicated to hating on me. There's the bathing suit picture, too. Good gravy, I'm, like, twelve in that picture! Is this even legal? There are other pictures that people have dug up from my past, probably from acquaintances who've long since stopped speaking to me.

This is worse than I imagined. Unable to stop myself now that I'm so deep in this rabbit hole, I open Benny's Instagram page on my phone and look over the comments on a recent picture he put up of me, in which he is pushing falafel toward my face and my mouth is hanging open midlaugh. Wordplay fan that Benny is, he captioned it "Feed the Recse-t." Somehow my stomach sinks even further as I see more of what I've seen everywhere else.

I know that Benny only uses social media out of obligation, to appease the bosses and keep up the "public persona," so it isn't necessarily a surprise that he hasn't responded to any of this stuff. But it also wouldn't hurt to see my boyfriend give some kind of eff-you to rufus1234 for calling me a "bucktooth bitch." I think even my old orthodontist would jump to my defense on that one.

I don't know if I really want that either, though. I don't know what I want, or what I should do with this discovery. My face is red and puffy and I can't believe I'm able to produce as many tears as I have the past couple of hours. My phone is still on Do Not Disturb.

It occurs to me that if so many FoF fans are aware of the overgrown man-children waging their one-sided war against clueless me, surely some of those closer to me know, too. Certainly Benny has seen, at a minimum, the comments on his Instagram. Natalie and Clara have both told me that they follow him and make heart-eyes at everything he posts about me. Presumably, Margie and/or others in marketing who handle the likes and comments on the videos I'm in are aware. Because he knows everything about everyone's business, I bet Aiden knows, too. Did he think if I smiled more, the problem would go away?

Goodness gracious. I want to throw things. It's all too reminiscent of the last time everyone turned on me. I feel the weight that I've carried around for four years come crashing back down on my shoulders. Added to it is the sense that I've been making things worse for myself by pretending that plugging my ears and saying, *"La la la I can't hear you,"* to others' opinions would keep them from falling on me.

And now I can't push away the overwhelming feelings from the meet and greet. It's an emotional pile-on as I think of each creepy man, each bold speculation about my love life, each uncomfortable comment or question that I know my male coworkers didn't get.

Eventually, I toss my phone aside and nestle into bed, rolling myself up into a little blanket burrito. I know this doesn't actually fix anything, but it feels like the stuff can't reach me as well through these layers of fluff. As I stare into the room watching daylight slip away through the sheer curtains, I find myself wondering how this ends. Do I somehow rise above? Or am I just going to get ruined all over again?

Chapter Eighteen

When there's a knock on my door later that night, I toy with the idea of not letting him in.

I know it's Benny. There's no one else who would casually swing by my hotel room, and he's been texting me for over an hour now and getting no response, so he's probably checking for signs of life. But who am I kidding? Of course I'll let him in.

I slide with zero grace out from the covers and onto the floor, stumbling across the room. I double-check the peephole because I do have a little self-preservation, then open it to see my handsome boyfriend leaning on the doorframe. His hands are in his pockets, an easy—if somewhat inquisitive—smile on his face, and lordy, it can't be safe to like someone this much.

"Reese's Cup," he says as he strolls in. "You been sleeping off the social overload?"

I shrug noncommittally as I return to the bed, folding my legs up underneath me. I don't know how to explain all of this to

Benny. He gestures to the spot beside me, his eyebrows raising as if to ask permission, and I nod.

"I've been wallowing," I admit on impulse as he settles down beside me.

"Wallowing? What's wrong?" His voice is soft with concern and he drapes his arm over the pillow that I'm resting against. I accept the invitation and lean against Benny instead.

I sigh in a way that I know is extra dramatic, but it feels good. "I broke the golden rule."

Even without seeing his face, I can tell he's giving me a strange look. "Treat others like you want to be treated . . . ?"

"The other golden rule. Don't read the comments."

I feel his arm tense around me and he lets out a short sigh. "Reese . . ."

I sit up on my knees and shift so I can look at him. "Why didn't you tell me it was like that, Benny?"

He reaches up to readjust his hat, his eyes drifting to the ceiling as if the answers I want to hear will be up there. "You said you didn't want to know about all that. Why would I shove it in your face anyway?"

Dammit. Fair point. "Okay, yeah," I say, my voice going softer. "But I . . . I didn't know it would be that bad. It's like high school again but intensified, and it doesn't feel good. At all."

"I'm so sorry, Reese," he says, meeting my eyes again as he reaches for my hands with both of his and laces our fingers together. "But honestly, I don't think you should pay it any attention. Like, go back to what you were doing by ignoring 'em—the good and the bad—because what do they matter? They don't. And they don't know anything about you."

"I know you're probably right; it's just easier said than done," I say. "I'm not invincible. It hurts to read such awful things, no matter who it's coming from."

Benny frowns. "I wish I could make it go away."

I give him a weak smile. "Me too. But I guess I've been through it before and came out on the other side. I have some experience in growing a thicker skin. Not thick enough yet, apparently, but I . . . I can probably get there. If you want to block anyone who calls me ugly on your Instagram in the meantime, though, I sure won't stop you."

"Dumbasses," he mutters. "Seriously, they don't know sh—"

"It's fine, Benny. I don't want to talk about it anymore," I say, though I don't know if that's the full truth. More like, I don't think we'll come to any brilliant conclusions tonight about how to make people on the internet be nice to me, so let's distract ourselves for a while. "How was dinner?"

"Eh, fine. Raj and Katherine got into it over whether the restaurant's burgers were fresh or frozen. She called him a foodie one-percenter, he said her taste is pedestrian, then Seb ordered bottomless margaritas for the table and that shut everyone up. Hey, have you eaten anything?"

I shake my head, turning around to glance at the clock. Eight-thirty already. Dang, time flies when you're having a one-woman pity party.

Benny releases my hands and claps. "All right. Up. We gotta rectify that right now. We can go out and find a place, or I can pick something up, or we can get room service, or—"

"Room service!" I burst out, definitely overeager. "I mean, if you want to. I've never gotten room service before. It sounds fun. Even more fun since it's not our money. Plus I'm already in my pajamas, sooo . . ."

Now that I think about it, I'm sure I look an absolute mess. I get off the bed so I can maybe do some damage control in the bathroom.

He laughs. "It's a plan. Check out the menu. I'm gonna see what's on TV. But hey—" He scoots to the edge of the bed and catches one of my hands before I get far. I meet his serious gaze. "You can tell me if you're not okay, or if you want to talk more. You know that, right?"

I smile at him. Bless his emotionally stable heart. "Yes I do. Thank you."

His face relaxes into that one-sided smile I love so much and he rests back against the pillows again, reaching for the remote to flick on the flat-screen TV.

A few minutes later, I've fixed my hair into something other than the blanket-burrito-caused rat's nest that it was and made my food decision. I feel like Eloise at the Plaza—or rather her less famous cousin, Reese at the Moderately Nice Chain Hotel—as I place my order and wait for it to arrive. When there's a knock on the door, I jump up and run for it before Benny can, returning with a big tray that I set between us on the bed.

We make a toast with our cans of Coke and then recline against the pillows as I tuck into my cheeseburger and generously share some fries—not the classiest of meals, but I had a hankering.

And while it's good, being comfy with one of my favorite people and demolishing a greasy mess of food, it doesn't quite erase the day. The crappy social interactions and similarly crappy internet lurking have left me with an unsettled churning in my stomach, this ominous feeling that I should've handled everything better and that worse things lie ahead. I still feel strangers' hands on me when I wish I could only feel Benny's. I'm rethinking every word I said and that was said to me, when I want to be enjoying this mindless early-2000s rom-com on the TV.

I want to ignore all the outside noise, to be present in this moment with this handsome boy in my bed. Instead, I'm all out of sorts. And expressing none of it aloud, of course. No, I opt for making snarky comments about the movie and how predictable it is, telling Benny how it's all going to play out even though we missed the first hour.

My predictions are spot-on, for what little it's worth.

"You could not have known he was going to leave Spicy Brunette at the altar for Cute Blondie unless you'd seen this before. I think I've been played," Benny huffs as he finishes off the last fry.

"Think about what you're saying, Ben Kenobi. Spicy versus cute. We're never supposed to like the *spicy* woman in movies, not for the romantic hero to end up with. He's supposed to go with the aw-shucks, girl-next-door type who was right in front of his face all along. Spicy gal never had a chance, bless her heart."

He scrunches his nose, mulling this over. "Then I have a dilemma, see," he says, and his feigned thoughtfulness makes me smirk.

"Oh, do you?"

"Yeah, because what if I'm into this girl who's cute but also spicy? Is she too good to be true? Can I really only have one or the other?"

I narrow my eyes at him, stretching one leg to nudge the room service tray with the now-empty plates out of the way and shift slowly in his direction.

"I don't know. A girl with multiple facets to her personality? Sounds fake."

Benny grins, his dimples projecting extra adorableness as he leans over to move the tray off the bed and onto the floor. When he leans back again, I scoot right up alongside him and push his cap off his head, running my hand through his curls.

"Oh, she's real," he says with a soft laugh, our faces so close I feel his breath tickling my skin. "I think, anyway. But just to be sure . . ."

Then his lips press into mine, and it feels like relinquishing so much of my tightly held control and letting my nagging worries fade as I sink into him. It's a blur of kisses and touches and affectionate whispered words even though we're the only ones around to hear them. My fingers twirling locks of his hair, his hand running up the outside of my thigh. My legs fitting around his hips as I climb into his lap. His lips on my neck, along my jawline. My palms dipping beneath his soft T-shirt, feeling the hard planes of those hard-earned abs.

I like the feeling a bit too much: not thinking, just acting, I run my hands up higher and the sound he makes as we kiss urges me on. It just feels so *good* and I like him so *much* and goodness, he's so *gorgeous,* and if I'm not gonna appreciate it, who will, right? My hands have roamed to his chest when he pulls his head back and raises his eyebrows, reaching for the neckline of his shirt. I nod, nearly as overeager as I was for room service, and he pulls his T-shirt up and over his head.

Lordhavemercy.

My eyes and my stomach and all things hormone-driven were not ready for this. It's like his torso is carved out of marble, for goodness' sake. I bring my lips back to his, in part to keep myself from sitting here gaping like a fool. But I also enjoy running my hands over this newly available territory, and all indications say Benny is having a pretty good time, too.

I let myself tip forward onto his chest and my legs stretch back so that I'm lying mostly on top of him. His hands have been making lazy rotations up and down my sides and when I move to this new position, I don't register that my own shirt has ridden up until his fingers reach the bare skin at my hips.

Goose bumps pop up immediately at his touch. His palms flatten along my exposed lower back and it feels so good, soothing even as it's putting me further on alert. But when his hands move up under the back of my T-shirt, thumbs hooking the hem to lift it ever so slightly higher, something changes.

It feels like all my muscles seize up, and I hear the angry, aggressive voices in my head—voices from my past, judging me for things I didn't even do. Online commenters who disapprove of everything I say and do, supposed "fans" whose leers make my skin crawl. It all puts so much pressure on me now, everything riding on my next move. If I go any further, let Benny in any more, am I easy? If I don't, will he think I don't like him? What about if—or more likely, when—we break up? I could have regrets. He could be angry, vengeful, tell people all the intimate details. Can I face that kind of fallout again?

Am I going to think about all this stuff for the rest of my life? I mean, damn, should I cut my losses and join a convent now?

Somewhere in the midst of my mental shitstorm, I've pulled my face back from Benny's. His hands have moved from my back to rest lightly on my forearms, which I'm using to prop myself up against his chest.

"Hey, where'd you go?" he says softly, searching my eyes.

I blink twice, shake my head. "Sorry, I . . ." I swallow heavily, not the least bit sure what to say. "I don't think I can do anything else tonight. I'm sorry, I—I thought I was good, but . . ."

I shake my head again, averting my eyes and pressing my lips tightly together. Benny doesn't move, or scoff, or start throwing things. Because he's *Benny*, not one of the monsters in my head. He's Benny, and he's different, and he's good. His fingers continue to brush my wrists, one of which still bears the outline of a phone number written on it by a total stranger without my permission. I feel his eyes on my face.

"It's all good," he says, and the breath I let out feels like a balloon of tension deflating inside me. "Anything you want is fine with me. I'm sorry if I—I mean, I didn't mean to make you uncomfortable. I never want to do that, Reese, so just tell me to stop and—"

I look at him and plant a light kiss on his cheek so abruptly it stops him midsentence. "You didn't do anything wrong, promise. But thank you for understanding." I shift so I'm lying beside him and rest my head on his shoulder, letting my arm drape over his stomach that—my screwed-up sense of self and sexuality aside—is still really, really nice to look at. "You're great, you know. I mean, I hope you know. And I appreciate you a lot."

Benny brings his arm up to rest over mine. "Right back at you," he says. There's a hint of something like confusion or maybe self-consciousness in his voice. Which, given the events of the past two minutes, is understandable. After another moment, he adds, "I'm gonna, um, put my shirt back on now."

I smile at him and try to think of something reassuring to say as he pushes his arms and head through the shirt's sleeves and collar. I don't want him to freak out or feel like he messed up or to leave with us on questionable terms. The issues are mine entirely, and I don't want him to get hurt because of my baggage.

Unfortunately, what comes out is, "I, uh . . . Slow. I need slow. Issues. Challenges. You know."

Excuse me, Reese Camden, do you even speak English? He definitely does not *know* whatever it was I just tried to convey.

But because Benny continues to be the greatest, he just clears his throat and says calmly, "What was that?"

I cover my face with my hands and blow out a long breath. "I'm a mess," I say, the words muffled.

I feel his fingers wrap around mine and pull my hands down so he can see me. Pretty sure I'm a brighter red than I've ever been, flushed head to toe with both embarrassment and residual hot-for-boyfriend feelings.

"You're not a mess," Benny says, placing a soft kiss on my forehead. "But do you want to tell me what's going on in your head right now, maybe with actual sentences?"

I do my best to pick out a few thoughts that have been dredged up from deep within me by today's events and explain them to him—about double standards, scrutiny in the comments I've read, and creepy guys at the meet and greet. He listens attentively, concern evident in his eyes as I tell him it wasn't his fault that I went into system shutdown at the least convenient time. It's hard to turn off all the noise, even when nothing feels better than being in the moment with my very attractive boyfriend.

As I talk, I've been picking determinedly at my cuticles because everyone knows how well anxiety-induced, DIY manicures turn out. Fortunately, Benny reaches over and stills my hands before I make myself bleed.

"Reese," he says, shifting so that he's facing me. I look up and his gaze is warm. Understanding. Relief rushes through me. "I don't blame you for that at all. I get it and it's okay—we're okay. This is all new to me too, all right? I thought we'd established already, I may talk a good game, but I've kissed, like, two girls before you. Ever. And one I missed and went full nose-kiss. You can't imagine what an improvement this is."

I let out a snort of laughter, and he smiles, but it falters. "Hey," he asks as if it's only just occurred to him, "what do you mean, 'creepy guys at the meet and greet'?"

Without really thinking about it, I pull my marked wrist to my stomach. Do I really want to open this additional can of worms? What good would it do now? The damage is done. He's not about to go track down my harassers and demand retribution. I think I'd rather keep this one to myself. Then it's only on me to let it go.

"Nothing," I say with a wave of my hand. "Just a lot of . . . enthusiastic fans. It was fine, really."

Benny does not look convinced, his eyes stormy. "Reese, if anyone did anything to make you uncomfortable, or—"

"Hey, I'm fine," I repeat, reaching up to place my hand on his arm. "Nothing I couldn't handle. No need for you to go Hulk-smash on anyone."

I give his bicep a squeeze with a teasing smile. It's true—

today wasn't anything I couldn't handle. Of course, my version of "handling it" is letting people pass me around like a rag doll without saying a word while internalizing a whole mess of feelings. But that's my choice.

"If you're sure," Benny sighs, and I nod decisively. He continues. "Listen, we can go as slow as you want and need. You set the pace forever for all I care. I just want you to tell me what's happening when you shut down so I can be here for you, because you don't have to work through it all on your own and worry yourself sick. I'm on your team. I'm the head of your fan club, the guy making all the 'Go Reese' posters. I should probably act cooler about it, but I like you so much and just want you to know it."

What started as a small, relieved grin from me is now a full-on, cheesy, toothy smile. I nearly can't believe that this guy is my partner, that he's really here right now, working through our first issue that could have turned into a whole awkward mess, not letting it get weird or tense.

This is what it should be like, when it's good. And this thing with Benny is so, so good, regardless of all the other voices hollering nonsense in my head.

Lunging forward, I throw my arms around Benny's neck and hug-tackle him so he falls back on the bed, letting out an *oof.*

"You're amazing," I murmur into his neck.

After his surprise wears off, Benny wraps his arms around my waist. "Back at you, Camden."

We stay like that for a bit, a mass of intertwined limbs, not kissing or talking, the only sound our breathing and Benny's hand making slow circles on my back over my T-shirt. Eventually, my neck gets uncomfortable at its funky angle, so I sit up and suggest we find a new movie to watch. Benny agrees and we land on a stupid buddy comedy, settling in under the covers and relaxing against each other to laugh at the dumb jokes and ridiculous plot. But the laughter gets more sporadic as we grow sleepier. Benny clicks off the lamp and I tug the sheets up higher under my chin.

Long before the credits roll, I'm conked out with his hand running through my hair and my drool running onto his shirt.

Chapter Nineteen

If most of the people in my life are right and there is indeed a higher power, then she must not be too mad at me for letting a boy sleep in my bed. Because in spite of us stupidly passing out without setting any alarms, Benny wakes up before the crack of dawn, which leaves plenty of time for him to get back to his room and for both of us to get ready for the day. If that's not divine intervention, I don't know what is.

Sorry, Mama.

I walk him to the door, unable to resist giving him a final peck before he leaves and I shut the door behind him. I go back to sleep for a few minutes, though I set an alarm this time. When it goes off, I roll over and grab my phone, tapping at it with eyes half-open till it stops blaring. But my eyes pop fully open when I see that I have more than a few unread messages from Benny.

Benny: Hey, so don't freak out but as soon as I left your room, I saw a couple other people coming down the hallway who may or may not have seen us kiss goodbye

Benny: They didn't say anything but they had *looks* on their faces ya know

Benny: But it was prob just because of my very obvious walk of (no) shame

Benny: Highly doubt they were FoF fans or have any idea who we are

Benny: You know, they prob thought I was your male escort, come to think of it

Benny: I give off lots of Sexy Escort Vibes right?

Benny: Anyway EVERYTHING IS FINE

Benny: I shouldn't have yelled that. Everything is fine

Benny: You went back to sleep didn't you

Benny: I'm heading to the fitness center to get a workout in but text me when you wake up again:)

This is fine. This is fine! I'm not going to freak out, even though whenever someone leads in with "don't freak out," it means that whatever comes next is definitely freak-out-worthy.

Those messages sure woke me right up. I get out of bed and start to gather my things for the day, shooting Benny a text to say that it's all okay. I shower, dress, and dry my hair, all the while feeling anxiety building in my chest, simmering, waiting for the other shoe to drop somehow.

In the end, I don't have to wait long. I meet Benny and the Friends in the breakfast area beside the hotel lobby. As we all walk to the convention center for today's full-cast cooking demo, Benny leans in to whisper, "Still doing okay?"

His face tells me he has an idea of the answer, but a growing part of me feels like I'm being ridiculous, so I smile. "Just fine, Bendy Straw."

He laughs, pretending to push me off the sidewalk.

When we reach the convention, the staff leads us to the green-room to prep for the demo. The concept is "Gourmet Game Day," and we're assigned different foods to work on in pairs. The stage, which apparently is gigantic, will have multiple ovens and stovetops and all of the ingredients we need to make the food with our own twists. While the rest of us are cooking, Aiden will play moderator and alternate between letting us narrate what we're doing, like we would in a video, and taking audience questions. The whole thing will be live on the UltiMedia home page, like a lot of the events happening this weekend, which makes me inclined to fake food poisoning, but everyone else seems so game that I know I can't bow out. We're given headset microphones to wear, along with special UltiCon aprons. Then, we get our assignments. Benny and I have nachos; Seb and Katherine are on chicken wings; Rajesh and Lily get potato skins. Nia will tackle pigs in a blanket on her own.

There's a brief break to hit the bathrooms, grab water bottles, check our reflections one last time, and see that, yep, the headset makes my hair look weird, then it's showtime.

We take the stage with as enthusiastic a reception as we had at the meet and greet, and it feels like being on a morning talk show as we smile and wave at the massive crowd. There are three sections of chairs set up auditorium-style and divided by a couple of aisles. When I turn to face the stage behind me, my mouth gapes so wide I'm surprised I don't accidentally swallow the headset mic. It's set up in two tiers, one sitting higher behind the other, which gives the audience a better view of the whole group while we're at work. Each tier has enough appliances and counter space for us all to be working on our separate dishes at the same time. And before the applause has died down, we settle in to do said work.

It's funny and chaotic at first, all seven of us trying to move around each other and gather all the supplies and ingredients we need, but we find a rhythm, with Raj, Lily, Benny, and me on the upper stage and Katherine, Seb, and Nia on the lower. Aiden fills the settling-in time by talking about Friends of Flavor in general, each of the different series represented by the chefs here today, and what each team is making.

Benny and I have claimed a corner of the counter next to a stovetop for our nachos. There's plenty to do: I'm chopping tomatoes, onions, cilantro, and jalapeños for pico de gallo while he works on the homemade tortilla chips. Yes, homemade tortilla chips. FoF acts like having any processed foods in a recipe would be akin to committing murder.

But to be fair, the tortilla chips look awfully good.

All of our mics have buttons so we can turn them on and off at will, and we were advised to try and keep them off unless we're talking, to cut down on excess noise. Across from us, Seb explains the differences between the three sauces he and Katherine are preparing for their wings—buffalo, garlic-lemon-herb, and teriyaki—along with a dry rub. Aiden must have decided we're ready enough to handle questions, and he makes his way down to the audience and selects someone from a show of hands.

"Sticking with the game day theme, what teams do you all root for?" asks a young woman near the front.

I peek over my shoulder to see Raj stepping away from his workstation and pushing the button on his mic. "Seahawks, obviously," he says to a few cheers from the crowd and the agreement of the rest of the Friends onstage.

"Any other Warriors fans here?" Benny cuts in, earning way more cheers because California, I guess. Aiden moves on to find more questions from the crowd.

I don't know if it's the pressure of doing this live in front of an audience or what, but I'm having trouble keeping my shit together. I'm dropping things and misunderstanding what Benny's asking me to do and creating messes left and right. The other Friends are ribbing me for it and people seem to find it funny, though, so it isn't a total wash.

"Oh lordy, I got cayenne on the microphone," I mutter, then hear it echoing around the room because I must've hit my mic's on button somehow. As the audience laughs, I hit the off switch so I can wipe the mouthpiece with a wet cloth without blasting everyone's eardrums out.

"There's a joke in there somewhere about your voice and hotness, but I need to think on it more," Benny muses under his breath as he adds some spices to his cheese sauce, poking his tongue out between his teeth. Unfortunately he seems to have tripped his mic's on switch, too.

There are more laughs and murmurs in the audience, and Benny turns his back to them with a grimace as he realizes his mistake. I roll my eyes in a big-enough way that everyone can see it, attempting to make it seem like this is all part of our act. It's not much more overt than his usual charm game, but having to react to everything he says with a live audience has me a little on edge.

When I turn my mic back on, I say in my most sarcastic, mamaw-like drawl, "Keep it up, Elizabeth Bennet."

The crowd eats it up like candy. The oven beeps and I lean down to take out the chips. I try to sneak a little taste while they're still warm, but of course the crunch echoes through the whole room in stereo. *Dammit.* I feel a new appreciation for the boom mics back at the prep kitchens that don't pick up every little breath we take.

"Reese's Pieces," Benny says in a warning tone just behind me, "are you sneaking samples of our nachos before they become nachos?"

I whirl to face him. "Oh, please, like you haven't been lick-ing cheese off your fingers when you think I'm not looking this whole time! Don't be a hypocrite, mister."

I've brought my face extra close to his and narrowed my eyes, and I can tell we're both working hard not to smile. If we were alone right now, I would kiss him.

"Now, children," Raj says in an exaggeratedly parental way. Then I hear Aiden's voice introducing another audience member to ask a question.

"Yeah, so, uh, Benny." The voice is deep and sounds on the edge of laughing about something. I look up to see it comes from a young dude-bro in a muscle tank, his vibe not unlike Benny's when I first met him. He's holding his phone in one hand. "Saw an interesting picture on Twitter, where it looks like you're kissing some blonde outside a hotel room. Reese, you know anything about that?"

My head jerks back in surprise. I don't make the connection at first, what he's talking about, what it has to do with me. Some murmurs start in the audience, all sorts of confused and amused as people pull out their phones to look. I take a step away from Benny, my eyes flitting toward him to see that he's frozen in place, jaw clenched tight.

The silence stretches on, but I don't know what I expect—a save from Aiden?

Instead, it's Katherine who speaks next. "What a weird and inappropriate question," she says bluntly. "Anyone have anything actually relevant to ask?"

That pretty much puts a stop to things. The room quiets and

a few hands raise. Aiden, snapping out of whatever stupor he was in when we actually needed him, rushes over to a woman who asks what kind of dough Nia is using for her blankets.

I'm blinking down at my hands as I break up a couple of too-large chips and start transferring them to the serving dish, unable to engage with whatever just happened. I feel a hand on my back and then Benny stepping close beside me. He double-checks that both our mics are off.

"Hey. Reese, look at me," he whispers urgently. "It must've been the people I saw in the hall this morning. I didn't realize they got a picture, but it's no big deal, okay? Forget about it. We didn't do anything wrong, all right? It's some misguided fan's dumb attempt to make something out of nothing. Are you okay?"

I avoid his eyes, trying to focus on the task at hand. I know logically that I should listen to what Benny's saying and not be bothered by a picture on the internet I haven't even laid eyes on yet. Apparently, the photo doesn't even show my face.

"I'm fine. Let's just focus on this. We can talk about it later," I whisper back, then move away, brooking no argument.

The Friends carry on seamlessly like nothing has happened, and Benny and I play along well enough. I'm shaken up, though, and he knows it. I don't joke around much during the rest of the demo, and he does most of the talking about our food. I thank my lucky stars that my coworkers can put on a good show.

The nachos are excellent, for what little that's worth, and of course the rest of it is, too. We get a huge standing ovation at the end and I smile and wave with everyone else, but I'm mostly relieved that it's over. I can run away.

Which I do quite promptly once we've stepped backstage. Aiden gathers us and lets us know that we're free to roam around and enjoy the convention as guests from here on out. Nia and Lily are stopping by the hotel first and offer to take our aprons with them so we don't have to hang on to them. I practically throw mine in Lily's face, then make my excuses about heading to the bathroom.

Except I bypass the bathrooms and keep on going, hightailing it down aisle after aisle in the massive maze of an exhibition hall, looking for a place where a girl can sit and have a long-overdue freak-out.

Eventually, I find a spot that'll have to be good enough. It's a couple of big watercoolers with stacks of cups surrounded by a handful of tall tables and barstools. The best part is there's only one other person hanging out there. I fill up a cup, down it, then refill it and take a seat with my back to the main thoroughfare so hopefully there's little chance of anyone recognizing me.

I almost laugh at the thought. *Life! It comes at you fast!*

Then, all settled in, I pull my phone out to double down on my do-not-approach vibe. Immediately confronted with all the familiar icons that I use to check the Friends of Flavor social accounts, my stomach sinks. Do I dare look at this incriminating picture? If I avoid it, pretend it isn't there, is it possible that it'll go away? If a tree falls in a forest and I don't see a picture of it on Twitter, did it really happen?

Delaying the decision of whether or not to look, I go to my texts instead. I've missed several from Benny, who's surely wondering where I ran off to. Guiltily, I skip those and pull up my messages from Nat.

Natalie: Hey babe, doing okay?

Uh-oh. This is Nat's Sincere Text Voice. The one she saves for when someone's died or one of her shows gets canceled. I don't like the sound of it.

Reese: Yeah I'm fine, you okay?

Natalie: Are you sure? I saw the picture on twitter.
And was watching your ulticon stream when that dbag harassed you

Natalie: I'll fly to California and kick his ass if you want me to

Natalie: Virtually kicking some asses in the comments in the meantime

Ah shit. So the tree really fell. It is *that bad.* My fingers are itching to close out of messages and go inspect the damage. My heart beats faster, anticipating the abysmal rush of my private business being exposed to the world, of a bunch of strangers talking shit about me. Have I become addicted to this oddly specific brand of self-destruction?

Who am I kidding? I'm too weak for this. Too weak to resist it when the button is right there. I know it'll hurt, but I'm afraid it'll hurt me more to sit here and obsess over what's going on without my knowing about it.

I bring up Twitter first and immediately see all the tweets tagging or hashtagging our channel name. Which, today, happens to be a lot of the same picture. It captures Benny from the side, in his clothes from yesterday, ball cap slightly askew. The way I'm standing plus the way his hand came up to rest on my cheek during our brief goodbye kiss make it so my face isn't visible. But the old county science fair T-shirt with holes in the armpits that I wore to sleep—that's quite visible.

I spare a moment to mourn the fact that of all the things I could have been wearing in a viral picture of me kissing my boyfriend as he leaves my hotel room at the crack of dawn, it had to be this. But only a moment. Because there are bigger things to mourn—my reputation, my dignity, my future at Friends of Flavor, you name it. I'd like to believe that all is not lost, but I know how it goes when there's just hearsay and speculation. And this is a picture—it's tangible proof.

Like a glutton for punishment, I start to scroll through the replies. What. A. *Wreck.*

There are, to their credit, a few people who defend us, saying that the picture is an invasion of privacy and other fans should leave the two interns alone. But way more vocal is the mob all fired up over the compromising position they've finally caught us in. Some tease or chastise Benny, but most have taken up their torches and pitchforks and begun a Reese Roast.

wait lmao he's def doing a walk of shame

LOL NIIICE, BENNY

knew she seemed easy

Reese lmk when you want better company

is that really what she sleeps in? #classy

He could do so much better smh

But like is anyone surprised the hot blond intern is a slut

She's been a skank forever, nothings changed ask anyone from our school

lolll he hit that

Shes prob sleeping w someone up top too right? Only way they keep her around

I drop my phone. It's like they're circling sharks and the blood in the water is the implication that a young woman has a sex life. Which I don't! It wouldn't be deserved either way, but still. I've got to be the most slut-shamed virgin there ever was.

I think for a second about going to watch the UltiCon stream of our demo, but figure I'd only be setting myself up for more of the same. So I sit there, letting the convention pass me by as I continue to stare at the wall and sip my water, thinking of all the damage this could cause. What are the other Friends thinking? Will Aiden be upset with us—or worse, with just me, while his bro Benny gets a fist bump? Will Margie question how serious I am about the job or lose respect for me entirely?

I rest my chin in my palm and close my eyes as if I can undo the events of today. But it's not like this mess can be fixed with another pep talk and impromptu movie night.

I don't know that it can be fixed at all.

Chapter Twenty

A couple more cups of water and one real bathroom break later, I nearly fall off the stool when a hand lands on my shoulder.

"Hey there," Benny says softly. "I've been looking for you all over. Found a good place to chill, I take it?"

I sigh, rolling my empty cup between my palms. "Honestly, this bar sucks. They don't even have juice boxes."

He smirks and settles onto the stool next to mine, then his expression turns more serious. "Reese . . ."

"Today's been a hoot and a half, hasn't it?"

"Where's your head?" he asks. He reaches out as if to take my hand or touch my arm before he seems to realize that might not be the best move right now.

"Attached to my neck still, far as I can tell."

Benny frowns at my attempted brush-off, and for a moment, I want to lean into him. I want to rest my head on his shoulder, let him wrap his arms around me, tell me that this isn't a large-scale repeat of my freshman-year drama. But then I remember myself. Remember that letting myself be vulnerable, trying the whole romance thing again, is what landed me back in this position. If I'd stayed firmly in the No Feelings Zone, none of this would have happened. So I straighten my spine, tip my chin up, and meet his gaze.

"I don't know, Benny. That sucked back there at the demo, and the stuff online sucks even more, and you can tell me that it's stupid and we shouldn't care what one loser speculates, but it still doesn't feel great to have your business broadcast to thousands of people. People who, by the way, already have *plenty* of opinions. But there's nothing to do about it now."

He looks away then, and I watch his gaze harden, see a muscle in his jaw tick. Benny isn't just worried about me; he is pissed in his own right.

"I feel like I should've been able to stop this from becoming a thing this morning. I—"

Just then, a group of people in hand-painted Friends of Flavor T-shirts appears beside the table seemingly out of nowhere.

"Benny!" they cheer, before noticing Sulky McSulkerson. "Reese!"

They tell us they're big fans and how much they enjoyed the meet and greet yesterday. One of them even boldly announces how ridiculous he thinks all the stuff about the picture of us is, and I nod in awkward agreement. Another of them apparently runs the Instagram account dedicated to memes about us and shows me one he posted of a little girl squish-hugging a tiny kitten. Over the kitten's head, it says "Reese, a sweet baby angel" in bold letters. Over the girl's head, it reads "Fans of Flavor protecting her at all costs."

It's one of those things that's so nice and unexpected and also feels so undeserved that it's all I can do to chuckle and tell them I appreciate the support. We continue to chat for a few minutes and pose for pictures, and I find I honestly don't mind, as baffling as it still is that anyone is this interested in meeting us. Their friendliness is a nice distraction, and it's also delaying the rest of the conversation I've decided I'd rather not have with my boyfriend.

But before long, Benny says, "Reese and I actually have to get going. We've been wanting to check out the gaming lounge."

Oh, have we? I glance at him in confusion, about to protest, but then he fixes me with a stern lift of an eyebrow that may or may not give me goose bumps. There's a voice in my head nervously trilling, *He's onto you! You're not getting out of this that easy!*

We say goodbye and give another round of hugs to our fans, then head in what I guess is the direction of the gaming lounge. Despite our strides being roughly the same length, I feel like I'm scurrying to keep up with Mr. Speed Racer. I'm about to ask if we're actually in a rush to get to the games when he starts talking under his breath without looking at me, so quietly that I have to strain to hear.

"I'm trying to find somewhere for us to talk."

"Can't this wait till we—"

"Oh my God, hi! *Amateur Hour,* right?" The excited voice cutting me off comes from a young woman who has stopped in front of us. Out of this whole big convention, how are we running into all the fans of our little cooking show?

Beside the woman is a man who looks slightly embarrassed by the whole interaction. Maybe I can just swap him and Benny real quick, save us both from the uncomfy conversations we don't want to have.

But since I don't think anyone else would be on board with that idea, I smile and make small talk and take pictures with Benny and the couple, and then they're on their way again.

"No, it can't wait. This way."

I make an *oof* sound in surprise as he takes my hand and tugs me away from the big exhibition hall, into a spacious, arcade-like room. There are a ton of huge TVs and projector screens with gaming consoles in front of them, and people are taking turns playing demos that appear to be based on UltiMedia shows—mainly their most action-packed scripted dramas. There are also arcade games and some VR headsets. My understanding of the gaming world is limited, but this seems like the fun place to be.

I don't know what Benny's plan is, as this does not look remotely private or quiet. But then, when I'm looking the other way, he tugs me again. I plop down into a fake car with two seats and steering wheels in front of a screen where the windshield would be.

"Um," I say, shaking my head as I get my bearings, "what are we doing?"

Benny shifts to face me from the neighboring seat, as if we're sitting in an actual car and about to have a meaningful conversation. "I want to continue our conversation. I want us to work through this together, and I—"

Suddenly, a head pops in through the side window. Or the hole where a side window would be. It's attached to a man in an UltiCon staff shirt.

"Hey, man, if you're gonna be in there, you gotta be playing the game. No loitering."

Benny lets out a frustrated sigh, but he faces forward and nods. "Thanks, man. Got it."

With that, Benny pushes the big red Start button on the faux dashboard. The man disappears and Benny puts his hands on the wheel to flip through the options for his car and course, gesturing for me to do the same.

I am beyond disoriented. I take my wheel and turn it to choose a green sports car and a beach town track. Then Benny hits another button to start, and okay, I guess we're racing now?

The tiny avatar with boobs larger than her head counts down from three and waves a checkered flag. It takes me a second to remember to put my foot on the gas pedal.

As soon as both our cars are moving, Benny resumes talking.

"You were clearly upset by that guy in the demo, and the picture taken this morning. You have reason to be—and I'm mad, too."

I scramble to find words *and* navigate this ridiculous race car at the same time. "Are . . . are we really debriefing now? Right here?"

"Yes," he says with certainty. "I know it's thrown you off and you're already trying to act like you can handle it on your own, but we're not doing that. I'm on your team, remember? I want you to tell me how you're feeling so I can help fix it."

My car hits a mailbox. Jesus take the wheel.

"Benny, I don't know what to say. This isn't your fault, and I don't think you can fix it. *Oh shoot fire,* there goes a pedestrian."

I try to right my car, hoping this game has a fake ambulance and fake hospital that can help the lady I just left in my dust.

"Are you upset because people basically know we're together now?"

"Well, yeah." The words come out before I can stop them, and I wince at my bluntness. "I mean, it's not *just* that. I guess if anything, I feel like I've had this coming from when I first started having feelings for you. Maybe by opening up that way, I've become more open and vulnerable in every way, and that's all the trolls need to see—any bit of weakness—in order to pounce and use it against me."

I see Benny shake his head in my peripheral vision. "So you think liking me has made you weak? I don't think I like that logic, Reese. Or understand it, even. I feel my best when I'm around you and I wish you felt the same."

Now I shake my head, swerving briefly into oncoming traffic. "It's not—that's not what I meant. I feel great around you, I do.

But with you, everything has changed for me. I had this whole plan to come here and start over at Friends of Flavor, to just be this badass, boss chick who puts in the work, impresses everyone, and gives them no choice but to take her seriously, then *boom*, the fall internship would be mine. But then I met you and we began *Amateur Hour*, and I started to . . . I don't know, laugh and smile and have fun and freaking *flirt*, even while trying to compete against you. And in a lot of ways it's been amazing, but it's also brought some negatives. I've lost focus on work. Legions of folks have come out of the woodwork and ganged up on me online. And now ol' sneaky tweeter posts this picture and tries to make our relationship some salacious thing, and you're getting carried around like a champ on the internet bros' shoulders while I'm being called trash."

I find myself feeling thankful that we're having this conversation under these absurd circumstances, because goodness, I don't know if I could've laid it all out there so plainly if I'd had to look him in the eyes. I already feel the tears threatening in my own, no matter how hard I try to hold them back.

Suddenly, Benny's hands drop from the wheel and he shifts around in his seat again to face me, laying one hand on my knee.

"Uh, you're gonna crash. Ohmyword you're crashing, you're crashing, Benny! You just drove off the bridge!" I yelp, as if that's what matters right now.

"I'll regenerate," he says calmly. "Reese."

I give him a sideways glance, then decide, hell, I might as well let myself crash for this, too. I look at him fully and let him take one of my hands in his.

"Is it really so bad for people to know about us? Do their opinions really matter so much? I mean, I get it. I wish I could push all the stupid double standards out the window, take all the name-calling and everything on myself because I don't give a shit anyway and you certainly don't deserve any of it. I hate that it's so stressful for you. But I think you're putting too much stock in the voices of a bunch of trolls. We're together—so what? You're beautiful, smart, talented, and some people are dicks about it, but who cares what they have to say? They're not the ones making Friends of Flavor's hiring decisions."

I have to look away, because the car crash on my screen is preferable to Benny's earnest face at the moment. I know he means well. I wish I could pat his cheek and tell him he's completely right and it'll all be fine if we stick to our values and keep smiles on our faces, that the haters don't matter, good always triumphs over evil, and all that. But I know better.

I take a deep breath as I shake my head. "Benny, you don't get it. You can't, because you haven't been here, because it's not you facing all the backlash. It hurts, and it feels personal. And it doesn't exist in a bubble. It would be hard for Aiden and Geoffrey Block, CEO, and the other suits to see all of this Reese hate and decide it's worth keeping me around over you. That is, even if they did like me better to begin with, which I'm pretty sure they don't. I've had Margie on my side so far, but when she sees the picture, will she think I'm just here to have a summer fling with the boy intern, that I'm not serious about the job? It would feel so shitty to lose it over all this. And it's like I can already feel it happening."

"Hey," he says sternly, squeezing my hand until I look at him again. "That's not going to happen. People will forget about the demo and the picture and it'll blow over in no time, but you deserve to be at Friends of Flavor and they wouldn't take that away from you because of this. They *couldn't*. Trust me, okay?"

I swallow. I do trust Benny, of course I do. But that isn't a promise he can make. It happens all the time—women get laid off, passed over for promotions, struggle to appeal to voters during campaigns, or generally get little respect because of factors totally outside their control. *She just wasn't likable enough. Her voice grates on you, you know? She's good at what she does, but she's so bossy. There's something about her that rubs me the wrong way, but I can't put my finger on it.*

She seems to care less about her summer internship than about getting in the boy intern's pants. Okay, so I haven't heard that one specifically yet, but it's totally plausible.

But I don't feel like explaining that kind of internalized misogyny to Benny right now. So I shake my head again, my frustration building. "You don't know that. Could you just—I don't know, trust me? Let me be upset? I'm not asking for much. You don't have to defend me on your Instagram from all the people who say hateful things. I'm not asking you to speak up on my behalf when a random dude harasses me in front of people. But if you could let me get angry in private, I'd appreciate it."

Benny holds up a hand. "Whoa, back up. Are you mad I haven't been doing those things?"

I set my jaw, not even sure what the answer is.

"Reese, they're not worth it. They want a reaction, and we don't have to give it to them. But if you've been upset about this, you should've told me."

"I shouldn't have to!" It bursts out of me like it's been on the tip of my tongue for a while. "You should recognize that you're the *Amateur Hour* darling—audiences love you, our bosses love you, you have all the power. There's no way you haven't noticed that. I know we're competing and you want the fall job as bad as I do, but it wouldn't hurt you to have my back more often."

His mouth drops open. He's clearly taken aback. "I—I've tried. I thought I did. I—where is this coming from? Are you just trying to pick a fight?"

I scoff. "Seriously? That's the way you want to play this right now?"

Benny folds his arms over his chest. Those arms that were so recently wrapped around me, making me feel warm, secure, cared for. Some of my irritation deflates, replaced by sullen disappointment.

"I can't do this right now, Benny. Maybe we should . . . I don't know, cool off. Stop trying to make us a thing when there's too much working against us."

"Reese, no—"

I hold up a hand, cutting him off as I try to climb out of this faux automotive cage. My eyes sweep over the screen one last time, where I see the race has ended, and despite neither of us actually finishing it, Benny and I are ranked ninth and tenth, respectively.

Ouch. A little too on-the-nose, computerized race car.

I finally make it out of the car and start walking through the arcade, unsure where I'm going except that it needs to be far away from the boy now following me.

"Reese, wait!" he calls.

I whirl around to face him, speaking in a low voice so as not to cause a scene. "Let me go, okay? We'll talk later. Just let me go."

The look in his eyes makes me feel like I've just kicked a puppy. Finally, he sets his jaw and gives a slight nod. The last thing I see is Benny reaching up to readjust the ball cap on his head, before I turn and stride away.

Chapter Twenty-One

Something I've started noticing whenever I'm feeling especially sorry for myself is the multitude of little signs that the universe doesn't give a shit. The empty box in the break room that once held English breakfast tea bags doesn't care that I got less than four hours of restless sleep last night and was counting on it for a boost. The puddle I step in on the way home from work doesn't take pity on me for walking alone, having lost my usual companion, who would probably make me laugh and forget all about my wet, squishy shoe.

The blue progress bar currently crawling across my computer screen, so slowly that I keep thinking it's stalled, has no concern for all the extra time it's giving me to dwell on my regrets and think of what I should have done differently. No, this upload of some new illustrations I'm sharing with Margie is just taking its sweet time.

It's a pretty quiet Tuesday afternoon in my sad little TV-tray corner. Margie is preparing to put some of my drawings up for sale as prints on Friends of Flavor's merch site. They drew up a special new contract for me and everything, laying out a payment structure for the rights to sell and use my art, and I emailed it to my parents' lawyer to review before I signed. It's both exciting and intimidating, these creations of mine being available for purchase—actually making me money— and landing in strangers' hands and homes across the world. But mostly exciting. If this is the only lasting impression I make at Friends of Flavor, it's something I'll be proud of long after I'm gone.

I haven't become any less confident that I'll be gone pretty soon. Since the drama at UltiCon over a week ago, no one's said anything to me about the picture or the incident at the demo. The only one who's even tried is Benny, but I've continued to tell him that I need space. We've filmed one new episode of *Amateur Hour*, in which Benny and I did our best at acting normal for the cameras while he destroyed me in a flatbread pizza competition (**Benny—5, Reese—4,** but who's counting?) before returning to our stilted noncommunication once filming was over. But mostly, Margie's kept me busy in marketing with a mix of social media engagement and working on my own designs on the clock. This has, for the most part, made it hard for me to dwell in my own head during the workday, leaving me to obsess over the trolls, my stalled relationship, and impending job decisions during after-work hours.

But boy, have I been busy obsessing on my lonely, Benny-less evenings and weekends. I've run our last conversation at UltiCon over and over in my head, what was said and what wasn't. I lie awake late into each night thinking of all of the ways I wish I'd communicated better and the things I wish I'd heard back from him. Between all that and the many ignored "please, let's talk" missives from the guy who may or may not still be my boyfriend, I've started to realize there's more for both of us to say.

And maybe, I think as I sit there feeling tired and sad during this lull in activity, it doesn't matter whether the universe cares about my problems. It only matters whether I care enough to fix them myself—to make the conversation that Benny and I clearly need to have happen. My eyelids droop millimeter by millimeter, in time with the speed of this file upload. When I lean back in my seat and stretch my arms over my head, the urge to yawn finally winning out, I feel a disconcerting series of pops from a few different places in my body.

Yep, that's it. It's time to take a lap and find Benny.

We'll figure out a time to get together, clear the air. I don't know quite what I want for our future, but I'm woman enough to admit I've missed him and that all the unresolved stuff between us is making me nutty. And kind of miserable.

I pass through Prep Kitchen 1 with no sign of him, and I'm about to turn in to PK 2, when I hear the familiar, booming voice of Geoffrey Block, CEO. *Ugh.* Since we met, I've tried to avoid him when I catch word that he's visiting the office, which feels too frequent for someone who lives two states away.

I'm about to retreat when I hear Benny's laugh. A laugh seemingly in response to something Geoffrey Block, CEO, has said. Or perhaps, I think hopefully, the older man has slipped on a banana peel. Benny could be laughing *at,* not *with.*

But when I peer around the corner like some kind of cartoon spy, I see Benny, Aiden, and the CEO, all fully upright and looking like the best of pals. I slink back out of sight, dread gathering in the pit of my stomach. Maybe it's not what it looks like. Maybe if I wait here just a second, the other two will go away and I can catch Benny alone.

The dread is quickly joined by fear, the two feelings ganging up on me and sending pinpricks down my spine. They're in my head, whispering, *This is when the other shoe drops.*

". . . and it'll be awesome, Benny, really. I bet it's such a relief for you, too," I hear Aiden say. Curiosity is fully piqued. Dread and fear remain.

"Indeed. I'm sure everyone here will be glad you're sticking around, son." This from Geoffrey Block, CEO, and . . . I'm sorry, *what?* Surely he is not saying what I think he's saying.

"Congratulations, big guy. Seattle's lucky to have you for the long haul," Aiden adds.

"Thanks, guys. Yeah, I'm really excited about it," Benny says, and I can even hear the smile in his voice.

What. The. Ever-loving. F—

"So for Thursday, we'll probably try a mid-afternoon slot for your livestream. Since it's a new format for us, we're still working out the details as far as which time draws the best audience without making you and the film crew stay late . . ."

I tune out the rest of Aiden's explanation as I turn and head back down the hall. I suddenly feel like I'm trudging through thick mud instead of across clean office tile, each step heavier as the conversation I just overheard sinks in.

They've totally offered Benny the fall internship. Already, and without a word to me. And from the sound of things, he's accepted.

I mean, I'm not surprised that it's him. I've been here for all of it, UltiCon and the online hate, the fact that Aiden seems to talk *at* me more often than to me while Benny is his little protégé, and Geoffrey Block, CEO, is hardly aware of my existence beyond my legs. I get it. Benny is charismatic, a great cook, beloved by audiences—he's the obvious choice.

But even knowing all this, it hurts. And it could just be the hurt talking, but I like to think that if I'd been offered the job, I would've talked to Benny about it before officially accepting. It's not like we're married, or even really dating at this point, but it would feel like the respectful thing to do, to give a little notice.

Maybe I'm being unfair. Maybe I should just be happy for him, this guy I care for so much even though we're not speaking. But I feel the sting in my eyes that says tears are imminent. I blink them back, trying to steel myself as I head back to marketing. I straighten my posture and attempt to hold my chin high, but it trembles, so I focus on my feet. One foot in front of the other, till I make it out of here at the end of the day.

Because after everything, I'll feel so stupid if I cry at work. Like a little girl who didn't get the part she wanted in the elementary school play. I have to handle this as maturely as possible, because you never know who is watching and what respect you might lose the moment you let them see you cry.

I *do* care about Benny, and I want every good thing to come his way. But if this decision was so instantaneous for him, if he sounded so purely happy about it without even a hint of dismay that his success means my loss . . . well, does he care about me?

He texts me about an hour before the workday is through.

> **Benny:** Hey, I know you've asked for space, and I'll keep giving it to you, but I have some exciting news I really want to tell you. Soon. Please, R? I'll throw in some ice cream on me if you'll walk home with me today

My stomach sinks. *Seriously?* That's how he's gonna frame it when he tells me that he got the job we've both been vying for? Honestly, I think I'd prefer an ominous "we need to talk."

I'm starting to shift from just plain sad to sad and fuming. I don't answer Benny's text. The more I think about it, the more confident I feel that if I try to have this conversation with him today, I'll say something I regret.

I push my chair back and stand abruptly, then march over to Margie's desk.

"Reese," she says before I can begin, taking her reading glasses off as she peers up at me. "Everything okay? You seem tense today."

At that, I realize my jaw has been clenched for who knows how long. I relax it and try to do the same with the rest of my face, neck, shoulders before realizing that, yeah, this is the kind of tension best left to a massage therapist. I guess when my internship is up, I'll have plenty of time to get it taken care of.

"Yes—I mean"—I shake my head, closing my eyes briefly in frustration—"no, I'm not feeling so great. Would you mind if I left a little early today? Just fifteen minutes or so."

Margie nods, her brow furrowed in concern. "That's fine, of course. Whenever you need to go. Let me know if there's anything I can do for you."

I nod, not trusting my voice to stay steady, and thank her. But not without bitterness. Surely she knows they've decided to give the fall spot to Benny. So why didn't she tell me? She wants me to think she's this supportive mentor figure, but when it comes to the difficult stuff, she's gonna leave it for me to hear it through the grapevine?

I shake my head as I gather my things. I've got to focus my anger on one person at a time, and right now, it's Benny. I'm able to slip out of the FoF offices without running into him, and even avoid an inquisition by Teagan, who's surely been wondering why her favorite intern OTP hasn't been walking home together lately.

But, of course, my luck doesn't last. The elevator of men-in-suits-plus-Reese seems to stop at every dang floor on the way down so that by the time I'm leaving the building, I'd guess I'm barely ahead of the guy I'm avoiding. I power walk the first few blocks back toward my dorm, but this city's hills are killer and it feels like every muscle in my legs is on fire before long.

I wouldn't have this problem if I was Benny, my bitch of a brain reminds me. *Because he works out all the time and is super in shape. On top of being handsome and nice and good at everything else, which is totally why he got the job and I never had a chance—*

"Reese!"

A voice breaks into my self-loathing spiral. I think I'm hearing things until the voice calls out again and I know without turning around that Benny has caught up to me. Because good freaking gravy, he can't wait a minute longer to break the "happy" news, can he?

"Hey," he says as he jogs up beside me, and it's gratifying to see that he's at least a little winded. "Teagan said you left early. Did you get my text? Are you all right?"

I bite down on the petty observation I want to make regarding the order of those questions. His big news is the most important thing to him right now, not my well-being. Not even after everything we've gone through together this summer, all the ways I've opened up to him and I felt he did with me. There's a lump forming in my throat again, of disappointment and dejection and the knowledge that I've failed, once and for all. I try to swallow it down, squaring my shoulders and looking straight ahead as I decide what to say.

"I know about your big news already," I start, pleased that my voice sounds stronger than I feel.

Benny's steps falter, but he recovers and falls back into step beside me. "Y-you do? Oh. Did Margie tell you?"

"I heard your conversation. I just—I have to say I'm surprised. I didn't think you would be so quick to toss me aside like that. Not after you've told me over and over again this summer that we're a team."

I can hear the confusion in his voice when he replies, "Oh. Reese, I—I'm sorry. You'll have your chance, too. I didn't think it would be that big of a deal, but I don't have to do it if you don't want me to."

My frustration definitely starts to show as I huff. "Seriously, Benny? You know that's not how this works. I heard the bosses congratulating you. They're thrilled to keep you around."

He steps in front of me then, walking backward uphill like he's a campus tour guide and I'm an inordinately angry prospective student.

"Yeah, honestly that's what I thought you'd be at least a little happy about. Or happy *for* me, even if you're mad at me right now," he says, his palms out in the "calm down" gesture that I hate coming from most people, but especially here, now, from someone who's been so good at validating my feelings in the past. "I thought this would be a good thing for both of us, so I'm kinda confused here."

I try to edge around him, but he catches my arm and brings us both to a stop in the middle of the sidewalk.

"I'm trying to be the bigger person here, believe me," I bite out. "But it might take me some time. It just felt . . . sneaky, the way it was all done in this meeting of the bro minds, how you didn't even talk to me about it first. I don't know, maybe that was too much for me to expect from you."

Benny jerks back as if I've smacked him. "What's that supposed to mean?"

I let my head roll back so I'm looking up at the sky, and try to keep my breathing steady. "I don't know, we haven't known each other that long, all things considered. Maybe I've put too high hopes and expectations on you, or started holding you to an unreachable standard."

"That isn't fair," he says, his own breath coming quicker. He's starting to look less confused and more straight-up angry. Join the club, bud. "I probably should have told you before Geoffrey and Aiden, but I was excited, and you've been ignoring all my attempts to talk since UltiCon. And I really didn't think you would take the news this way. I thought it was a good thing and truthfully? I think you're overreacting."

The little porcupine quills that I imagine live just beneath my skin, primed to shoot up and protect me at a moment's notice, are at the ready now. Except they feel more like Wolverine claws in this case, and Norberto Beneventi's about to feel their wrath.

"Overreacting, huh? *Love* to hear that. Sorry I'm not over the moon, shooting rainbows out of my eyeballs because I'm so delighted for you. Sorry I'm not a selfless little woman whose only goal in life is to see her man shine, that I have real feelings and ambitions for myself."

"Reese, for the love of—" he shouts, throwing his hands up in the air and walking in a tight circle before returning to stand in front of me. He adjusts his cap with a long-suffering sigh. "You know what? I think you've been waiting for this. I think you figured out that there was more to say after our last conversation, and you know this is not that big of a deal, but you've been scared for so long, and angry, and the world's been unfair to you. And I bet whether you realize it or not, you've been waiting for the first excuse to get rid of me for good. You're used to being alone and it's easier than letting another person in, so all you needed was the smallest hint that something may not be perfect and boom—no more Benny. Am I right?"

I scoff, moving to pass him for real this time and not stopping when his hand brushes my shoulder. "You just know me so well, don't you? Please, tell me more about how I'm feeling, why I do the things I do. But you'll have to send it in another message, because I don't have to stay here and listen to it."

I hoist my bag farther onto my shoulder and stomp away from him, my own fury nearly blocking out his parting words.

"Go on, then. Maybe you can move back across the country. See if running from your problems works the second time around."

His words reverberate through me as I turn the corner, out of his sight, and I have to press myself against the concrete wall beside me to keep from crumpling to the ground. Those words hit their mark, that's for sure. I feel them rip through my chest, through the layers of pride and stubbornness I've built up to make people think I'm okay.

But nothing about this feels okay, and I'm not sure how it ever could again.

The last of the hard outer shell I thought I'd constructed so well is shattered. The first tears fell as soon as I walked away from Benny, and they've been unstoppable since. Holed up in my sad, tiny dorm room, I pull out my meager supply of sandwich fixings for a sad, tiny dinner for one. The tears continue as I change into pajamas long before the sun has set and crawl into bed, feeling more sorry for myself than ever. They keep on coming as I pull out my phone to tell Clara and Natalie about what happened, and they only pour harder when I find a bunch of texts and missed calls from Benny.

Somehow, I know the messages won't be hateful. If I know the boy at all, he probably regretted the last thing he said to me before the words were even out of his mouth. Still, I read them with one eye shut, as if that will ease whatever potential blows await.

Benny: Reese, I'm so sorry. Please call me back.

Benny: I shouldn't have said all that. You're allowed to feel how you feel

Benny: I wish we could talk about this on the phone or in person but since there's probably a better chance of you reading these in the meantime, I'm gonna keep sending them

Benny: I keep going over everything we said and I feel like there's some kind of disconnect

Benny: What I was excited to tell you is that I finally talked to my parents this morning and it actually went well. I told them I'm staying in Seattle. They aren't thrilled or anything but they didn't seem too mad at me either. I hope eventually you might be happy about it too

Benny: Please let's talk about this. I want to know everything you heard or think you heard. I want to make it better. I'll be here whenever you're ready

Hell's bells.

I don't know what to make of all this. On the one hand, he wasn't excited to tell me about getting the fall internship. But does that mean he didn't get the fall internship and I didn't hear what I think I did? Or I heard right, but he wasn't excited to tell me that part? Or he wasn't *going* to tell me that part?

I'm not sure what the answer is. But Benny was also onto something when he said that I'm scared. I've been wrong about people before, in super-damaging, life-altering ways. It isn't hard for me to believe that I've put too much faith in Benny all this time. I can't determine which of my instincts to trust in these circumstances. There are the ones that have told me for years to assume the worst, especially of guys. To look out for myself because I can't be sure anyone else is going to.

But then there are the instincts that I've had about Benny, the ones that told me that despite first impressions and superficial appearances, he is the real deal. He is worth trusting, worth believing, worth loving—

Whoa. Did I just think the L-word?

I throw off the covers, feeling the need to get moving. So much is happening in my mind right now that I'm not able to pick out any one thing and address it. I want to *do* something, *make* something, just to feel capable.

The kitchen.

I can go to the dorm kitchen and cook something. I've kept the sandwich-fixing stash close by for days I'm feeling lazy, but most of my grocery haul lives in the kitchen, with a full-size fridge and stove and other necessities for cooking real grown-up food. What better time to flex the culinary muscles I've honed this summer? To do it all on my own, because I'm a capable, independent woman who darn well *can*?

I don't even bother to change out of my pajamas—I've gotten the sense there aren't many summer residents or at any rate not many who have the same schedule as me. I rarely see anyone else around. I grab my laptop and phone as I head out the door and up the stairs.

Once in the kitchen, I scan the fridge and cabinets and communal shelves for provisions other than my own. I think I'll just be able to make do and satisfy a craving. Something that feels like comfort and family and warmth—biscuits.

I wish I had my mamaw's recipe on hand, but with the time difference, she's surely asleep by now, so I work off memory. I don't have every ingredient I think I'll need, but substitutions exist for a reason, right? And leaving out a quarter teaspoon of this or that shouldn't make much difference.

Just as I've gathered everything on the counter, a call comes through from Natalie.

I pick up on the second ring. "Hey, what's up?"

"Ugh, I've been in the barn for six hours. Six. Hours. I'm using you as an excuse to get away, told my parents we made plans to talk. You know they wouldn't deny you anything."

It's true. Her parents have always had a soft spot where I'm concerned, for reasons beyond me. While Nat dials Clara on three-way, I start measuring out flour, salt, and baking powder. Normally, I'd sift them together, but I can't for the life of me find anything to sift with.

"Hello?" comes a raspy whisper on speakerphone.

"Uh, Clar? Have the pressures of nerd camp made you a chain smoker?" Nat's tone tells me she's cracking herself up and in spite of my still-watery eyes, I'm fighting a laugh too.

"Hold on," Clara hisses. A few seconds later, we hear what sounds like a door shutting and heels clicking on hard floors. She clears her throat and continues at a normal volume. "Sorry, mock trial practice. I'm on the defense team."

"We can talk later. No one needs to go to mock jail on my account," Nat offers.

"Nah, I have co-counsel. He's kind of an idiot and I've done all the work so far, so he can handle a few minutes on his own," Clara says. "Maybe. So what's up?"

"Hey, Clar," I call, making my presence known. I've just poured the dry ingredients into a mixing bowl.

"Oh, hey, Reese. You okay? You sound kind of sniffly."

"Uh, hay fever," I mumble as I start to stir.

"Hay fever, my left ass cheek," Natalie snaps. "I was waiting for my backup to ask you, but you can't fool us, Reese Camden. You've been feeling feelings and they've been leaking out your eyeballs and you're gonna tell us all about it."

"That was . . . crude, but you're not wrong. I don't feel like talking about it, though, not yet anyway. The best thing y'all could do is distract me with something else."

"Are you still mad at Ball Cap Benny? Do my Louisville Slugger and I need to have a li'l talk with him?" Nat asks.

I give a short laugh. "No, if anyone could use that, it's probably me."

She sighs. "Reese, whatever it is, I think you should just talk to him. Boy is clearly obsessed with you, and I know it's been hard seeing how he's treated differently from you, and the internet and your coworkers have giant bromantic crushes on him while you're consistently getting shat on while doing the same job just as well"—I'm about to cut her off because, good gracious, does she have to toss so much salt in these fresh wounds? But I wait it out—"but it seems to me like he's trying, and if you tell him to jump up and defend you, he'd sure as hell ask how high and if you'd like a cup of tea while he's at it."

As Nat talks, I am trying my best to cut butter into the dry ingredients with a fork. It's slow going and I'm not even sure it looks right, the tiny shavings curling and piling up on top of the white snow drifts in the bowl. I'm also sidetracked by what Nat has said, which has the tears stinging at the backs of my eyes again.

Clara chimes in, "I obviously don't know what's going on either, but I agree, Nat. Reese, I love you to death, but you have a habit of taking on too much on your own. You've come so far, and you just need to keep communicating and letting others help you when you need it. You've put yourself back out there in the biggest way this summer, and your other mother and I are just so proud, right, Ma?"

"I tell you what, Mama, if I was any fuller of pride, I'd be fixin' to burst." Natalie lays the accent on extra thick, diffusing the seriousness of the message, but the love and sincerity are there.

"I don't deserve y'all," I murmur, fighting this latest wave of emotion. My mamaw's biscuit recipe does not call for salt water. I win this time, though, and clear my throat before I speak again. "Okay, no more Reese drama. Update me on y'all's lives before Clara has to save an innocent from facing the prison industrial complex."

Natalie launches into a story about how she's trying to negotiate a lemonade stand merger for a few kids she babysits who live in the same neighborhood, because "patrons can't decide which stand to support, so they're not buying from anyone. All those profits down the drain with the unsold lemonade!"

Meanwhile, Clara—notoriously tight-lipped about anything love and dating—has a suspicious amount of good to say about a pretty redheaded court justice at camp. Then Nat asks how badly Clara wants to bang her gavel, and Clar uncharacteristically starts yelling at her for being inappropriate.

I'm distracted with laughing at my friends' bickering as I pour milk into the mixture. I remember Mamaw stirring everything together with a fork. I'm feeling impatient and find a hand mixer in one of the drawers. If I keep it on a low speed, that could be more efficient than a fork, right? Mixing ingredients is literally what it's for.

I plug it in and push the lever to the lowest setting, but it's immediately clear I've made a big mistake. Flour explodes into the air in a butter-flecked cloud, with milk splattering on its heels. It goes all over the counter and, more upsettingly, all over me. It's the macaron video all over again, but wetter and dustier this time, especially because I'm too shocked to turn off the mixer right away. When I finally do, I can barely move. It feels like moving would mean spreading the mess even farther, and I don't know how the heck to start cleaning it up.

A bit too much like my life as a whole.

"Reese, did a bomb just explode or a plane take off in your room or something? Both? Houston to Reese, come in, Reese?" Nat's voice is touched with humor but a bit of panic, too.

"I'm using a mixer," I say shakily, even though the mixer is more using me. I feel the tears threatening their return, and I make a quick excuse to get off the phone and save my biscuits. We all know it's not the biscuits I'm upset about, but my friends let me go anyway with promises to keep them updated if I need anything.

I wipe my face and hands with some wet paper towels, thinking how bonkers it would seem to Early Summer Reese that I'm wishing Benny was here to laugh at me and brush flour out of my hair. I finish the recipe as best I can, though the dough's consistency is not quite right. I flew too close to the culinary sun, trying to skip the fork mixing. I'm definitely adding an excess of salt with my stray tears. But I keep trying, using a glass in lieu of a biscuit cutter to make some misshapen, liquid-y lumps on a pan.

When I ultimately pull a dozen half-charred, half-dough mounds out of the oven, it's just as well. This proves it. I am not a chef nor a baker. Benny is the real talent. He deserved the fall internship all along, and I was kidding myself to think otherwise. I'm still wiping tears from my eyes as I pitch all of my efforts into the garbage and head back downstairs to shower and change into clean pajamas.

I send Benny a text before bed saying we should talk soon, but I need a little more time. In my current state of frustration and confusion and disappointment I don't want to say anything I don't mean and make an even bigger mess of things. And okay, maybe to some extent I'm putting off what feels like the inevitable, once-and-for-all end of this thing between us. Because even if today's showdown was based on miscommunication, I'm still stung by what he said and the ways he's shown that he doesn't quite understand my feelings. I'm in over my head on the relationship front as much as on the career one. Maybe it'd be better for both of us to cut ties before we get even more attached than we already are.

The pesky L-word pokes at me from the back of my mind.

When I settle in under the covers, I think of how my mamaw once told me that one of the reasons she and my papaw have stayed together so long is that they never go to bed angry. I know she probably meant angry at each other, not angry at their circumstances or angry in general. But goodness, if I tried to live like that, I'd be in for even less sleep.

I'm tired. Tired of getting the short end of the stick. Tired of the judgments that surround me. Tired of trying to make myself lesser so that others are more comfortable. Tired of being angry when my efforts never pay off anyway.

Chapter Twenty-Two

There was a day in March some years back when I clearly remember waking up, going down to the kitchen for breakfast, and stopping in my tracks, thinking, *My dad must have been in a terrible car wreck.* He looked an absolute mess, eyes blearier than I'd ever seen on a human, face weary and basset-hound-level saggy, hobbling around with his shoulders slumped and one hand on his back like everything hurt. He had not, however, been in a wreck. It was only that the University of Kentucky men's basketball team had lost the national championship the night before. And that was how I learned the word "hangover."

When I go to the bathroom and glance in the mirror first thing the next morning, I look worse than my dad post–March Sadness. And never did a drop of bourbon pass my lips. Would I feel any better if it had?

Oh good *gravy*, Reese, pull it together.

I brush my teeth and wash my face, doing my best to make

amends to my skin, which, between the crying and carelessly falling asleep with makeup still on, is none too happy. Plodding back to my room, I consider what I should do about the Benny situation. Something about the ten hours of sleeping like the dead has left me feeling calmer and less angry than I did yesterday, despite how much worse for the wear I appear.

Back in my room, I stick my oatmeal in the microwave and start practicing aloud what to say when I go into work, like a woman who is totally fine and stable.

"Hey, Margie, can I talk to you about something?" Hmm. Too ominous? Or just enough to fit the situation?

I'm going to talk to my bosses about quitting *Amateur Hour.* I already know I'm not being kept on, and if there's no need to impress people at FoF anymore, is it worth all the online abuse? I think not. Whatever happens with Benny and me behind the scenes, it's his show now. It sounded like they were already making plans to start filming him solo, so he can just have it all.

I'll go back to helping Margie in marketing full time for the last few weeks, if they'll let me. I'll fade from public memory. The trolls will have nothing to troll about anymore, and maybe they'll start leaving Friends of Flavor alone. I won't apologize for anything, but I also won't continue to cause a stir, however unintentional my stirring has been thus far. It's going to be painful in the short term, but hopefully better for everyone going forward.

Now the challenge is to be able to talk about this like a mature adult and without bursting into tears.

"I'm so appreciative of the opportunity y'all—*you all* have given me, but I feel it's time that I should step back." Do I sound too self-important? Like I think I'm the president of Friends of Flavor?

What will I say if they ask why? *The pressure's become too much. I'm a sore loser. The internet is a terrible place to be a girl. Your CEO is a douche canoe.*

Might need to keep workshopping my answer.

When I get tired of hearing myself talk, I head into the office a bit earlier than normal, deciding I should bite the bullet while I still feel the momentum. I stop by marketing first but Margie isn't there, so I head for Aiden's office, avoiding eye contact with the few early birds bustling around the kitchens.

As I turn down the hall to the big boss man's office, I nearly run smack into the bigger boss man. Geoffrey Block, CEO. My, unbeknownst to him, nemesis.

"Watch out there, young lady," he says, laying a hand on my arm. I could point out that he's the one who was looking down at his phone, but it'd be as worthwhile as laying blame on a brick wall.

"Sorry," I say instead. *So strong, so empowered. Kill 'em, girl.*

"Ah, Benjamin's sous-chef," he says with a nod and a knowing glint in his eye.

Ex*squeeze* me? My jaw feels like it comes unhinged as it falls open. Not that there's anything wrong with being a sous-chef, and lord knows, especially after last night, that I am far from being an actual chef. But doesn't Mr. Important know it's called *Amateur Hour,* not *Professional Chef and His Li'l Lady Friend Hour*?

Plus, Benny's name is not Benjamin, it's *Norberto,* but telling Geoffrey Block, CEO, that would probably be more of an offense to Benny than to the old man.

The CEO's nose twitches and his gaze drifts like he's smelling something. Probably the smoke pouring out my ears.

"Huh, someone's making something good. But they usually are around here, right? Ha." It's the Ken-doll laugh again. "What's your name again, sweetheart?"

Oh, this son of a charred-dough biscuit—

"Reese. My name is Reese," I say curtly, hoping to end this before I combust.

He looks surprised, like he's never heard my name before in his life. "Like the actress, huh?" He looks me up and down in a way reminiscent of the cookout, but it's somehow ickier in the close quarters of the hallway that's empty save the two of us. "I see it. You're like that one movie of hers, except instead of following the guy to law school, you follow him around the kitchen, right? Ha."

Rest in peace, my jaw. It has fallen clear off my face, not least because this man missed the entire point of the *Legally Blonde* films. I'm gonna have nightmares about that fake laugh.

I feel my mouth forming shapes as if to respond, but no sounds are coming out. Which is good, because the ones I'd like to make would be guaranteed to get me fired. After what feels like two hours but is more like five seconds of me standing there unresponsive, Geoffrey Block, CEO, lays a hand on my shoulder.

"Well, I'm out of here—meetings off-site for the day." His hand slides all the way down my arm and gives my wrist a squeeze before he lets go and steps around me to walk away. "Good to see you, kiddo."

I murmur a less-than-heartfelt goodbye, then continue to stand there gaping for a few moments, going over the exchange in my head. *Young lady. Sous-chef. Sweetheart. Kiddo. Following the guy around the kitchen.* I feel the path Geoffrey Block's hand took from my shoulder to wrist as if it's burned my skin. I feel his discomfiting gaze on my face, my body.

If I hadn't run into him, I would have marched straight into Aiden's office and carried on with my plan. Bowing out gracefully, fading into the backdrop, eventually allowing everyone to forget I was ever here.

But now I feel utterly patronized, and a tad violated. Talked to like I'm an idiot, touched as if my permission to do so is irrelevant. Good mother-loving gravy, I could spit on that man. I imagine his words and actions coming from the anonymous internet commenters, from the smug dude-bro at the UltiCon panel who was so proud of himself for outing my supposed hookup with Benny. I hear them in my head from my former classmates, from the boy who treated me so terribly a few years back and shook up my world. And it makes me want to puke.

I don't know what to do. I don't *want* to quit, but what other option do I really have? It might be time to accept that this is the way of the world. That I was never gonna win this summer. That even with a guy like Benny in my corner, I still only have myself to rely on, and once again, I've failed me. I'm about to take a step forward, to continue on and deal with the guilt and confusion later, when a voice stops me in my tracks.

"Why do I have a feeling you're about to do something stupid?"

I gasp, both because I didn't know anyone was behind me and because the person speaking is Katherine.

I turn slowly, my eyes meeting her intense gaze. Her arms are crossed and her stance is all power and self-assuredness.

"Um . . . I—I—" I start. Then, because I guess that's just how this day is gonna go, my chin wobbles and my eyes well up. In a matter of seconds, tears are pouring down my face.

In the hallway.

At eight in the morning.

In front of my number one role model.

"Come on," Katherine says, taking me by surprise as she reaches for my hand and starts pulling me behind her. I keep my head down to try to hide my blubbering and let myself be dragged along, praying to whoever's in charge of these things that we don't run into Benny.

Katherine finds the nearest room I can safely cry in and shuts the door, then flicks on the light. Because this is Friends of Flavor, it's a pantry full of food.

At least it's a spacious pantry, though, so we duck around

a row of shelves and sit on the floor, almost hidden from view should anyone else come in. As good a spot as any in the office to sit and be pitiful. Which I am, as I cry openly now, letting the tears fall and soak my face and shirt. The No Feelings Zone has been completely invaded by enemy forces, demilitarized, made into a monarchy in which emotions have sovereign power, the whole nine yards. I know I'll likely be red and puffy for the rest of the day, but I don't imagine that Margie will say anything.

Of all the people to be sitting here as I sob pathetically on the floor, it had to be the strong, badass woman I've spent years idolizing and still have to work up the nerve to talk to.

"Sorry, I should probably just go . . . ," I sniffle, starting to get to my feet with no actual destination in mind except *away*, but Katherine holds a hand out.

"Sit," she says, and because I would stand on my head if she told me to, I sit back down. "Is this about your job or your boyfriend?"

My watery eyes widen and I gape at her for a few moments.
"I—he's not—"

"Girl, please. We all knew even before that picture on Twitter. There are no secrets here; someone should've told you guys that your first day. So which is it?"

I blink a few times, taken aback by the turn of events. "Both?"

Katherine nods and folds her little legs up to her chest. Neither her stature nor the position make her any less intimidating.

"Why don't you tell me about it."

She doesn't make it sound like a question. And she doesn't look surprised when I start talking, though I myself am surprised as all hell. I relay the entire convoluted story to her, starting with the events of freshman year and ending on how I fought with and may or may not have dumped the best guy I ever met, had a creeptastic run-in with FoF's CEO, and now feel like I'm letting down my best friends, our feminist idol, and essentially all women everywhere.

After ten minutes of rambling, I wonder if Katherine was hoping for more of a two-sentence summary. Too little, too late.

Katherine's expression hasn't changed and when I'm finished, she doesn't tell me I'm crazy. She doesn't shake her head, get to her feet, and leave the room, never to set foot in a pantry again.

She gives a single nod that somehow conveys deep understanding and wisdom that the likes of me will never possess, then angles her body more toward me.

"So obviously that's a lot," she says, in an understatement of epic proportions. "And I mean it with zero judgment and only your best interests in mind when I say that, long term, I recommend therapy. I've seen a therapist for fifteen years, and therapy will change your life."

I blink in surprise, as if this warrior has shown me a chink in her armor. Yet it doesn't make me see her as any less strong and powerful. If anything, I'm even more impressed and feel like saying, "Yes, my queen, I will leave in search of a therapist this instant." But before I can respond, Katherine goes on.

"In the meantime, can I first say that letting me down should be the last thing on your mind? I mean, the *very* last. Someday I hope you get over the desire to please most everyone else except yourself, but at the very least, take me off the list of people to please immediately. I don't give a shit how you live your life if you're doing the best thing for you. That being said, you're not."

She pauses for a moment, letting the words sit there between us. I'm able to get out, "Wh-what?"

She raises her chin, somehow looking down her nose at me even though she's still a few inches shorter while seated. "You heard me. Setting aside your boy problem for the moment—which, for the record, I think will work itself out because the boy is a lovesick puppy—I know the online haters are hard to deal with. Yours have been especially bad, but we all get haters. I can't tell you how many dumbasses bombard my personal social media and email with their opinions on how I look, how I talk, how I could be so pretty if I smiled, how a woman shouldn't act like I do. I hate to say that you get used to it, because I know that doesn't help right now, let alone the fact that you shouldn't have to, but you *will* get used to it."

I sigh in frustration, tears pooling in my eyes. "I don't mean to be all 'why me' . . . but really, why me? Why go after a random summer intern on a cooking channel so hard?"

Katherine shrugs. "I mean, that's probably just it. These same losers certainly hate a lot of what Oprah says and does and stands for. But if they tweet their opinions at Oprah, what does she care? She'll likely never meet them and if she does, who gives a damn? She has zillions of fans and runs half the world, and a few idiots aren't changing that. But a random summer intern on a cooking channel is an easy target—not a 'big' celebrity with tons of fans, and much more accessible. They feel like they can be the macho crusaders who take you down and then pat themselves on the back, one less silly woman feeling free to have fun and be herself on the internet.

"Reese, you probably know this to some extent, but this stuff happens *all the time.* And not to minimize your experience, but it's more frequent and usually worse for women of color and others who are marginalized. Nia, Lily, even Seb and Raj? They've had people trying to run them off Twitter and out of their jobs for years. I'll bet you can find comments on any of their videos telling them to go back where they came from because they have skin that's not white. They're all from, like, Illinois and Nebraska and other white-bread middle-American states. Makes no difference. Bigots are bigots."

I know this, of course, from my hours and hours of button clicking and "taking out the trash" in comments on others' videos. People are vile without any goading. I just see less of it these days because I'm busy with *Amateur Hour* or designs, and it's easy not to dwell when it doesn't feel personal. I recognize how messed up that is, though, to not be affected by hate until it's pointed right at me.

"What about Aiden and Mr. Block?" I sniffle. "It's clear

neither of them take me seriously, that they basically see me as Benny's pretty, brainless assistant. I can't imagine any way to fix that even if I do get past the online stuff."

It shouldn't much surprise me when Katherine rolls her eyes, but I still raise an eyebrow in question. Then she murmurs something that would definitely have my mother washing a grown woman's mouth out with soap.

Louder, she says, "Reese, I hope you have many fulfilling and wonderful work experiences with a multitude of inspiring leaders and managers in the future. But more than likely, you'll start to see a pattern that the world's most powerful people are often the world's biggest assholes."

My jaw, having only just reattached itself following my encounter with Geoffrey Block, falls a tad. "O . . . kay?"

"I mean to say, never take the suits' word as an accurate reflection of reality. And definitely never take it as a reflection on yourself. I've gone toe to toe with Block on so many things over the years. I know of at least a few times early on that he tried to get me fired. Probably the only reason he hasn't is that viewers and the other Friends like me too much. *Fuss-Free Foodie* crushes it in ratings. My blog's super popular. I've made myself invaluable to the brand. But the guy is a creep and, unfortunately, short of him doing something so over the line that the other suits couldn't possibly ignore it, he's here to stay.

"But all the rest of us here like and respect you and we have your back. We're your coworkers but I feel like the other chefs would agree that we want to be your friends and supports, too. All that to say, if someone's being a jerk to you, feel entitled to push back. Or if you're uncomfortable doing that, tell one of us and we'll do it for you. We've all been there, especially Nia, Lily, and me."

I hope I properly mask my inner fangirl freak-out at the suggestion that we're *friends* and nod, swallowing the fresh wave of emotion Katherine's words have brought on.

"Anyway, the internet is a cesspool, we have some dirtbags in charge, and you and I don't have it nearly as bad as a lot of people. I don't know what all is happening with the fall internship, but I believe you're counting yourself out too early for things that shouldn't even be a factor. Don't let yourself be swayed by stupid internet trolls and men too up their own asses to recognize that an eighteen-year-old girl's looks and actions and love life have no bearing on her professional abilities. Don't be a martyr because the shit you've faced in the past has convinced you that you don't deserve better this time around. You deserve it all and you should let yourself go after it."

She drops that last statement like a bomb, and I sit in silence for a moment wiping at the tears on my cheeks. Everything she's saying just sounds so . . . smart. And refreshing. And empowering. Because she's Katherine, and she knows what she's doing.

"So. You staying in the game?" she asks.

The feeling that I have right now is the exact opposite of what I felt after running into Geoffrey Block, CEO, or after hearing him and Aiden talking to Benny. I am peeking back out from my hidey-hole and finding that what looked to be endless gloom and doom outside was actually a passing summer storm. I'm finding out that maybe I was wrong, that there *is* another path I could take, and that path is brightly lit and has good people to walk with me along the way.

"Yes," I say finally, and we both smile as Katherine takes my hand and we shake.

Then she says, "Great. I have an idea. And it's going to require backup."

She pulls out her phone and starts tapping out messages, presumably to the "backup" she referred to, not looking to me for an answer. But once again, it wasn't really a question.

Chapter Twenty-Three

The next afternoon, it's standing room only in Aiden's office. He and Geoffrey Block, CEO, are leaning against the edge of the desk nearly shoulder to shoulder, facing a semicircle made up of Margie, Nia, Lily, Teagan, Katherine, and me.

"Feminism . . . with Flavor?"

Geoffrey Block, CEO, says the words like the flavor in question is battery acid. He looks cornered, and he kind of is. This meeting was a bit of an ambush, thanks to Margie waiting until the last minute to tell the two men that she had some guests joining their after-lunch huddle. She didn't want to leave them any time to speculate on what we wanted or come up with some canned response to any request we might make.

Getting Margie as our ally was the second-best plan Katherine pulled together yesterday. The first, she's about to explain.

"Yes. The title is negotiable, though we think that one's pretty clever. But the point is that Friends of Flavor has an opportunity to be a leader in the online community by showing that we stand up for women. For years now, our colleagues—especially our female colleagues—have faced near-constant attacks and vitriol in response to simply existing as confident women in our videos. It has been notably worse as of late, and particularly directed toward the youngest and least experienced of us, making her first impression of working in this industry an unfavorable one. With Feminism with Flavor, the women of Friends of Flavor and our allies will show that we won't back down or hide ourselves away and therefore reward the temper tantrums of a small faction of trolls. Rather, we will double down, starting a dedicated video series that, in addition to carrying out our main purpose of sharing recipes and food prep as entertainment, will highlight important women's issues."

Nia chimes in, right on schedule. "We have a list of potential guests, from scholars to media personalities to professional athletes, who we can invite on the show to cook with us, and as we cook, we will have informal interviews and discussions about their experiences with feminism, gender discrimination, working in their respective fields as women, and so on. The goal is to educate and, of course, entertain viewers while also sending the message that women are not here to appease any and all critics. We will not be silenced. And Friends of Flavor cares about amplifying our voices."

Aiden looks thoughtful. Geoffrey Block, CEO, looks like we just asked him to take his pants off and hang them as a flag atop the Space Needle.

We formed this proposal, which has been tabbed and stapled and highlighted and is currently resting in the hands of Margie, Aiden, and Geoffrey Block, CEO, in less than twenty-four hours. To be fair, Katherine had a lot of her own scribbled notes already compiled when she called the rest of us together.

Shortly after Katherine and I finished what I think of as our brain-to-heart (the former hers, the latter mine) in the pantry, Lily and Nia showed up and joined us in a floor huddle. Katherine gave us the rundown of her vision, an idea she's had on her mind for years and was finally motivated to set into motion after seeing what I'd been going through this summer from the sidelines. Apparently, she noticed me much more than I'd thought. I asked if we could loop Teagan in, because she does a lot more in her admin role than she gets credit for, and I thought she'd love a chance to help with a woman-powered project. My suspicion proved correct, as Teagan was already bouncing in her seat when I told her about it. Nia suggested we propose it to Margie and see whether she would be willing to back us up with Aiden and the suits if we came up with a detailed plan. Margie's exact words, when the four of us approached her at her desk a few minutes later, were, "Oh, hell yes."

Immediately after work, Nia, Lily, Teagan, and I piled into Nia's car and met Katherine at her apartment on the northwest side of town. The drive was similar to the one Benny and I took to Golden Gardens on our first date, where we'd walked along the beach. A pang of missing him hit me again, and I knew I needed to figure out what to say to him soon.

But first, there was other business to attend to.

At Katherine's place, we ordered burritos and drank wine—which was only allowed after I swore I'd never accuse them of corrupting me—and discussed our ideas for the project. Within a few hours, we had our proposal fully fleshed out. And thus, Feminism with Flavor was born.

Now, though, standing in the silent office, it feels plausible that I've made the mistake of counting this particular chicken before it had the chance to hatch. A tiny part of me is tempted to say, "Look, y'all, thanks for trying, but we can go back to the original plan of me quitting, that'd be way easier for all involved, no skin off my nose, best of luck to ya."

But I look at the confident expressions on the faces of the strong women around me, and it makes me want to be stronger, too. So I keep my trap shut. The silence has become tense and almost awkward as the boss man of all boss men skeptically eyes his packet.

"Forgive me, but," he begins, and I know this can be going nowhere good, "what about the men who watch our channel? Do we really want to look so biased? We can't alienate half our viewership."

I see Katherine open her mouth to respond, but then I must enter some kind of alternate reality in which I think I'm the best one to take these questions, as I open my big mouth and beat her to the punch. "Who's to say they'll be alienated, though? Men watch plenty of TV shows and movies led by women. Or if they don't, they certainly should. We've been put through five million *Fast and the Furious* and James Bond movies, for goodness' sake. And if they're opposed to watching and learning from women, because they think we're boring or don't get our perspectives, well, I reckon they're part of the problem."

I fold my arms over my chest defiantly, then lose my remaining nerve and avert my eyes from those of the CEO. When I look at the other women instead, they're all staring at me with some measure of shock, some looking amused and impressed on top of that.

Katherine is the first one to shake herself out of it and narrows her gaze on Geoffrey Block, CEO, once more. "It may also be of interest to you that if this series doesn't happen at Friends of Flavor, I plan on hosting it on my personal site, the Kat's Muse. I have advertisers who have long expressed interest in helping me launch my own videos, but I've been reluctant to take any of FoF's thunder. I would feel obligated to make it clear, though, that I was only hosting the series because this channel had rejected the proposal."

My jaw drops along with Katherine's figurative mic. She kept that little contingency plan from us yesterday, but *damn.* Of course she had a secret weapon in her back pocket.

Lily pipes up, "And if you all didn't know, men do not make up half of Friends of Flavor viewers. More like thirty percent. Meaning women are seventy percent. Maybe worth looking at who's really getting alienated."

Well *okay*, Lily. For someone who spends so much of the time off in her own mental universe, she sure knows how to pop back down to earth and spit facts when needed. Other than the sounds drifting in from the kitchens and the hall, it's quiet. No one even bothers trying to talk Aiden onto our side, I assume because his opinion doesn't matter when we have Geoffrey Block, CEO, involved. I watch the hard expression on the older man's face as he slowly flips through the proposal again, though I don't think he's reading it. He's probably just stewing on how all the feeble womenfolk of the office somehow managed to paint him into a corner.

Finally, after what feels like hours but has probably only been minutes, Geoffrey Block, CEO, looks up with a pinched scowl on his face and speaks. "Let's go forward with the new show. Margie, Aiden, schedule a time to get together with the ladies and figure out next steps. Now if you'll excuse me, I need to step out and make a couple of calls."

Once he leaves, Aiden follows close behind him, leaving the rest of us on our own in his office. There's a beat of silence before the celebrating starts. All of us cheer and hug. Even the ever-stoic Katherine is clapping with a wide grin on her face.

I register with some surprise, after everything that's come to pass this week, that I am truly so happy. And despite how it felt in the midst of the saddest of pity parties, I was never alone. I have a pretty strong team backing me up.

This team of badass coworkers. My team of supportive

friends, Nat and Clara. The team of my family, who love me unconditionally and who I owe a phone call or two.

My team with Benny, if there's still a chance for us.

"Thank you," I whisper as I give Katherine a hug. She hesitates, then wraps her small arms around me in a crushing hold. It wouldn't surprise me to learn she has the same workout regimen as Benny.

"Don't thank me," she says. "You deserve it. We all deserve it."

"Nice job, Camden," Margie says with a small smile, patting me on the shoulder as I release Katherine. "Glad we'll have you around a while longer."

My brain is a bit too scrambled by the excitement of the past twenty-four hours—and especially the past twenty minutes—to parse her meaning, so I just look at her with my brows knit together. "What? I'm not—I mean, Benny got the fall internship."

Now Margie looks at me with confusion. "Pardon? I just meant that I expect we'll be keeping you around for Feminism with Flavor at least. No one's been selected for the internship spot yet, though I know Aiden and Geoffrey have had their eye on Benny. They have him doing his own livestream on Italian cooking today, starting any minute now. I believe their story is that they're testing a new format and everyone will do a livestream on a specialty of theirs at some point, but between you and me, I think it's a kind of a solo screen test for your costar."

I'm reeling from the "we'll be keeping you around" bit and don't have time to process it before Katherine leans in. It's the only time I've ever seen her in eager-gossip mode. "Mmhmm, and from what I've heard, Benny's been reluctant to do it without you."

I freeze, my mouth gaping. He . . . They . . . *What?* My eyes flit back and forth between the two women, as if one of them is gonna throw out a "just kidding!" any moment now. When they don't, my heart starts to beat even faster.

He doesn't want to do his live show without me. He was never taking the fall job without telling me. He still wants me around. He might still want *me.*

The churning in my stomach that's been pretty consistent for days is now more like the exciting kind, the all-my-dreams-might-be-coming-true-at-once kind. Lily, Teagan, and Nia join our circle, looking totally unsurprised in a way that suggests they're also aware of my current relationship predicament.

"Maybe you should go check on him," Nia says with a mischievous glint in her eye.

"Calm his nerves," Teagan adds, her eyes wide and innocent, but she's not fooling me.

But I've been fooling myself, right? It's clear I completely misinterpreted things. All they offered Benny was one solo live show, one he's apparently not thrilled about. What he *was* thrilled about, however, was finally working up the courage to talk to his parents and let them know he plans on staying in Seattle. Staying with *me.* And he just wanted me to be excited, too.

Even the small, prideful part of me that wants to be mad at the ways he called me out, how he didn't totally see my perspective, knows that he was more right than wrong. He's been trying his best since the start. I still have my own damage, my own shit to work through. But maybe I was too hasty in thinking I'd have to do it without him. I have another teammate, if I'd just let him be one.

The L-word. It's there again. Poke, poke, poking at me.

"I—I should go find him," I say.

All five women nod with an enthusiasm that would be funny if my mind wasn't already with somebody else right now. I turn on my heel and dash out the door.

Once I'm in the empty hallway, though, panic seizes me. An endless scroll of what-ifs and worst-case scenarios threatens to unravel in my head. I shoot off a frantic text to Nat and Clara.

> **Reese:** SOS y'all were right about Benny, there was a big misunderstanding between us, mainly my fault, he's done his best and I really want him back
>
> **Natalie:** How is this an SOS!!!!!
>
> **Clara:** yes! this is the best news
>
> **Reese:** But what if I screw it up what if he doesn't want me anymore what if what if what if
>
> **Reese:** Can we 3way call please
>
> **Clara:** don't think you need to. you know what to do, you're not going to screw it up, trust your instincts you smart and beautiful girl

Natalie: No I can't call I'm clipping my grandma's toenails

Clara: I'm bathing my pet lizard

Natalie: Guess you'll have to handle this one on your own LIKE RIGHT NOW GO DO IT GO GET YOUR MAN

Clara: you are woman hear you roar!

I laugh, shaking my head at this ridiculousness. It's clear the mama birds have decided this is the time to push their cowardly baby bird out of the nest.

Reese: Y'all are no-good dirty liars but I get the point

Reese: Here goes nothin

Chapter Twenty-Four

My heartbeat is pounding in my ears as I continue through the Friends of Flavor offices. I want to find Benny before he starts his livestream, to tell him how I feel and patch things up so I can at least take that stressor off his plate and then wish him luck for his first time filming alone. I get to the whiteboard at the head of the hallway connecting the kitchens, where the filming schedule is listed each day, and check the time, confirming that Benny's show should start in exactly two minutes.

I think of him in PK 2, where we spent so many hours goofing around and filming together and falling for each other. I picture him introducing his first show on his own, and I . . . I can't help it. I know it will probably hurt to watch, knowing he may be hurting and my not being able to do anything about it yet, but I have to see. To support him. To try to discern anything I can about where his mind's at on all things Reese Camden.

And if he actually seems totally fine and done with me, maybe it'll help me move on, too.

I sneak around to the corner of the kitchen, out of Benny's line of sight. My view is mainly his back, along with Charlie filming and Aiden overseeing it all. Benny's voice is relaxed, but the line of his shoulders is . . . stiff. Tense.

Not totally fine and done with me, then? Oh, sweet Norberto.

Returning my focus to what Benny is saying, I realize that he's not introducing the prep part like he normally would.

"So, today is a little different, for a lot of reasons. As you may notice, my partner in crime, Reese Camden, is not here."

I flinch at my name being brought up first thing. I can't help it. I thought I was going to be the blond elephant sitting at the edge of the room. He's just dragged me right into the middle.

"That's kinda shitty, to be honest. For all of us. There's no way I'm gonna be any good without her beside me."

Wait, *what?* Aiden's shocked, slightly horrified expression probably mirrors my own. He's waving his hands wildly like, *What are you doing? This isn't what we planned.* Behind him, some kitchen assistants and Seb have trickled in to watch, and I see Margie weaving through them to stand next to Aiden and Charlie. So many people to witness this bizarre spectacle unfolding.

Benny goes on. "So in her honor, I prepared something special. You'll have to excuse me if this is a bit unconventional. Or don't excuse me. Honestly, I don't give a shit."

Oh. My. Stars. What is he doing? Aiden's eyes are about to pop out of his skull and it feels like mine are doing the same. Clearly Benny knows nothing of my intentions to resolve things with us, nor that I'm staying on at FoF because of the new series. Of course he doesn't know yet; I barely know what's going on. Bless his heart, he's talking like I've died. Or rather, like the show killed me off and he's my disgruntled number one fan.

I see Aiden lunge for the camera, presumably to shut it off less than two minutes into the livestream, but Charlie—Charlie! Quiet, grumbly, couldn't-care-less-about-anything Charlie!— puts an arm out to stop him. Then Margie—Margie! My solemn boss turned champion of women!—leans over and whispers in Aiden's ear before laying her hand on his shoulder and pulling him back a couple of steps.

What on God's green earth is happening?

Meanwhile, Benny has kneeled behind the counter and when he stands back up, there is no Italian food nor any relevant ingredients in sight. Rather, he's holding an elegant, three-tier cake on a cake stand. He sets it on the counter, and the cake is nearly level with the top of his ball-cap-covered head. It's flawlessly frosted, white with intermittent swirls of light and dark brown, each layer topped with brown crumbles of . . .

Reese's Cups?

Lord. Have. *MERCY.*

I need to step away. I should if I know what's good for me. Either that, or run into the kitchen and shut off the camera myself before Benny does something stupid.

But I don't.

"I made this cake for today from my very favorite candy in the whole entire world, Reese's Peanut Butter Cups."

I feel more than see Katherine approach my side. She murmurs, "So, now might be a good time to tell you that I, uh, let slip to Charlie about our talk yesterday."

My attention is divided as Benny goes on. "And this cake, my friends, has a lot of meaning to me, and I couldn't imagine making anything else for my first livestream. Apologies that I didn't show you the process of making it, but it's only because I wanted to ensure I'd have the time to walk you through the many facets that make this cake so special. Let's get started, shall we?"

"Katherine, what did you do?" I hiss.

"Nothing! Nothing. But Charlie might have told Benny. Who, rumor has it, might feel like he hasn't done enough to support you in a, er, public way."

I cover my face with my hands, leaving my fingers open to peek through them. "I swear, this office has more busybodies than my papaw's church choir."

"First, as you can see," Benny continues, "this cake has layers. It has the layers that are visible but also so much depth within. It's so much more than meets the eye. So much more than you, the viewer, see through your computer screen, through whatever it is that this cake allows you to see about itself. So much more than people who casually glance at the cake in passing would notice. You can't even begin to imagine what's contained inside.

"Obviously, this cake is beautiful. I mean, you could stare at it all day. It's gorgeous. It makes you want to lick its face—"

I press a hand to my mouth to keep in a laugh of disbelief. Tears are pooling in my eyes, though from good feelings or humiliation I can't tell, and I blink furiously to keep them at bay. After the past few days, my eyes barely need an excuse to start leaking.

"—its surface, that is, and it clearly knows how to present itself. I mean, *damn*. What a stunning cake. But you know what? That stuff is just icing and a few crumbled candies. The cake's real power is in its substance. For one thing, it's taught me so much. It was a process making this cake, getting to know its ingredients, what it is and what it comes from and what it wants to be, and I learned a ton from it—more than any one cake has ever taught me about myself, and life, and cooking. Did you know a cake could do all that? I sure didn't, at the beginning of this thing."

"Oh my God," says Teagan, right in my ear. When did she get here? Is anyone at FoF actually working right now? "Oh my God, *ohmyGod.*"

"Another component it has, see, is the chocolate. The chocolate is this unbelievable deliciousness that everyone wants and is lucky to come into contact with. It's sweet, it's light, it's of the highest quality and best flavor. Just so much sugary goodness there."

Benny turns over the piece of a Reese's Cup he's holding between his thumb and forefinger. I've given up trying not to cry.

"But here, it's complemented by peanut butter. Peanut butter, it's got protein, right? So it has a lot of strength. A little saltiness, a little punch—this peanut butter won't take your shit sitting down, y'know? Because peanut butter has been through a lot to get here in its current form. A long process, a whole lot of grinding and pressure and struggle, to come out as smooth and complex and amazing as it is."

I see that Raj, Nia, and Lily have wandered into PK 2 and are standing with Seb and the others, watching with expressions ranging from confusion to astonishment to pure enjoyment as Benny gets more and more spirited. About cake.

About clearly much more than cake.

"Now, even with all it took, even with all that these ingredients had to go through, all the heat it's taken to make the cake what it is, people might not be fans of this cake. While it's objectively incredible, perhaps the greatest cake that has ever existed, it's still gonna have haters. There are those who might watch this video and feel the need to comment on this cake, and tell it that it's not as special as it is, or point out what they think are flaws. People will disagree with chocolate and peanut butter being delicious, a stance that is plainly wrong. Others might suggest that Friends of Flavor would somehow be better off without this cake, or that my limited experience making decent Italian food somehow make my presence here more valuable than this cake's.

"Well, I'd like to make it clear that those people don't know a single fucking thing."

Gasps echo through the room, including my own. Did he just say that? Live?

"They don't know about this cake, they don't know how wonderful it is. They've never seen something so purely good, so unobjectionably awesome. They feel intimidated and inferior, because they are inferior and always will be. They don't have anything on this cake and they know it, so they sit behind their computer screens or stand behind their oversize egos and tear it down to try to prop themselves up. But they'll be lucky if they ever cross paths with a cake like this one and it dares to spit in their direction."

While he's in the middle of this portion of his rant, which has devolved into near shouting and erratic hand gestures that have him close to knocking the top layer off his precious cake, I feel a hand on my back. I turn and see Teagan, her eyes gleefully wide and her mouth in a shocked smile. A small crowd of people from the office has gathered behind us and Katherine, enthralled by this shitshow.

She leans in and whispers, "Oh my God. Okay, Reese, as much as I don't want this to stop, I think you might have to cut the boy off."

I give a shaky laugh, brushing the tears off my cheeks as I turn back toward Benny. Taking another glance in the direction of the camera, where Margie and Charlie show no signs of ending filming and Aiden might be in an actual state of shock, I decide she's right.

Benny has slowed down somewhat and seems to need to catch his breath, but he continues to talk. If the boy can do anything, it's *talk*.

Okay. I can do this.

I slowly cross the room toward Benny, deliberately avoiding looking at my bosses or Charlie and his camera or the who knows how many others who have gathered to watch this train wreck live.

"So before you pass judgment on this cake, maybe take a look at yourself and what's going on in your own screwed-up life that's given you a warped perspective on an innocent, beautiful, phenomenal in every way—"

I lay a hand on Benny's shoulder and when he turns toward me, his mouth falls open in a perfect circle, dark eyebrows wrinkling his forehead under his cap. He is flushed and startled and so, so handsome. It's the first time I've looked at his face since we were on a city sidewalk and I was walking away from him and goodness, I've missed it. I step closer and he searches my weepy eyes.

"Sounds like a pretty good cake," I manage with a soft smile.

"The best," he breathes.

I step closer still, just a few inches from him now. "I'm a little sweeter on the baker, to be honest."

His eyes close and his chin tips down for just a moment, and he exhales on a laugh before looking at me with so much warmth and intensity.

"You have no idea how good it is to hear that," he murmurs, and then he's kissing me hard, one hand in my hair and the other wrapping around my waist to pull me to him. I bring my arms up around his shoulders, barely registering the cheers and applause in the packed kitchen before I pull the cap off Benny's head. I hold it up to cover our faces from the camera, as our kiss goes on much longer than I'd ever want my mama to see.

When we break apart, Benny whispers, "I love you, Reese. And I'm sorry for not making that totally clear before now. I want to be with you, and support you, and fight for you—"

"I love you, Benny." I hadn't said it out loud before, for fear that this would end and I'd be heartbroken. But it appears that will not be the case. And I'm so, so certain that I love him.

"Woo!" he shouts, lifting me by the waist and twirling me around. Then, since the camera is still rolling—perhaps a sense of "what do we really have to lose at this point?" on Charlie's part—he yells, "I LOVE REESE CAMDEN! Who wants cake?"

The room fills with the sound of laughter and excitement for what is most certainly the wildest livestream that will ever grace the Friends of Flavor channel. Aiden looks like he could keel over any second. Margie, calmly amused, pushes a stool behind him and urges him to sit. Even Charlie is laughing as he turns off the camera and the Friends of Flavor staff pour into the frame to cut and claim pieces of Benny's Reese's Cup cake.

The scoreboard I've carried in my mind for most of the summer starts to scroll wildly through numbers on both Benny's and my sides, like a malfunctioning slot machine, both of our scores getting higher and higher, all the way toward infinity. Because somehow, regardless of who's the better chef or the fan favorite or the bosses' preference, we've both won.

I go stand in a quieter spot off to the side with the man of the hour, or perhaps the man who has made me the woman of the hour, my arms around his waist and my head upon his shoulder.

Speaking just for Benny to hear, I ask, "How did they not stop you at 'frankly, I don't give a shit'?"

I feel a laugh rumble through his chest. "Charlie's a romantic at heart, really. I knew Aiden would flip—hoped you wouldn't, wherever or whenever you saw it—but I'm mostly surprised Margie let any of it happen."

Glancing in the direction of that familiar frizzy gray braid, I smile. "Don't underestimate Margie."

"Hmm." After a pause, he says, "So, you heard me say I'm sorry, right? I hope that's clear. What I said the other day was stupid—you're so strong and you've handled everything that's been thrown at you like a boss. I wish I'd been better at sticking up for you this whole time. I know you don't need me protecting you or anything, but I want to be beside you, however you want me."

I place my hand on his chest, leaning back to look at him. "*I'm* sorry. I jumped to the worst conclusions because I was scared. It's been hard for me to believe that this can actually be a wonderful thing, you and me. That there's no catch. But I believe in *you,* and I've missed you something awful. Plus, no one else has ever made an entire cooking show that's basically an extended metaphor for how great I am, in the most excellent and most public display of affection I've ever seen."

"Wait, that's what you thought I was doing? Ah, this is awkward. You're great and all, but my Reese's Cup cake is next level. You should try some."

I pretend to shove him away, but he holds me even tighter and kisses my forehead. "So, Reese Camden, teammate and all-around wonderful person whom I love . . ."

"Oh lordy."

"Assuming they don't fire me outright once everything settles down, are you ready for these last few weeks as costars? I know I may have looked like a calm, cool, and collected professional doing this by myself, but I definitely prefer working with a partner. With you, specifically."

I look into his eyes, biting my lip to stall the grin that threatens to break through. "I'm ready. But I have a feeling that our time as costars is far from over."

"Really?" He gets a confused pout on his face. "Are we still talking in Benny-and-Reese-are-in-love code?"

"No, literal costars," I say, laughing. "Long story, but all signs point to both of us sticking around Friends of Flavor a little longer."

"Okay, Magic 8 Ball girlfriend, let me know when you want to clue me in." He eyes me with suspicion, but I'm not going to tell him everything right here and now. "You're lucky I like you."

"Love," I correct.

"Right. I really hope the lunch rush at Beneventi's ran late today."

I frown. "Why?"

"So my family didn't end up watching my first livestream. C'mon, let's get some cake."

Epilogue

"**H**ey, everyone, welcome to *Feminism with Flavor.* I'm Katherine, and I'm here with Dr. Teresa Novak, an OB-GYN, outspoken advocate for women's reproductive health, and *New York Times* bestselling author of *The Lady Doctor.* Today she's also my sous-chef as we prepare chicken cacciatore. Dr. Novak, thanks so much for joining me."

"This is so badass," Benny whispers as we peek around the entrance to Prep Kitchen 3, a few yards behind the camera filming Katherine's episode.

"She's even more perfect in person," Natalie squeaks from beside him.

"It is, and she is," I agree with a smile. "But we should probably make ourselves scarce before—"

"Beneventi, Camden. Two interlopers. What are you still

doing here?" Aiden's voice snaps behind us, as quietly as one is capable of snapping.

"Leaving now," I say as we scramble to grab our things and head toward the exit, hoping my more respectful response drowns out Benny's snickering. "See you Friday!"

Natalie and Clara, who are in town for fall break, trail Benny and me as we pass the chefs and kitchen assistants carrying on the usual hustle and bustle of the Friends of Flavor office. I know them all by name now and exchange smiles and waves with a few as they mix ingredients, organize pantries, clean kitchens, take dishes out of ovens and set others on burners, sneak bites of each other's food.

There's a reason why Benny and I always want to stick around even after we've finished our work for the day. A reason why we eagerly stayed after our summer internships ended, when the suits offered Benny the fall culinary internship to continue *Amateur Hour* and step into more of a chef's role, and me a part-time permanent position to film with Benny and launch the new series with the women of FoF.

This place feels like home.

Helping develop *Feminism with Flavor*—from designing our logo to coordinating guest spots and everything in between—has given me more of a sense of belonging than I can recall ever having. It's the coolest thing to be a part of, and we're only a few episodes in. Since we rotate which of the female chefs, plus amateur me, hosts each one, I hadn't been able to see Katherine filming yet. Benny, arguably the biggest fan of our new show, was eager to sneak in and get a glimpse of Nat, Clara, and me after we finished filming our own video today, which we've dubbed "Take Your Friends to Work Day."

As it turns out, my boyfriend unwittingly played a big role in the series having such a successful launch. The livestream in which "an amateur baker quickly devolves into madness and cake metaphors as he tries to win back his girlfriend," as one news anchor described it, went viral in an even bigger way than Benny getting hit with a salmon. It boosted Friends of Flavor's subscriber count significantly, though many of the new fans have probably been disappointed with how little romantic drama 99 percent of our content entails.

Still, the buzz was great for bringing public attention to the channel as a whole, and Benny and, more reluctantly, I, even gave a couple of interviews in which we talked about the hate that women online receive and plugged our new, woman-centric series. This led to an outpouring of support, so much that the anti-Reese mob has been all but drowned out. And any uncertainty that Aiden and Geoffrey Block, CEO, still had about *Feminism with Flavor* or about me was swept away in the resulting wave of sponsorship and advertising interest.

The four of us manage to squeeze into the elevator outside of Friends of Flavor, our brightly colored coats serving a stark contrast to the businesspeople's blacks and grays. We keep talking the whole way down, Nat and Clara chattering excitedly about seeing the prep kitchens in real life, meeting Rajesh and Nia, how much they enjoyed today's *Amateur Hour* episode. Normally, the only sounds on this ride are the soft tapping on phone screens and occasional throat clearing. But instead of feeling awkward or nervous about upsetting the peace and quiet, I'm more comfortable in this spot than I've ever been.

"Tacos for dinner? We talked about taking y'all to that new place on Forty-Fifth," Benny says over his shoulder to my friends, taking my hand as we walk out of the building and onto the busy downtown sidewalk. I suppress a grin at his "y'all," a new addition to his vocabulary that he doesn't even seem to notice. Nat isn't gonna let it slide, though.

"Oh, were *y'all*, Norby? How fun!" she teases in an extra-thick accent. He reaches out and flicks the side of her head, which is more or less the essence of their relationship. I'm not sure he'll ever fully forgive me for telling my friends his real name.

"But it's a Wednesday," I answer his original question as I peer up at the sky. We're firmly out of the dreamy summer weather, and the clouds are threatening a drizzle anytime now.

"It's Tuesday somewhere," he says. Traditionally, we only eat tacos on Taco Tuesdays, when a lot of our favorite places have special deals. Which is to say, we eat tacos on most Tuesdays.

"That is plainly untrue," I say with a smirk. "What if we go to the dining hall tonight? I need to use my meal plan more. I can even buy dinner for everyone with my flex points. *Pleeease?*"

"Oh, all right," Benny says, sighing. "But they'd better have broccoli casserole."

The food snobbery of the other Friends has definitely rubbed off on the two of us, which has made dorm life a challenge. I've had to instate a "no negativity" rule when I bring Benny along and buy him food with my points. So now he only talks about the foods he *does* like there, which are basically any made in a giant casserole dish that taste like only a grandma could make them.

Though not Benny's grandma, as she's Italian and therefore in a different league cuisine-wise. I've had his parents' home cooking a few times now, first when his mom came and stayed in his tiny studio apartment with him for a week after he moved from the Seattle U dorm. She was worried about his ability to feed himself as he relocated and settled in while simultaneously starting part-time classes at culinary school and working at Friends of Flavor. This was in spite of Benny's protests that most of his days are spent doing nothing but cooking and eating. I was excited to meet her, though, and even more so when I had her homemade manicotti with cannoli for dessert, and subsequently found a way to have dinner with them every night that week.

We've also been down to see the rest of his family in San Francisco, on the rare weekend when neither of us had other plans. I quickly learned that Benny's brothers (a) are every bit as beautiful as he is, which he really loves to hear from me, and (b) will never let him live down the Reese's Cup cake episode, which they were streaming live on every TV in their restaurant.

My family has not yet admitted to watching it, and they have been strongly encouraged not to. At least not before they meet Benny in person, when he comes home with me for Christmas.

So far, he's surpassed expectations for in-person meetings with the two other most important people in my life. We picked Natalie and Clara up from the airport when they got in last night—one of many reasons I'm thankful for a boyfriend with a car now in his possession—and their ease around each other has been blowing my mind. With our limited space, we've divided and conquered, with Clara crashing on my dorm room futon and Natalie staying on Benny's couch. So far, Nat is freaked out by Benny's cleanliness and he by her "snoring like a freight train." Secretly, I think they're both thrilled to have the chance to grill one another without me present.

"So picky, Benjamin. Maybe you've got that cap screwed on a little too tight—you seem irritable," his temporary roomie teases.

"Careful, Nat, he knows where you sleep," Clara warns, glancing up from her phone with a smirk. She's been glued to it so far, texting Jessie, formerly known as the pretty redheaded court justice from camp and now known as Clara's long-distance girlfriend. She still gives us the bare minimum as far as relationship updates or even a basic rundown of what Jessie is like, but she seems happier than I've ever seen her, so I don't complain.

"Gimme a break, the people love the hats," my boyfriend sighs with mock exasperation. He still wears his backward caps in the kitchen; he tried to go hatless one time on *Amateur Hour* and that episode's only comments were about how goofy he looked. But he knows how much I like his curly hair, so on days we're not filming, he sets it free.

Benny does a lot of things to make me happy. He cooks for me often, naturally, letting me act as quality control for anything new he's learned in class. He keeps a pitcher of sweet tea in his fridge at all times, usually with lemon wedges in a dish beside it, ever since I taught him my mamaw's way of making it. He gives the best neck massages when I let school stress get to me—not that I have much frame of reference when it comes to neck massages, but his are amazing.

He also keeps me adventuring, pushing me gently into trying new things that are out of my comfort zone or that break down my shell a little more. But he's always the first one to pull me back in, to tell me that my feelings and fears and freak-outs are okay, and talk to or hold me or whatever I need until I feel all right again. His favorite thing is talking about our feelings. I'm working on that one.

I still have a lot to work through, of course. I probably always will, because who doesn't? But these past few months have been transformative, through the job and my relationships, the falls and the recoveries. I've found my people—Benny, capital *F* friends and lowercase *f* friends from my dorm and classes, a therapist recommended by Queen Katherine herself, and the folks back home who have been with me from the start and for whom I have a new appreciation now that we're long distance. And it's with all of their help that I'm finally finding my way.

Which is ironic since currently, in a city where two of us have lived for almost half a year, I'm pretty sure we're lost.

"Aren't most of the buses that take us toward UW going to be back that way?" I ask hesitantly, pointing in the direction we came from.

"Little predinner detour, Reese's Cup. Come on, let's catch this one!"

I raise my brows in confusion but turn to my friends with a shrug before the three of us jog to keep up with Benny. He pulls my hand, my backpack bouncing against my puffy coat. We hop onto the crowded bus just before the driver closes the door and scan our ORCA cards as we claim standing spots in the aisle. It's a bus route I'm not familiar with and I watch out the window, curious as to whether Benny actually knows where we're going.

I ask him as much and he shrugs, the look in his eyes conveying that there is a plan, but he will not be telling us. I just hope that whatever it is, it'll leave me enough time to write my sociology paper that's due tomorrow.

We ride through the Belltown neighborhood, shifting a bit at each stop as people get off and on. Benny and I share a few Seattle fun facts with our guests as we go. Then, finally, he pushes the red button to signal we're disembarking at the next stop.

Right by Seattle Center. Hmm . . .

We follow Benny off the bus and when he takes my hand again, Nat and Clara dramatically clutch each other's hands. I stick my tongue out at them, but Benny doesn't notice as he leads us through what seems like equal parts post-workday locals and tourists. We walk farther off the busy rush-hour streets, down the tree-lined sidewalks that run in and around this museum-filled corner of the city. We could be headed toward anything from the Imax theater to the big public playground that usually smells of popcorn or cotton candy or whatever food the vendors are selling that day. Benny pulls me along until he comes to a stop . . .

. . . right underneath the Space Needle.

"Ooh, this looks familiar." Nat rubs her hands together eagerly.

"I hope you don't mind that I prepurchased tickets." Benny gives us all his classic lopsided smile that still makes me want to kiss his face off every time.

But instead, I blink at him in a mix of surprise and confusion. "Um. Okay? I mean, thank you, I've been wanting to do this since I got here, but—but I thought we agreed that we'd wait till someone's parents came for a visit and offered to pay for it."

"Oops, I forgot," he says in a flat tone that tells me he didn't. "Anyway, let's go before we miss our window!"

I laugh and look at him like he's lost his mind, but he's turned and is skipping to the entrance, and my friends are following, and I figure I'd better get a move on. He already has the tickets, after all.

The ticket taker scans Benny's printed confirmation and sends us up the ramp, which is bordered on each side by walls printed with the timeline of the Needle's construction and stories of its history, interspersed with screens showing footage of the

Needle through the years. It's actually pretty fascinating, learning about this iconic spot in my new home, a spot I know embarrassingly little about. We spend a few minutes reading the stories and watching the videos as we wind our way around and reach the photo spot. Well, three of us do. Nat doubles back to rush Clara along.

Once she's with us, we stand in front of a green screen to take a photo that will be superimposed over whichever Space Needle background we choose. Benny arranges us in a ridiculous prom pose with his arms around me from behind, mine around Nat, and Nat's around Clara. While I won't know until I go online and look at it later, I'm almost positive they were all making ugly faces.

Then we're at the elevator, and I get nervous for the first time. I remind myself it isn't even as tall as the building where Friends of Flavor's office is. But the elevator there isn't glass and looking straight out into open air. Nor does it have a friendly operator letting you know exactly how high and how fast you're going. I lean back against Benny nervously, inviting the prom pose this time as we soar higher and higher and my stomach feels less and less cool with it.

But when we reach the top, it isn't so scary. Well, the indoor part isn't, with a little café and seating that basically feels like you're in any other tall building. I think about just plopping myself in a chair and enjoying the view from here, but then Nat and Clar are the ones pulling my hands, and I guess that's how we're doing things today.

Ever so reluctantly, I follow them out into the air that feels a *lot* cooler and breezier than it did on the ground. I look up, still surprised there's no rain yet. But then I look out, and oh my stars. It feels like I should be able to see the whole world from up here, though I'm mainly looking at downtown Seattle, the bay, and, in the distance, a glimpse of Mount Rainier.

Benny appears at my side again and places a hand on my back as we slowly follow Clar and Nat around, pointing out all the recognizable sites and landmarks as we go.

"You can't quite see it, but straight over that way is Golden Gardens, where I had my first official date with one Reese Camden and took a picture of her that may or may not be my phone background," Benny says, and I laugh as I follow the direction of his pointing finger.

"Wow, are you, like, obsessed with her or something?" Nat scoffs.

"Completely," he declares.

Clara shrugs. "Not the worst choice."

"Y'all keep me humble," I say, giving my friends' cheeks a pinch.

A few minutes later, the other two have drifted off and Benny is pointing a different way. "There's my apartment building."

I squint and it takes me a minute to spot the little blue concrete box on the north side of town that houses a bunch of tinier boxes, one of which houses my boyfriend.

His finger moves farther upward. "On a clearer day, you're supposed to be able to see Mount Baker over there, up near the border." I nod, duly impressed and also beginning to wonder if Benny has reverted to nervous information-dumping. I thought we were long past that. But then he guides me so we're both looking farther to the west, across the water where several ferries chug along. "And you know what's in this direction?"

I chuckle, feeling like I'm being quizzed. "What?"

"The fancy-pants cabin with the hiking trail along the coast where the girl I'm super in love with kissed me for the very first time."

There's a flutter in my stomach and a smile splits my face. I feel Benny's arms by my waist and I pull them tighter, all the way around me, and lace my fingers through his. His chin rests on my shoulder, his cheek pressed to mine as we both face the least cluttered view the Needle has to offer.

Then he goes on, "You know, I realize we haven't discussed what our official anniversary is, but it's been three months today since we kissed for the first time, which everyone knows is an important monthiversary. So I wanted to do something special, and coming up here came to mind because I've felt about this high up in the air for every moment since discovering, officially, that you were feeling the same as I was."

Lordhavemercy.

The stomach flutter is more like the roller-coaster stomach-swooping that I've had around Benny from the beginning, but in the best way. I twirl to face him and wrap my arms around his neck, so close our noses nearly touch.

"Norberto Beneventi," I say, and he narrows his eyes a moment before smiling softly again. "You are sweet as all get-out, and I do indeed feel every bit as in love with you, so much that I'll excuse the total cheesiness of your alleged reason for bringing me up here."

"Hey, I thought it was pretty . . . *gouda*." His face goes mock-stern, lips twitching with the effort to suppress his smile. I can't possibly do the same, already letting out a snort-laugh.

"God, that note was some of my best work, wasn't it?" I say through the subsiding giggles.

"Could've used a few more props from the pantry, if you ask me. Some of us put a little effort into asking their cute coworker out," Benny answers as he pulls me closer.

"Don't worry. I brainstorm new puns every time I go in there on an ingredient run. Keeping a running list for future date invitations."

He laughs. "Good. I expect you'll have a while to work through them all, you know. Months"—he kisses one cheek—"years"—then the other—"maybe even longer"—then lands a kiss on my nose.

"Sounds like a plan to me," I answer with a smile.

Then I kiss him full-on, with all the mushy, soft, vulnerable, madly-in-love feelings I have in me, not caring one bit if the whole world sees.

Acknowledgments

When I was fifteen and determined to be the next Disney Channel star, I would sit in chemistry class and draft awards-show speeches in my lab notes, listing everyone I would thank. This is probably why I did so poorly in chemistry, but I also think it was good practice for keeping gratitude at the forefront while my dreams have changed and come true. I have so many folks to be grateful for in bringing this book to life, starting with:

My incredible agent, Laura Crockett. You have loved this story so well, found it a home in the middle of a global pandemic (!), and continue to be the most supportive, dependable ally. From the first time we spoke, I knew you understood the heart of my book and, through that, understood me. I feel so lucky to have you and Team Triada.

My wonderful editor, Hannah Hill. You've been a delight from the get-go, when you sent pictures of your quarantine baking in homage to Reese and Benny and I thought, "When should I tell her that I'm actually terrible in the kitchen?" Your brilliant editorial feedback brought out the best in this book while also feeling like a warm hug, and for that, you are magic.

The rest of the team at Delacorte and Random House, who have been a lovely, welcoming publishing home, including Beverly Horowitz, Barbara Marcus, Tamar Schwartz, Colleen Fellingham, Dominique Cimina, John Adamo, Regina Flath, Cathy Bobak, Heather Hughes, and Alison Kolani. Extra thanks to illustrator Ana Hard for the beautiful book cover of my dreams!

Auriane Desombre and Susan Lee. You were the first total strangers to read a thing I wrote and tell me it was good, and as such, you were the first ones I sort of believed. Thank you a million times over for choosing me as your Pitch Wars mentee, sharing your wisdom and experience, and being the sweetest friends.

Elora Ditton, soul sister and Nancy Ditton to my Sherlock Hill. Thank you for being equally game for a meltdown or a celebration, whichever I need at any given time. Your clever way with words inspires me constantly and your friendship is a gift.

Claire Ahn and Thais Vitorelli. You are both so thoughtful with your writing craft and generous with your love and support. I'm always *clutching* you tight from afar.

My PW '19 mentee class. One of the best parts of this journey has been sharing it with all of you. Special thanks to Anita Kelly for being a gentle listening ear and partner in romance obsession, and Kate Dylan for your wealth of publishing knowledge and perfect balance of optimism and snark.

Many other authors who have encouraged and inspired me, especially Rachel Lynn Solomon, who read and edited my first-ever hideous query letter and somehow still became my (much-loved and cherished) friend, and Martha Waters, one of my first historical romance faves who is now an excellent pen pal and writerly ally.

Some of the amazing friends who have cheered me on at each milestone—thank you to Katie and Aaron Cambron for giving the first feedback on this book and being both my best pals and my one (1) successful matchmaking effort; Megan Wall for your endless belief in me and excited-puppy brand of love; Barton Lynch for being my most loyal blog reader and the funniest person I know; Maggie Garnett and Jillian Madden for making me want to write the kind of books that you would staff-pick; Stephanie Robinson and Laura Wiltshire for pushing me to dream impossible dreams; Lee Kiefer for being Olympic-level at friendship and indulging my attempt at a Sports Story; and Ana Bahrami for getting me into fanfic circa 2009 and believing in my writing ever since.

My family. Thank you to my parents, Michelle, Ron, Brad, and Ginny, for your unconditional support in all my pursuits and for instilling in me a love of books before I could even read; my sister, Brianna, for the inspiration to live boldly and use my voice; my not-so-little brothers, Julian, Grant, Reagan, and Max, for keeping me young and humble; my grandparents for spoiling me with biscuits (Sheryl), sweet tea (Joleen), and love (all of you); and the rest of my partner's and my wonderful extended family.

Stephen. Thank you for being my one and only since we were

Reese and Benny's age, and for always picking up my slack in our real world while I work on fictional ones. Everything I know about true love and partnership I've learned with you by my side.

Every reader who's picked up my book. Thank you so much for giving this story a chance! I hope it brought you laughs, smiles, and/or food cravings.

Finally, Chris Fannin—I wish you'd been able to read this one, and hope to help your legacy of beautiful storytelling live on.

About the Author

KAITLYN HILL is a writer, reader, and sweet tea enthusiast who believes that all the world is not, in fact, a stage, but a romance novel waiting to happen. She lives with her real-life romance hero in Lexington, Kentucky.

thekaitlynhill.com